Gaia's Revenge
By
Patrick J. Fleming

Dedication

To my amazing wife, Sue, my love, my best friend,
my partner, my "Pearl of Great Price",
my *Anam Cara,* and my constant inspiration.
Without her loving and affirming challenge,
I would never have become a writer,
and this book would never have happened.

Gaia's Revenge

Double Rainbow Books

"If we fail to take care of the Earth,
it will surely take care of itself
by making us no longer welcome."

James Lovelock
Creator of the "Gaia Hypothesis"
The Revenge of Gaia

"Blessed is the one who reads
and blessed are those who listen
to this prophetic message
and heed what is written in it,
for the appointed time is near at hand."

The Book of Revelation 1:3

Nada. Their adobe-style chapel stands on a ridge of the monastery property overlooking the communal library, kitchen, and dining room, and the fifteen or so small wooden hermit cabins.

These are scattered in curving lines along the sides and ridges of the sandy hills that roll across the hundreds of acres of monastery property. A long adobe bridge connects the chapel to the communal central building, affording soul-stopping panoramic views of the Sangre de Cristo mountains towering above the chapel and the immensity of the San Luis Valley below.

Sr. Clare McCulloch—a seventy-two-year-old, white-haired Carmelite nun—is praying inside the darkened chapel, below a large, dramatic, dark metal Cross with a modern, yet realistic, over-sized corpus of Jesus hanging in agony, while at the same time extending his arms to embrace everyone who enters the chapel.

Surprisingly flexible for a woman her age, Sr. Clare is sitting Buddhist-style in the lotus position on a cushion on the stone floor. She is short and compact, dressed in a heavy blue sweater and jeans. Her feet are bare so she can feel the Earth, her back plum-bob straight, and her hands cupped open atop her knees in a meditative position.

In a barely audible whisper, she repeats her centering prayer over and over, "Lord Jesus Christ, Son of God, have mercy on me" clearing her thoughts and bringing her deeper into the Nothingness she longs for. She has been sitting, meditating like this for almost an hour, as she does daily, a palpable peace and presence slowly growing within her.

At 3:55pm, Sr. Clare's peace is shattered by a sudden, unbidden vision of a series of horrific events. The vision seems to unspool in her mind for an hour, but only five minutes goes by when she cries out in terror and faints onto the floor. The last, most intense image of the vision has overwhelmed her mind, and her brain shuts down. She lays on the floor, breathing rapidly at first, and then gradually more slowly. She lies there for over an hour, unconscious, until Fr. David, a priest of the Nada community, comes to the chapel for his prayer hour. He tries unsuccessfully to awaken Clare, but does manage to pick her up and lay her on a cushioned pew. He runs off to knock on several hermitage doors to get help from other community members.

Five miles from the Nada chapel, further south along the rocky, dusty road of the Baca Grande Grant, past the house with a sign in the front yard advertising the "Village Witch," skirting a little closer to the base of the Sangre de Cristo mountains, stands the Haidakhandi Universal Ashram and its temple of Devi, the Divine Mother Goddess.

The temple complex, with its two onion domes, looks like a small Hindu temple lifted from an Indian village, and incongruously air-dropped into the American West. There is a meditation garden surrounding the temple populated with statues of various Hindu deities and a couple of Catholic statues of the Virgin Mary.

At the center of the temple, sits the stunning statue of the divine mother goddess, her four arms holding various symbols of blessing and instruments for the battle against evil. She has an exceedingly pale, bejeweled face. She is dressed quite sexily in what looks like a sports bra, her midriff bare, and a flowing cotton peasant skirt dyed in a rainbow of colors.

Aavani Chakrabarti, the tall, thirty-five-year-old Indian-born leader of the ashram, is dressed very similarly to the goddess. She is strikingly beautiful, sitting alone, praying in the lotus position on the floor below the divine mother goddess. A pot of incense fills the temple sanctuary with fragrant smoke that sometimes swirls around the figure of Devi. Aavani is spending her Holy Hour before the divine mother goddess. She alternates between Hindu chants, songs, and quietly whispering her personal mantra over and over again.

At 3:55pm, Aavani's devoted gaze at the divine mother is interrupted by an intrusive flood of horrendous images of death and destruction. She can no longer see the statue. The hideous video plays in her mind's eye, filling her with intense dread. It is reaching an intense, fearsome climax, when she screams and falls over face-first onto the temple floor. She moans a brief prayer, "Divine Mother, save us," before she loses consciousness.

Aavani's scream is heard in the ashram community house, and three women and two men run over to the temple. They find her unconscious and groaning on the floor before the statue of Devi. Their attempt to waken her is not successful, so they lift her up and carry her to her room in the community house. They debate what to do and are on the verge of calling the doctor in Alamosa, when Aavani awakens.

She cannot speak, but writes, "I am okay. I have been given a vision from our divine mother goddess which I cannot yet speak of."

One of the women devotees sits by Aavani's bedside holding her hand. The rest go to the community room, and quietly discuss what has just occurred with their leader.

Six miles further up the road, sitting on a small plateau on the side of the mountain, with a view of the starkly dramatic Great Sand Dunes National Park and Preserve thirty miles to the south, Crestone Mountain Zen Center is an oasis of solitude and simplicity. All of the buildings and their interiors are austerely simple, devoid of anything like the almost-garish ornamentation of the Hindu temple and the Catholic symbolism and statuary of the Carmelite monastery. The meditation room is an unadorned, wood-paneled rectangular space dimly lit and windowless. There are no views of the mountains to distract from focusing on the breath and clearing the mind of every thought and image.

Rev. Mark Krummanocker—a forty-year-old gay minister from the Metropolitan Church of St. Louis, who is a little overweight and lumpy—is sitting on his meditation pillow during the afternoon meditation. He struggles to get comfortable and focus on his breathing. He keeps wondering whether Buddhists have the same kind of backs and butts as Christians do. His back hurts so much from sitting on the thin meditation pillow on the floor he can hardly stand it.

He struggles to focus on his breathing and yet his mind is mostly consumed with worry about whether he will make it to the end of the meditation hour without fainting or embarrassing himself in some way. Mark is surrounded by a few fellow retreatants and by the male and female community members. The latter are mostly German Buddhists who the American guru and founder imported, because he found his American disciples too undisciplined, in his opinion, to make good Buddhists.

Mark came to the Zen Center on the recommendation of his Jesuit psychotherapist to recover from the trauma of a mass shooting and hate crime at his church in St. Louis. Five months prior—on the first Sunday of Advent, at the 10am service—he had been winding up his sermon when a lone gunman, dressed all in black with black body armor, burst in with an AR-15-type semi-automatic rifle.

He began cursing and yelling anti-gay slogans, "God hates homos!" and "I'm sending you faggots to hell where you belong!"

Then he walked coldly and methodically down the main aisle of the church toward the sanctuary, spraying bullets left and right into the parishioners in the pews, his eyes as dark and dead as a zombie. Twelve of Mark's parishioners were killed instantly, and twenty were wounded, six critically. Mark escaped death only because he instinctively

loud the lines from one of his favorite poets, Gerald Manley Hopkins:

> The world is charged with the grandeur of God.
> It will flame out, like shining from shook foil,
> It gathers to a greatness, like the ooze of oil crushed...
> And for all this, nature is never spent;
> There lives the dearest freshness deep down things.

With about ten minutes to go in the 3-4pm meditation hour, Mark is finally getting comfortable sitting on the meditation pillow. His back stops distracting him. He is able to focus almost entirely on his breath. He enters a state of empty-mindedness and palatable bliss. This is what he had longed for. After five minutes of near-nirvana, Mark's mind is suddenly assaulted with a vision of unimaginable horror and disaster. He struggles to focus back on his breath, but the onslaught of images is too powerful. The same black cloud of fear that had stricken him during the shooting, and nearly every day since, engulfs him again. He feels like he must be going crazy.

Maybe this is what they mean by a nervous breakdown? he thinks. Intense fear erupts from deep within him like a super-heated pyroclastic flow of white-hot terror. He senses he is losing control of his mind, as a primal scream shoots up his throat and bursts out of his mouth before he can stop it, shattering the silence of the sitting room. Mark then faints, writhing on the floor for several minutes as if having a seizure. He screams once more and then lies silent, motionless, sprawled on the floor appearing dead.

His fellow meditators are shaken out of their silence, and rush to help him. Several of them try to restrain him while he is rolling and moaning on the floor. One leaves to call 911 and summon the Crestone ambulance. An older man continues to sit in meditation on his pillow in the corner of the sitting room, remaining as calm and detached

14

as if this drama was an ordinary part of his daily meditation. When Mark finally lies still, one of the monks checks his pulse and breathing. He tells the others he is still alive, but unconscious.

The ambulance arrives thirty-five minutes later, staffed by local volunteer EMTs, one a tall, long-haired hippie and one a diminutive, but muscular young woman in a tie-dyed t-shirt. By this time, Mark is awake and sitting up. He can't talk, but otherwise seems quite alert and functional.

The EMTs examine him thoroughly and ask a lot of questions. Mark can only respond in writing. They think he might have had a stroke, because of his inability to talk, but there are no other stroke symptoms. They tell him they want to take him to the nearest hospital in Alamosa, at least an hour away. Mark shakes his head. When he continues to resist, they call the town doctor to consult with him.

Mark's meditation guide, Gisella, talks with the doctor and explains Mark revealed to her he recently experienced a mass shooting at his church. She suggests he may have experienced a traumatic flashback, not a stroke. Mark nods. So, it is decided to simply bring Mark to his room, and keep him under observation. Gisella sits with him till nightfall when he falls asleep, then checks on him several times during the night.

Chapter Two

The next morning, speech returns to all three visionaries, Pastor Mark, Sr. Clare, and Aavani. Although they refuse to talk about what happened to them, or what they saw in their visions. The Nada community and the ashram respect their silence, and assume they experienced profound spiritual ecstasy, which was beyond words to describe. Mark and the Zen community believe his experience was a PTSD episode of some kind. Gisella makes Mark promise he will call his psychotherapist when he returns home. Mark readily agrees.

After resting for a couple of days, Mark leaves the Zen Center for the long drive from Crestone to the Denver airport to catch a plane back to St. Louis. As he drives north through the wide-open, arid San Luis Valley with the procession of Sangre de Cristo peaks looming to his right, the images of his vision keep trying to intrude into his thoughts.

Fighting the intrusive pictures and rising anxiety tightening his throat and chest, he tries to focus on the scenery, and on slowing and deepening his increasingly rapid, shallow breathing. He keeps telling himself either he is going crazy, or this is a new bizarre symptom of his PTSD which he never heard of before. Neither possibility is very comforting.

After climbing out of the San Luis Valley, crossing over the long, gradual Poncha Pass, Mark descends into another mountain valley dominated by the high Collegiate Peaks, now stretched in a row to his left. The gruesome images fade away as he is caught up in the grandeur of these mountains marching like dark sentinels in a further procession up the valley toward Buena Vista.

He then winds through a range of low mountains, until he sweeps around a corner, and the vista suddenly opens up to the vast expanse of South Park, an immense prairie bowl entirely encircled by high, snow-covered peaks. He is stunned by the immense scene suddenly unfolding before him, and almost runs off the road.

He steers back onto the road, and is regaining his composure when the vast openness of South Park suddenly cracks his mind open again to the fearsome images of his Zen Center vision. They flood his mind and overwhelm him. He is afraid he will crash the car, so he quickly turns onto a gravel National Forest service road, swerving and fishtailing for a quarter of a mile until he can bring the car to a halt.

A video montage keeps swirling through his mind. The images are all he can see. South Park and the surrounding mountains become a black screen across which the bizarre and frightening PowerPoint slides maniacally play over and over in his mind in rapid succession. He cannot stop them, and feels he might pass out again with the horror and fury of what he is seeing.

Again he thinks, *I must be losing my mind! Maybe the horror of the shooting finally has unhinged me? Maybe now I am wholly at the mercy of these psychotic hallucinations.* He has the mordant thought, *Thanks a lot, God! You certainly picked a fine place for me to have my mental breakdown. In the middle of nowhere, surrounded by cattle, antelope, a few deer, a lone coyote, and a lot of nothing. There can't be a therapist or a psych unit for hundreds of miles.*

Then a surprising thought spontaneously pops into his mind: *The images really have nothing in common with what I experienced during the shooting, and are, except for*

Being a contemplative community of hermits, her community respects her solitude and leaves her alone. But they are puzzled and concerned. Only Fr. Paul, at fifty-one, the youngest and newest member of the community, stops by once a day for a few minutes to make sure Clare is alright.

Clare still has little idea what her vision means, only that it was very frightening. She seeks some answers in scripture. She finds herself attracted to John's apocalyptic images in the Book of Revelation. There is an eerie resonance with what she saw just a few days ago. *But what does that mean?*

She knows Revelation is a difficult book to interpret, often misused by fundamentalist Christians to forecast all sorts of God-awful, supposedly End-times events. She recalls from her scripture classes that Revelation's highly bizarre, apocalyptic images and events are actually symbols of hope for the early Christian church in a time of turmoil and persecution. In its original meaning, apocalypse simply meant an unveiling of a deeper reality in order to clear the way for something new. The events she saw were similar to what John described, but they did not seem symbolic. They seemed very real. Clare also had the sense that what she saw was a foreshadowing of actual events which would begin happening in the not-too-distant future.

She kept questioning herself. *How could that be? What was revealed was so extreme, how can it be real or about to happen? And why was it revealed to me? I'm just a little old nun, living in the middle of nowhere. I have no power or position to do anything about the vision. So why, if it is real, was it given to me?*

Clare receives no answers to her haunting questions. Sometimes she grows frustrated and attempts to debunk and dismiss the vision, instead focusing on her daily routine and prayers. Her thoughts keep circling around to her wish, *Maybe it will just fade away?* But, it doesn't.

On the fifth day after her vision, Fr. Paul stops by Clare's cabin and this time asks if he can sit down and talk a bit. He has some news. It turns out that Cassandra—the village witch, who is also the town gossip—recently talked to her friends among the Carmelites, at the ashram, and at the Zen Center.

She learned that Aavani and one of the retreatants at the Zen Center, a minister from St. Louis, both had very similar experiences during prayer at precisely the same time on the same day. Like Clare, they both lost consciousness and temporarily lost their power of speech.

Cassandra's Zen friends explained the minister's collapse as probably a psychological event related to a trauma he had endured. Being a witch, Cassandra had other thoughts.

How can this be a coincidence? Three dramatic spiritual experiences at the same time on the same day? This happened at exactly the same time, seemingly in exactly the same way, just a few miles from each other at three different spiritual centers here in our little, middle-of-nowhere Crestone. Something magical must be going on here. But what?

Cassandra put herself into a trance, employing one of her ancient witchcraft rituals, seeking an answer. She sensed her quest was being blocked by some spiritual power and at first she cannot move in any direction in her spirit. Strangely, the only thing that eventually does come to her are vague images of a troop of mountain gorillas in the tropical volcanic mountain ranges of Rwanda.

They are a family group, consisting of infants, children, mothers, and a large silverback male. They are running through the dense forest, appearing to be trying to escape from something. Then, Cassandra sees a shadowy group of armed men pursuing the gorillas. She assumes they are poachers, intent on killing them. The poachers are getting close to the gorilla band when a dense, green-tinted mist surrounds the men and the gorillas. When the mist clears, the poachers are all lying on the ground dead. Something has rescued the endangered gorillas.

After she comes out of the trance, Cassandra is puzzled and disturbed by what she has just seen. *What was that all about?* she wonders. *Have I been watching too many National Geographic shows? And what does it have to do with these strange events here in Crestone?* Cassandra hears no answers, until the thought arises from her inner source of deepest spiritual intuition, *Maybe these Crestone spiritual experiences have something to do with the global crisis of species extinction?* It is only a wisp of intuition, and then it is gone, leaving Cassandra still unsure what to think about what happened with her friends and the minister.

Cassandra did not meet the minister, but she had known both Clare and Aavani for many years. She knew them as solid, truly spiritual women, with their feet on the ground, and their souls in touch with the Great Mystery. They would never make up anything. Besides, how could they have coordinated their experiences with each other, or with a minister they had never met?

Something truly remarkable is happening here, she thought, *I need to let the whole spiritual community in Crestone know, so we can help Clare and Aavani discern what is going on in the universe that something like this would happen.*

So, Cassandra calls everyone she knows: Fr. Paul at Nada, her friends at the ashram and at the Zen Center, the communities of monks at the four different Tibetan Buddhist temples, and at the baroquely colorful Bhutan Buddhist temple, the priests and sisters of the Japanese Shumai shrine, the various New Age practitioners whom she knows, and the part-time female Episcopal priest who holds Sunday liturgy in the charming mountain cabin chapel in a grove of Aspens in the middle of town.

Cassandra even calls her friend Sue, the secretary of the Baptist church. She is fascinated by the news but suggests it would be best if she didn't tell her boss, the very traditional Baptist minister. Cassandra also decides not to call the Love Has Won group over in the nearby, scruffy little town of Moffat.

She has been wary of them ever since some townspeople were arrested in 2021 for illegally transporting the body of their deceased religious leader, "Mother God" Amy Carlson, and setting up her mummified body like a shrine in a back bedroom, wrapped in a sleeping bag and festooned with Christmas lights and glitter makeup applied around her empty eye sockets. This was too much even for an open-minded, inclusive witch like Cassandra.

Soon everyone in town and in the spiritual groups scattered among the foothills knows the story. Everyone wonders, *What manner of phenomenon can this be? It must mean something profound, but what? What could it signify? What does it portend?*

There is much gossip and discussion, but no one has any answers. Everyone in Crestone and the Baca Grande is mystified.

When Fr. Paul tells Sr. Clare all of this, she is first quite peeved and then shocked. She is upset everyone now knows her story. And then she realizes the full import of what Cassandra had found out and is stunned. Aavani had a parallel experience at the same time as her vision. At the very same time something strangely similar happened to the minister at the Zen Center.

What in God's name is going on here?

As she thinks this, her face grows very pale, and a deep primal shudder ripples through her body like the seismic waves of an earthquake coursing through the heaving ground.

This can't be coincidental. This means what I saw is real. This is a message that has been revealed to me and

in a general way what each of us experienced that day? Not the particulars or any detailed description of what we saw, because that seems to be forbidden, but some idea of what happened in the vision. Otherwise, how can we know if we were given the same thing, much less what in Devi's name it means?"

Clare smiles at the reference to the goddess, Devi. She had always enjoyed learning from Aavani about the Hindu pantheon. She loved it even more when Aavani swore irreverently in Sanskrit. She wished she remembered enough Latin to swear in that ancient Catholic language.

After more thoughtful silence, Clare agrees, "Yes, we must at least tell each other something about the visions we were given. It has to be significant that this vision happened to both of us at the same time on the same day. And that we were both put into some kind of ecstatic trance, and lost the power to speak for several hours.

So, why don't I go first? What I saw was terrifying. I saw many horrible events happening all around the world. Many people were killed. All of the events were natural catastrophes, but they were so extreme and unusual, and so calamitous, that they seemed outside of the natural order. I had the feeling that all of humanity was somehow at risk. I also had the sense that there was a plan and a force behind these events, but it wasn't clear to me what the plan or force was. Only that it was something very powerful, and potentially destructive.

Is it God? Is it the devil? I have never much believed in the devil, but there certainly seemed to be some evil energy involved in these events. I simply don't know where this awful vision came from. Do you, Aavani? The catastrophes I saw built up to a crescendo that was just overwhelming. At the end, just before I passed out, I thought I heard a voice, a woman's voice, say to me, "Tell no one, except the Chosen One, who will be shown to you, what has been given to you in these revelations. More will be revealed to you in time."

Aavani, in a trembling whisper, responded, "Oh my God, that sounds almost exactly like what I experienced! What does that mean? How can this be? Are we going crazy together? Did we both see the same God-awful disaster movie, and these are the flashbacks? Is this the result of too much prayer and too much time alone?"

Now raising her voice, Aavani almost shouts, "What the hell, Clare! What the fuck (she says this in Sanskrit) is this? And what the fuck (switching to Hindu) are we supposed to do with it? We both were told not to tell anyone. That's not a problem for me, because my community at the ashram would probably want to call a shrink and have me locked up if I told them."

She pauses, looking frightened and perplexed. "So, Clare, my friend, what should we do with all of this? I haven't a clue and I'm scared."

Clare looks intently into Aavani's deep brown eyes, taking her friend's hands in her own.

"I don't know either, my dear. I have learned, though, that when there is no clear path forward, or when life is chaotic and confusing, the best thing to do is slow down, shut up, pray, and listen."

Aavani nods assent, and they both agree to spend the next week in solitude, fasting, and prayer, and meet again in a week to share what they heard in their souls. They hug once more, Aavani with tears in her eyes. Then, she returns to her ashram.

That week there is a series of extreme natural events happening one after another around the world, all reported in the international media.

BBC World News: "We received a report from Uganda that yesterday a troupe of hungry chimpanzees attacked, killed, and actually devoured 11 children in two different villages. Ugandan authorities are at a loss to explain this

27

unprecedented series of horrific attacks. There are reports though that the chimps' normal habitat has been heavily altered by encroaching human development, and their natural sources of food have been seriously threatened, perhaps causing them to go on this deadly rampage."

CNN: Breaking News: "Late this morning an immense flock of starlings, thousands of sooty shearwaters, and an equally large "murder" of crows dive-bombed and attacked people coming to the weekly Farmer's Market in Bodega Bay, California. Initial estimates are that twelve people were killed and forty-five injured. Reports from the scene describe grotesque injuries: eyes plucked out, carotid arteries ruptured, bodies with multiple puncture wounds, and puddles of blood oozing out onto the town's streets and sidewalks. Surviving victims describe being suddenly mobbed by dozens of birds at once. "It was like I was being struck by a whirling tornado of birds which came out of a totally clear, blue sky," said one of the victims, who was able to escape her avian attackers only because she was close to her car, and was able to run back to it, and close the windows on the marauding birds."

Vice Online News: "More than 5,200 people were attacked by magpies in Australia in 2024. This exceeds the number of attacks in the previous record year of 2020 when there were 4,600 magpie-on-human attacks. At least 800 of these attacks have resulted in injuries, some serious. For the first time, this year there were also twelve deaths related to the attacks.

The magpie attacks seem to be increasingly vicious. One especially gory magpie attack took place in southeastern Victoria last month, when 72-year-old Paddy Dyer had both of his eyes violently gouged out by a magpie while enjoying his lunch outside his favorite neighborhood restaurant. Dyer had blood pouring out of his eyes as he was rushed to hospital for emergency eye surgery. Doctors were concerned he would lose his eyesight. During the surgery Mr. Dyer went into cardiac arrest and could not be revived. The chief surgeon reported it was probable the heart attack was induced by the stress of the bird attack and the substantial loss of blood. Authorities are searching for the offending magpie with the intention of euthanizing it, as they have done in other recent attacks.

Dr. Gertrude Kominski, professor of animal behavior at the University of New Hampshire, told Vice the magpies in these 2024 attacks had displayed uncommonly vicious behavior, which she suggested they may have developed as a result of habitat loss and shortage of food.

"Something strange is happening in their environment and in their interaction with people," said Dr. Kominski, "Twenty-five years ago, when I first began studying magpies, I never came across a single case like these attacks."

Des Moines Register: "Another devastating derecho, even stronger than the 2020 derecho, hit Iowa yesterday afternoon with widespread 100+ mph winds reported all across the nearly 300-mile line of storms. Top winds of 150 mph were recorded in Des Moines and Cedar Rapids. As in 2020, grain elevators were toppled; roofs of houses, schools, hospitals, and businesses were sheared off; and hundreds of semi-trucks were blown off the highways and overturned, in many cases their loads spilling. Hundreds of thousands of trees have been toppled and power lines blown down all over the state. An estimated 550,000 households are without power. Rescue teams are still sifting through the wreckage at numerous sites, searching for missing people. The current death toll stands at forty-five and is expected to climb. Thousands have been left homeless.

The new corn crop, planted just a month ago, was flattened and fields flooded. Farmers, many of whom lost most of their crops in the storm of 2020, are hopeful they can replant—as long as there are no more storms, and the

in Napa and Sonoma counties. Many homes are in the path of the fires, and mass evacuations involving an estimated half a million people are in progress. Several wineries in both counties are threatened by the fast-moving wildfires, notably DeLoach Vineyards in Sonoma and the historic Buena Vista Winery in Napa.

While Bay Area residents were focused on the amazing light display in the sky and on the threatening fires, a plague of millions of purple sea urchins snuck in under cover of darkness, and invaded San Francisco Bay. Having devoured 95% of the kelp beds off the California coast, their population has exploded. Warming California coastal waters and a mysterious disease have decreased the number of their predators causing the purple urchins to multiply exponentially. They then proceeded to devour their favorite food, bull kelp, almost to extinction, having reduced the once-lush kelp beds to denuded undersea barrens. Scientists have come to call them "zombie urchins" because they continue to live in vast numbers on the coastal ocean floor, although they have eaten almost all of the kelp and are essentially surviving in a state of near starvation.

This zombie invasion of millions of purple sea urchins caused several parts of the Bay to actually turn a bright purple for several hours. By midday, the urchins began to die en masse, poisoning the water, and sickening thousands of residents with the stinking gas clouds they emit as they die. The initial estimates are that several dozen people may have died from the clouds of poisonous gas emitted from this almost suicidal die-off of the purple urchins. The mayors of San Francisco, Oakland, Berkeley, and other Bay area communities have scheduled a joint news conference for 5pm this afternoon to provide more details and a plan for recovery from both disasters."

Anchorage Daily News: "Breaking News: Mount Edgecumbe, a long-dormant volcano sacred to the Tlingit people, located sixteen miles northwest of Sitka, Alaska, has suddenly erupted with multiple explosions and a pyroclastic flow aimed at Sitka. An urgent order of evacuation was issued. Thousands of residents have fled into the surrounding forest and are reported to be safe. An estimated 350 people are missing, some presumed to have been overcome by the incredible speed of the cloud of very hot ash, lava fragments, and gases which flowed from the volcano over Sitka Sound into the city of Sitka.

A number of buildings are reported to have been destroyed or set on fire, including the historic Sitka landmark, St. Michael's Orthodox Cathedral. The governor of Alaska has called up the Alaska National Guard to assist in search and rescue. The Coast Guard and U.S. Navy are also sending ships to Sitka to support the disaster recovery effort. Mount Edgecumbe had long been thought to be a totally dormant, dead volcano, seen as simply a harmless, attractive feature of the Sitka skyline."

These events happen sequentially every day for a week with unprecedented frequency.

Scientists declare that although unusual, they are just random, albeit coincidental, events. The Presidents of the US, Russia, and Brazil claim the stories are fake news staged by "tree-huggers" and other climate extremists, questioning—despite the video footage—whether some of them even happened at all.

Environmental leaders around the world are puzzled but wonder aloud to the media if at least *some* of these events are related to global warming. One environmentalist, Dr. Thomas Keating, is quoted as saying: "Are these signs that the Earth is finally being pushed completely out of balance by our actions? I don't know yet, and I don't quite see the connection, but maybe that is what is happening."

Another climate scientist, Dr. Christy Brennecke, also comments on the extraordinary events of the week: "It looks like our apocalyptic chickens are already coming home to roost, way sooner than we thought. We are seeing environmental impacts now that we thought we would only see fifty to a hundred years in the future. Every day now I'm feeling less like a conservationist and more like a coroner, as I study species moving toward extinction and eco-systems devolving into a death spiral."

Chapter Four

Sr. Clare and Aavani have been following these stories on the internet. Very much the modern hermitess and nun, Clare checks her computer daily before evening prayer. Aavani has been spending a great deal of time meditating in her temple before the statue of the divine mother goddess and praying for guidance. She too checks the news in the evening before the final prayers of the day with her ashram community. Both women are stunned to read what is happening around the world and how it parallels their visions. When they meet again on Saturday, they both remark how they were struck by the similarities between what they saw, and what was reported in the news.

Clare comments, "What I saw and what happened this week around the world are frighteningly similar. Scientists, politicians, and climate change deniers are all saying these events are just tragic coincidences and normal natural catastrophes. But what I saw in the vision was Nature turning against human beings, and seeking not the end of the world, but the end of humanity."

Aavani blurts out, "Oh my God! That's what I saw too. What the holy fuck is going on? I saw how millions of people are going to die soon."

The two women decide to share a few details of their visions without revealing the whole revelation. Their descriptions match exactly. Then, they sit in silence for several minutes till Clare says to Aavani, "Can you say something obscene in Sanskrit please? I'll try to remember how to curse in Latin or maybe Gaelic. That's the only thing I can think to say right now."

They both laugh and go to Clare's tiny kitchen to brew some tea.

"Did you bring any Irish whiskey with you, Aavani? I think I need a Jameson, something stronger than just tea to help deal with this." They both laugh again.

Over tea, they continue to discuss the situation and what they should do about their visions. They are still not sure they are not both suffering from some kind of shared hallucinations.

Aavani says, "Maybe one of the potheads from town slipped us both some very potent weed, or maybe even LSD, in gummy bears or brownies, or something like that, as a prank?"

Clare shrugs her shoulders and adds, "Who knows? But I can't remember eating or drinking anything before my prayer time."

"I can't remember eating anything either," Aavani responds, "I usually fast for at least a couple of hours before I go before Devi. Besides, what are we supposed to make of all these catastrophes in the news? Maybe they validate that what we saw is real and is actually starting to happen?"

They sit with this for a while, silently sipping their tea.

Then Clare breaks the silence, "I just had an idea. I think we need to talk to the minister from the Zen Center and see what he experienced. It's still strange to me that he passed out at the same time we did. Maybe, if he will talk to us, we might get confirmation for our visions. Or, if his experience is different than ours, we will find out this is just about two friends with identical outlandish imaginations. Or we are simply going crazy together. If that's what's going on, do you think we can get adjoining rooms in the shrink-tank?"

They both laugh at this. Aavani takes Clare's hands, and responds, "If there is anyone I would want to go crazy with, it would be you, Clare. Whatever this is, I'm glad we are in it together."

Clare says, "Let's call our good Village Witch. Cassandra will know the name of the minister, and how to contact him. Then, we can see if he will meet with us."

They call Cassandra, who instantly replies, "I knew you would be calling me. Of course I know his name! Rev. Mark Krummanocker. He is the pastor of the Metropolitan Church of St. Louis, Missouri. I sensed you would need to talk to him."

Clare takes the information and they immediately call Rev. Krummanocker. They tell him they are visiting St. Louis, and would love to meet him, since he had been in Crestone so recently, and had stopped by the ashram during his stay and met Aavani. Wanting to be hospitable, Mark agrees to meet with them at his church, but sounds a little wary on the phone. Clare and Aavani don't reveal to him the real reason for their trip.

The next day, after saying their goodbyes to their communities, and Aavani to her Zen boyfriend, Pieter, Clare and Aavani pile into Clare's old green Subaru Forester and begin their road-trip to St. Louis. They drive up the San Luis Valley, their sacred mountains processing northward on their right. Clare had often imagined that the great line of Sangre de Cristos was like a monumental stone sculpture of protestors marching for peace, civil rights, and the future of the planet. They stop at the top of Poncha Pass, turn south to look back down their immense valley, and say goodbye to their home.

They both have a vague feeling of dread about leaving the sanctuary of Crestone and the Valley. They often talk about the unique, sacred place Crestone is for both of them. Crestone, the Sangre de Cristo mountains, and the San Luis Valley have been a place of holy sanctuary for Clare and

Aavani for much of their adult lives. They both accepted the oral history that the area had been an especially spiritual place for Native Americans because that was their own experience as well.

It was land that had been holy and sacred to the Ute tribe long before the Europeans arrived. They often summered there, hunting, soaking in the mineral hot springs scattered around the valley, and walking up the steep pathways into the mountains for vision quests. Other tribes were welcome to enter the valley to hunt and pray. No tribal warfare was allowed. It was seen by all as a place of peace, refuge, protection, and Spirit. The Great Spirit kept a lodge in the Valley and abided there always.

Chapter Five

Clare and Aavani came to the sanctum sanctorum of Crestone along life pathways that were both labyrinth and maze. Clare grew up the middle of five children in a fairly poor but close-knit Irish Catholic family on a small, rocky farm just outside of Belfast, Maine. Her parents were both devout Catholics. So, it surprised no one when Clare decided to join the convent and the sisters of the Society of the Holy Child Jesus just after high school.

Like many Irish Catholic families, her parents never talked about sex, acting as if it didn't exist and the fairies had brought the five children. Clare had dated little during high school and was seemingly not bothered by the prospect of a lifetime of celibacy. She breezed through the novitiate and subsequent formation with little in the way of the doubt or vocational crises most of her fellow candidates seemed to experience. She had always been an excellent student, and easily transitioned to her studies at Boston College, double majoring in education and theology.

Upon graduation she was assigned to her order's school in South Boston, St. Bridget's Catholic school. She loved teaching the mix of Irish-American, Hispanic, and African-American students in her fourth-grade classroom. She thought she had found her niche, and would be happy with this ministry until she died.

But community life was challenging. Living with eight other sisters of all ages and personalities proved to be the most difficult part of her vocation. At an early age she was appointed the superior of the local community of sisters at St. Bridget's. In this role she often had to mediate personality conflicts between sisters. The worst came one day when she was called out of her classroom to the emergency room of the local Catholic hospital, where one of her elderly sisters was being treated for a severe bite on her right ear which another senior sister had inflicted during a fight over the last blueberry muffin. The ear had nearly been chewed off and was hanging on the side of Sr. Anne's head like a soggy potato chip.

Clare was mortified. She had to talk to the ER doctor and nurses and explain the community situation to them. She pleaded with the hospital social worker, who was called to the ER, not to make an elder abuse hotline call. She also had to convince Sr. Anne not to press charges against Sr. Clarice when the Boston police arrived to investigate the incident. Clare could only imagine the scandal if the story of a nun biting another nun's ear nearly off got into the media. She managed to convince everyone she would handle this matter back at the convent.

This was the last straw for Clare. She decided right then and there in the ER, as she watched her sister's ear being stitched back on, that it was time to move out and live alone in her own apartment. Maybe it was also time to move out of South Boston and go back to school for her masters or even a doctorate. She loved being a teaching sister. She loved her students. But she was starting to question the rest of her life in the community. The work was wonderful, and some of the sisters were as well, but she was growing increasingly restless, discontented, and lonely in her everyday personal life.

She called her Mother Superior the next day, and asked permission to move to an apartment and make plans to go back to school. Mother Julian had already heard the embarrassing story of the ear-bite and was very sympathetic to Clare. She told Clare she would have to get the Community Council to approve her request, but she was fairly certain permission would be granted. Clare's response was, "Soon, Mother, soon! I think I may lose my sanity and maybe my faith if I don't get out of that house ASAP. Thank you, Julian, for being so understanding."

In a few weeks, Clare moved into her own apartment near Boston College and enrolled for the upcoming semester. She was surprised this change did not make her happier. She was certainly relieved to be away from quarreling sisters, but still felt desperately lonely at times. She often felt a vague restlessness and a yearning for something unnamed and intangible that seemed to be missing. She was now thirty-three and wondered if she was simply in an early mid-life crisis. She reminded herself that thirty-three was a bad year for Jesus too.

Maybe the emotional emptiness I am feeling is the cross I must bear to somehow grow spiritually?

She thought this must be so, but the thought gave her little solace. When the semester began, she poured herself into her studies at Boston College as she always did. The academic work, with its rhythms and demands, was reassuring to her. Or at least it was a welcome distraction. The Fall semester passed uneventfully.

In the second semester, she signed up for a course titled *Christian Cosmology* taught by a brilliant, inspiring, very entertaining, very handsome professor named Avery Deloitte. Clare overheard the gossip from a few of the younger women in the class that Prof. Deloitte was forty and recently divorced. This didn't mean very much to her since she was a vowed celibate. She just enjoyed his witty, warm teaching style and the view of the cosmos he was opening up for her.

Mid-semester, Clare found herself at a loss for what to focus her semester paper on, so she asked to see Prof. Deloitte privately. He scheduled her for an hour that turned into four. The conversation's focus started with what she could write about, moved onto the fascinating questions of the Big Bang, various cultures' Origin Stories, the bizarre world of Quantum Physics, and the great mystery of God's role in the Universe in the light of modern cosmology.

They both found the conversation very stimulating and couldn't stop after the allotted hour was up. They moved on to share some aspects of their personal lives, and soon discovered they had much in common. At the end of the four hours, Avery suggested to Clare that they meet again sometime soon over coffee to continue discussing her paper. Clare found she couldn't say no.

She went back to the library to study, but she couldn't concentrate. She kept thinking about Prof. Deloitte. She gave up and returned to her apartment hoping to find some distraction there. She got out one of her prayer books, but was distressed to discover she couldn't pray either. Emotions and yearnings she had never let herself feel before started to stir inside her. All she could think about was Avery, how she felt with him, and how she could arrange to meet with him again.

She called him and told him she had some more questions about her paper—which was only partially true—and could they meet again soon? Avery agreed, and they arranged to meet in an off-campus sports bar near Clare's apartment. Once again, they sat there for hours talking. It became evident that Avery was as attracted to Clare as Clare was to him.

A mad, passionate affair ensued. They both knew this was crazy. Avery realized it was inappropriate for him to be having a relationship with a student—and a nun to boot—although Clare was certainly not a young, starry-eyed co-ed. He also recognized it was too soon after his fairly traumatic divorce. Clare felt very guilty about breaking her vows. But neither could stop themselves. Neither *wanted* to stop.

Clare felt more alive than she had in years, probably since her first few years as a nun. She wondered how something that felt so good, and had so revived her spirit, could be so supposedly wrong. There were even a few times in their frequent lovemaking at her apartment, when she experienced an intense, oceanic feeling of union with Avery, with God, and with all of Creation as she climaxed.

This feeling continued in the long after-glow lying in Avery's arms.

She had only experienced this twice before when her meditation led unexpectedly to an ecstatic sense of being uplifted by her soul into a feeling of deep communion with God and with all things. Clare was surprised to discover that sex could be so soul-stirring and spiritual, and so like prayer.

About ten months into the affair, both Clare and Avery began to talk about where their relationship was leading them. They both felt deep love for each other. Avery suggested marriage. Clare said she could very much see marriage with him, and hopefully raising a family together, but was conflicted because of her vows, and because there was so much to being a sister she still loved.

She was very torn and sunk back into the low-grade depression that had brought her to Boston College in the first place. Reluctantly, she decided she needed to meet with Mother Julian and reveal to her what was happening. Clare was surprised at how understanding and caring Julian was when Clare revealed her affair. Julian did not scold or judge her. She didn't tell Clare to end the affair. Julian's only suggestion was that Clare give herself more time to think about the situation and discern how she was being called.

She recommended Clare go to the Carmelite community in Crestone, Colorado, for at least a month, and meet with Fr. Robert, the founder and Superior of the community, for spiritual direction. Julian described how she herself had gone to Nada when she had been struggling at one point in her life and how clarifying and restorative it was for her to have time there in the mountains.

With a mysterious smile, Mother Julian ended their meeting by saying, "You know, Clare, you are not the only sister who has fallen in love at some point in her life."

With both Julian's and Avery's support, Clare made arrangements to spend a month at Nada. She soon fell in love with the Sangre de Cristo mountains, the San Luis Valley, her little hermitage, and the men and women of the Nada community. Fr. Robert was an excellent spiritual guide. He helped Clare see that either path she took was in God's Will, because both marrying Avery or remaining a teaching sister were pathways of love and Spirit. It was up to Clare to discern and choose which one fit her best and would be the most life-giving. That would also be the way that would bring her closest to God.

Toward the end of the month Clare was startled to realize neither of the two paths seemed right for her. The call beckoning her most powerfully was to remain at Nada and become a contemplative sister in this unusual community. The ecstasy she had felt both in prayer and during sex with Avery was a foretaste of union with God. That was her ultimate calling. Becoming a hermitess at Nada, she began to realize, was the best way for her to seek that union. She felt great peace at her decision, even more peaceful than she had felt when she first decided to become a nun.

Fr. Robert, who was just as surprised as Clare about her choice, suggested she try the life at Nada for one year before making a final decision. She agreed. Then she made flight arrangements through Alamosa and Denver to return to Boston and explain her decision to Avery and Sr. Julian. Clare bought a roundtrip ticket and had not left Crestone since her return flight.

Until now.

Chapter Six

Aavani's journey to Crestone was equally as indirect and surprising as Clare's, yet a great deal more traumatic. She was born the oldest of six children to a poor Hindu family in Kolkata, India. They were Dalits, one of the lowest caste, also called untouchables. Her father died when she was ten. Her mother struggled to keep the family together, but ultimately could not manage it.

To stop being a burden on the family, Aavani left at the age of twelve, and began to live and beg on the streets of Kolkata.

One day she was spotted on a street corner by Sr. Nirmala, one of Mother Teresa's sisters, the Missionaries of Charity. Sr. Nirmala tried to befriend Aavani, but Aavani resisted. Her mother was a devout Hindu, and had warned her about Catholics and other Christians who would try to proselytize her and steal her Hindu heritage. Aavani was uncomfortable then when a Catholic sister in a white sari-like habit with brilliant blue stripes on the edges of her veil approached her. She ran away.

Sr. Nirmala persisted in trying to reach out to Aavani. She could see Aavani was strikingly beautiful and was beginning to blossom and develop. She was very concerned a child sex trafficker would notice her and lure her off the streets with the false promise of a better life. She had seen this happen with numerous other young girls and boys alone and desperate on the streets of Kolkata. But Aavani would never let her get close, running away each time Sr. Nirmala approached to try to talk to her.

One day, Sr. Nirmala just stood back unnoticed in the shadows of a narrow alleyway watching as Aavani begged from passing American and British tourists. Then she spotted two Indian men she suspected were child traffickers. She watched as they stood and stared at Aavani, sizing her up as if she were a prize heifer, calculating how much they could get for her at market. She watched with apprehension as the two men approached Aavani, put some money in her begging cup, and began to chat with her. Aavani appeared spellbound by what they were saying.

When she started to walk off with the two men, Sr. Nirmala leapt into action, picking up the long skirt of her habit and running across the street to intervene. She had never done this, although she had witnessed such abductions before. This time she was determined to stop it. She stopped the men in their tracks, told Aavani who they were, and what they would really do with her.

"Don't believe their promises. These are evil men! They will not take care of you as they said. They will turn you into a sex slave, and sell you off to some pimp who will traffic you, and maybe even ship you off to some other country like America or Thailand. Once you are in their hands, you will never be able to escape. Please do not go with them."

Sr. Nirmala took Aavani's hand and said gently, "Come with me, and I will find a safe place for you."

When Aavani hesitated and pulled her hand away, the men grabbed her and began forcefully carrying her off. To everyone's surprise, including herself, Sr. Nirmala ferociously attacked the men, beating them with her fists and her heavy day-bag. After they get over their initial shock, the men easily pushed Sr. Nirmala to the ground, and continued to carry Aavani off.

At that point a policeman happened on the scene, saw a nun on the pavement, and two men roughly pulling a girl down the street. He shouted at the men to stop. When they looked back, and saw a policeman, they let go of Aavani and ran.

Sr. Nirmala and the policeman rushed over to Aavani who had been thrown by the men into a filthy gutter as they fled. She finally realized what almost happened to her. So, when Sr. Nirmala proposed to her and to the policeman that she come with her to one of Mother Teresa's homes for children to hide her and keep her safe, she accepted meekly.

She lived at the Missionaries of Charity home for the next six years all the way through high school. She came to love Sr. Nirmala and the rest of the sisters, becoming a leader among the other children. The sisters soon recognized Aavani was quite bright and enrolled her in excellent schools. Aavani was very happy during this time at the home. Her most prized possession from those years is a picture of her and Mother Teresa, who visited the home one day when Aavani was fourteen, posing in front of the home. Mother Teresa has her arm around Aavani, and they both beam at the camera, their faces lit with broad, joyful smiles.

When she finished high school and turned eighteen, she had to make plans to move out of the children's home, and find a job. The sisters hated to see her go, but Aavani had already exceeded the age limit of the home by a couple of years. The sisters had hinted through the years that she could become one of them, but Aavani could never envision herself as a nun, despite her love for the sisters.

She had found a job, but had not yet moved out, when one day on her way to work, she was accosted by two men. They stopped her and tried to talk her into taking a job with them at their financial services business in Mumbai. They promised her high wages and a wonderful place to live, but this time Aavani knew their cruel game.

She attempted to walk away, but they seized her and began dragging her away. The sisters had taught Aavani martial arts and self-defense, so she fought back. She kicked one of the men in the groin, doubling him up in pain, and then karate-chopped the second man in the throat. He stumbled off struggling to get his breath through his smashed windpipe. Aavani ran back to the safety of the home.

After that incident, the sisters and Aavani decided it was not safe for her to remain in Kolkata or anyplace else in India. Her beauty and youth were too much a magnet for the sex traffickers always on the lookout for attractive, young women who were vulnerable because they had no family to protect them.

Sr. Nirmala suggested they send her to one of their houses in the States where she would be much safer, and she could apply to an American university. It was decided she would live at one of the Sister's houses in New York, and attend Fordham University on a scholarship.

Aavani's years in New York were exciting and liberating. She discovered her low-caste background did not mean anything to Americans. She felt she could live the American Dream and become whatever she wanted. She was attracted to feminism and worked to empower herself in a way Indian women could not. She now thought of herself as an Indian American—even a little as an Indian-American princess—and less and less as a poor girl begging on the streets of Kolkata.

Her studies at Fordham went well. She loved the academic life and the free spirit of an American campus. She decided to pursue a career as a researcher and professor in Economics, specializing in creating economic development programs for women in third-world countries. Her path seemed set in an exciting new direction. She was almost grateful she had been the near-victim of sex traffickers, because it first brought her to the sisters, who had become her family, and then to America, which was providing her a once-unimaginably good life.

The only tear in the fabric of her life was men. She moved out of the convent at the start of her Junior year, and got an apartment with two girlfriends from Fordham. Once away from the sisters, she began dating. But her relationships with men were a disaster. She vacillated between keeping any man she dated at arm's length emotionally, or quickly glomming onto the men in a desperately dependent way. Either bipolar relationship state always chased men away fairly quickly.

The former cohort would give up on Aavani in frustration. The latter would flee from her in fear of being swallowed alive by her neediness. Sometimes, Aavani would alternate between the two extremes with the same man, eventually leaving him totally confused and exhausted.

However, her dark, haunting beauty provided her with a steady supply of men willing to try to navigate her emotional maze. This continued through all the years of working toward her doctorate and even after she began to work as an assistant professor at Fordham.

Her American roommates watched all of this with some amusement, but with growing dismay, recommending that she see a therapist. Aavani realized her problems with men probably stemmed from both the trauma of almost being sex-trafficked and the loss of her father at a young age.

She did not trust men and believed they would leave her or were just after her for sex. Or she felt a desperate need for a man in her life to fill the empty hole left by the early death of her father.

But she was still Indian enough that she was skeptical of the American, especially the New York, predilection for going to a psychotherapist for every personal life problem. Instead, she decided to consult with the pujari of the Brooklyn Hindu Temple which she had begun to attend regularly.

Aavani deeply respected and loved the sisters who rescued and raised her, and several times she came close to converting to Catholicism. Something always held her back. It seemed to be the memory of her mother's devotion to her Hindu faith and particularly her mother's deep bond with the Hindu goddesses, especially Devi. Aavani also did not want to lose touch with her Hindu roots and Indian culture. She felt very American, yet still very Indian.

After she moved out of the Sisters' house, she tried various Hindu centers in New York, finally settling on the Brooklyn Temple. She began meeting with its lead pujari, or priest, about her men problems. He actually recommended a few therapists he worked with, but then suggested she first take some time off and live in an ashram for a month to deepen her Hindu faith and have the time to think through her problems. He suggested the Haidakhandi Universal Ashram in Crestone, Colorado. Aavani agreed and arranged to spend a month there after the Spring semester.

Like Clare, Aavani quickly fell in love with Crestone, the mountains, the Valley, the temple, and the ashram community. Daily prayer and meditation in the temple before the statue of Devi brought her great peace. She felt she had come home. She thought about her problems with men a lot, but the urgency of finding answers about this gradually waned. It felt as if something else even more primal was filling the hole she had long felt inside. Her mother's fondly remembered devotion to Devi was rekindled within her and began to grow.

Aavani extended her stay at the ashram for another month. Then another month after that. After six months of extensions, she resigned from her position at Fordham, and decided to become a full-time member of the ashram. Eventually, she became its leader and main teacher. In time she also met a man, Pieter, a German Buddhist monk from the Zen Center, who she grew to trust and slowly allowed to grow close and intimate with her.

She neither pushed him away nor clung to him. She allowed the relationship to slowly ripen into a great love. They became soul companions, best friends, and lovers.

Aavani sometimes missed the vibrant, intense life of New York City, but she could never imagine leaving the quiet sanctuary of Crestone.

Chapter Seven

After crossing Poncha Pass and leaving the San Luis Valley, Clare and Aavani stop at the overlook park just above the valley of the Arkansas River, still in the central mountains of Colorado.

From the overlook, they can see all the way south to their Sangres, and all along the line of the Collegiate Peaks and the Sawatch Range stretching south to north from Mount Shavano to Mount Harvard and Mount Yale. Just across the valley from them is Mount Princeton, with its snow-capped main peak buttressed by two secondary peaks shrugging like giant, muscular shoulders on each side of the central peak.

Clare remarks to Aavani, "Princeton has always been a mystical mountain for me. It looks like God the Father pulling me toward him to wrap his arms around me in a cosmic embrace. I just love it here at the overlook. I could sit here for days, just soaking it in."

There is a long silence till Aavani speaks, "I see what you mean. I can feel it too. Except for me, Princeton feels female and I feel embraced by the divine Mother Goddess, the Earth mother."

Clare giggles softly, "Well, here we go again, Aavani, Hindu versus Catholic. Will the religious wars never cease?

I'm right, you're wrong. You're right, I'm wrong. Will these human divisions ever end?"

They both giggle knowing there is no real difference between them. Clare finally says, "All of us blind people are just describing a small fraction of the great elephant, aren't we?"

Aavani nods and smiles. Then they both look south to their mountains, the Sangres, to say goodbye. They notice for the first time a burgeoning cloud of smoke rising from a new forest fire on Methodist Mountain just above the town of Salida. It is still Spring, and yet the fire season is already starting. Clare and Aavani leave the overlook, turn east onto U.S. 285, heading toward Denver. After winding through a couple of small, open parks and around various rock formations, they round another bend and the vast expanse of South Park opens up before them.

Pulling off the main highway onto a gravel side-road—unbeknownst to them, the same spot where Mark experienced his flashbacks and panic attack a few days earlier—they sit in awe at the splendor that surrounds them.

The sky is intensely blue with occasional puffy, white clouds casting moving shadows onto the high, snow-covered mountains encircling the Park. The Park itself is an immense, open, high-altitude prairie, undulating 360 degrees—most of it treeless—to the borders of its enclosing mountains.

A small herd of antelope graze in the distance. A larger herd of cattle nearly surround their car. A lone coyote sniffs the ground intensely, hunting for prairie dogs. Back on U.S. 285, a steady stream of cars, SUVs, campers, and trucks head west, fleeing the crowds of Denver, intent on creating new, if smaller, crowds in the mountains.

Other than the human auto-traffic, the scene reminds Clare of the description of the Peaceable Kingdom of God described in the poetry of Isaiah, "The wolf will live with the lamb, the leopard will lay down with the goat, the calf and the lion and the yearling together; and a little child will lead them."

She recites this scripture to Aavani, who wonders, "What will happen to all of this beauty and harmony? Is it all threatened by what we have seen in our visions?"

Clare does not respond. They both sense an invisible, dark, foreboding cloud descending on them. The cloud weighs increasingly heavier as they descend from the mountains into the urban sprawl of Denver. The sudden transition from the mountains to the Great Plains and into the fast-paced swirl of Metro Denver has always been jolting and painful for Clare, like leaving a peaceful chapel and stepping out onto a loud, insanely busy New York street. It is even more painful today as a palpable atmosphere of apprehension and dread fills their little Subaru.

They drive through the suburbs of Denver, and out onto the great open plains of eastern Colorado and western Kansas on I-70, the mountains gradually disappearing behind them in the rearview mirror. They talk sporadically of their life and the people they love back in Crestone, but mainly they drive through the great emptiness of Kansas in silence. They are both aware of the coal-pitch gloom descending on them, enveloping them like an invisible weighted blanket.

They both decide not to comment on what they are feeling, sensing no words could dispel the growing spiritual darkness, mirrored by the gathering night shadows they drive into as the sun sets behind them on the open prairie.

They spend the night in a cheap motel just off I-70 in Junction City. Both Clare and Aavani have a restless night's sleep, disturbed by both the noises and smells of a nearby pork-packing factory and by another onslaught of nightmares about their visions. Their dreams are also infiltrated by the ominous thump-thump of heavy army helicopters taking off from nearby Fort Riley for night maneuvers. They both awake fatigued and irritable.

Over coffee and breakfast, their smartphones tell them the Missouri River is flooding ahead of them and threatening to close I-70 just west of Columbia, at the Missouri River bridge. They gulp down their breakfast, and rush to get back on the road to try to beat the flood and the highway closure. They agree Aavani should take the wheel because she is the faster driver.

Getting in on the driver's side of Clare's Subaru, Aavani jokes, "You Catholic nuns are awfully slow drivers. It must be because you learned how to drive in those cumbersome old habits. Must have gotten in your way of pushing the pedal to the metal. Me, I learned how to drive in India where everyone drives like bats out of hell. So, hold onto your wimple, sister, here we go!" as they roar up the on-ramp onto I-70 and quickly accelerate to a ninety-mile-an-hour cruising speed.

Clare makes the sign of the cross, looks at Aavani, and laughs.

When they reach Mid-Missouri, just west of the river-bluff wineries of Rocheport and the university town of Columbia, the interstate descends into a Missouri River floodplain, which has now become a broad lake. Traffic is down to one lane with walls of sandbags several feet high on either side, holding back the brown, silt-laden water on either side, some of it seeping onto the roadway itself. To the north, a line of black, grey, and white thunderheads threaded with frequent lightning threatens to add more water to the flood. Thunder reverberates through the flooded river valley, several times shaking Clare and Aavani's old Subaru.

Traffic comes to a complete halt in the middle of the floodplain while frantic highway workers scramble with Bobcats, forklifts, and hand shovels to shore up one of the walls of sandbags that is leaking and threatening to collapse. Clare and Aavani grow increasingly anxious that they might not make it through, as the minutes tick by.

After about forty-five minutes, a harried-looking, grizzled Mo-Dot worker walks up to their car to tell them the river is still rising rapidly, and they will probably have to close the interstate in the next hour. He seems to be a supervisor, because he is just watching the crews work to save the temporary levee.

Looking away from them at his leaking, almost-toppled-over sandbag wall, the obviously stressed highwayman starts talking and rambling absently as if in a trance, "This looks like it's going to be much worse than '93. I was here for that one too. I thought it couldn't have flooded any worse than that year. It was supposed to be a once-in-500-year flood. But here we go again. It's been raining nearly nonstop for three weeks now. These big storms keep jumping from one spot to another, from west, to north, to the east and then back to the west again. Even a big river like the Missouri can't handle all this water.

In the '93 flood the river scoured up an enormous amount of sand from the river bottom and dumped it on my fields. It practically turned my cornfields into sand dunes. Took me three years of bulldozing and restoring the soil before I could get the land back to production. Looks like it's going to happen again with this damn flood. I don't know if I can go through that again. I might just give up on my land and wait till I can retire from this frigging highway job. I don't know what the hell is happening to this world. Seems like the disasters are getting bigger and coming more often."

While they wait anxiously to see whether they are going to get through to St. Louis, Clare and Aavani chat and joke with the Mo-Dot supervisor, trying to cheer him and themselves up a bit, although they are feeling the same sense of foreboding he expressed, and are asking themselves the same question, *What the hell is going on?*

They are grateful and relieved when the traffic finally starts to move, and they can inch past the high sandbag walls and creep onto the narrow, four-lane bridge over the swollen Missouri River. Once past it, Aavani hits the accelerator and they are able to speed on toward St. Louis.

Clare makes the sign of the cross again. This time seriously giving thanks that they got through the flood. They barely make it in time. Thirty minutes later, Interstate-70 closes behind them. The high, dark clouds to the north and now to the east toward St. Louis foretell of more storms and rain to come.

Chapter Eight

While Clare and Aavani drive into another ferocious thunderstorm sweeping into St. Louis, Chooky—a marine biologist whose full Tlingit name is Chookaneidi—is aboard a trawler in Southeast Alaska studying the songs of humpback whales.

Chooky has a doctorate in marine biology and a masters in linguistics and is testing her theory that humpback songs constitute some sort of language. She has developed a computer program utilizing the latest advances in neural networks, a form of Artificial Intelligence (AI), that she hopes will be able to decipher some pattern or communication system in the humpbacks' eerie vocalizations.

As part of this research, Chooky has spent the last three weeks in the spectacular mountain- and forest-rimmed water-world of Southeast Alaska with her boyfriend, Woosh—whose full Tlingit name is Wooshketaan—aboard his fishing boat, the *Raven*.

Chooky and Woosh have known each other since childhood, growing up together in the tiny, remote coastal village of Pelican, Alaska. They became an item in high school and had been in and out of a relationship ever since. Now both thirty-three, they reconnected a year ago when Chooky returned to Alaska after being away in the Lower 48 for graduate school for six years.

Part of their bond is their shared Tlingit Indian heritage. Both feel they live in two worlds at once, the world of Tlingit myths and customs and the world of Western ways and beliefs. Because of her scientific and academic training, and her long time away from her roots, Chooky feels especially torn between these two worlds. Reconnecting with Woosh has helped her to begin re-grounding herself in her identity as a Tlingit. The Tlingit matrilineal family structure has also helped restore her sense of feminine power after fighting for years with the lingering patriarchy of American academia.

Their hometown, Pelican, is a magical place to be a child. A remote fishing village named after its founder's favorite fishing boat, it is built along a narrow shelf of land on the fjord-like Lisianski Inlet. Pelican's boardwalk and some of its buildings—including the fish processing plant, a few homes and the town's only restaurant—are perched over the water, atop the wharves extending out into the harbor. There the local fishing fleet of about two dozen fishing trawlers is moored. There is one lodge that attracts a few adventurous tourists, but most of Pelican's 222 inhabitants are connected in some way to the surrounding sea, and employed in catching its fish, mostly salmon and halibut.

The town is a self-contained world, bounded by the ocean, mountains, and almost-impenetrable temperate rainforest of Chichagof Island, one of the largest islands in the watery, mountainous wilderness of Southeast Alaska. The only way in or out is by boat or plane. Chichagof is situated just below the icy water entrance to Glacier Bay National Park and Preserve. The island has the highest population of bears per square mile of any place on Earth, many of them the fierce and unpredictable Alaska Brown Bear—which are actually oversized Grizzly bears pumped up on salmon-fueled steroids. There are many more bears than people on the island.

The bears regularly saunter through the town, terrifying the tourists. But there is actually a détente of sorts between the bears and the locals that reflects the pervasive atmosphere of harmony between nature and humanity. The bears and humans mostly give each other a wide berth and have learned how to live with each other. So, there are surprisingly few bear-human incidents in Pelican.

The only disturbance to the natural harmony on the Lisianski Inlet is the two large, barren scars on the otherwise heavily treed mountainsides across the inlet from town: open reddish wounds gouged by played-out goldmines.

Chooky and Woosh delighted in roaming widely all over this children's paradise. They were real free-range children, before there was such a concept. Sometimes, they rambled about in small gaggles of children. Often, it was just the two of them. Occasionally they explored alone, undeterred by the bears, wandering the woods pursuing various fantasy adventures. They fished and swam in the harbor or in the protected inlet behind their school. They walked the forested trails, and bush-wacked along the tumbling mountain stream that provided the town both fresh water and hydro-electric power.

Although they were from two of the only four Tlingit families in Pelican—the rest of the population were Caucasians of various sorts—they played freely with all of the other children, with little to no awareness of any differences in skin color or heritage.

Several times a year, they had the thrill of accompanying their fathers on their trawlers during fishing season. As they got older, they worked as crew on their fathers' boats, when they weren't occupied by school or by their other job, working together at the Lisianski Inlet Café, the combination restaurant and general store on the wharf overhanging the harbor.

Out on their fathers' boats they often sighted humpback whales spouting, spy-hopping, breaching, and feeding. On some occasions they were able to witness the extraordinary sight of the humpbacks hunting in coordinated groups, corralling shoals of fish with circles of bubbles, and then bursting to the surface underneath the ball of fish with their huge gaping mouths wide open.

Chooky and Woosh were often close enough to these humpback feeding eruptions that they would be drenched by the splash it caused or by the water the whales spouted as they surfaced. They both loved the thrill of being so close to these amazing, massive creatures. Other times they would encounter pods of orcas on the hunt, or dolphins, sea otters, bald eagles, osprey, and myriads of sea birds of all kinds. All this kindled a deep love and respect for nature, especially the sea and all of its creatures.

As they got older, their love for nature and exploring the outdoors together also kindled a love for each other. By eighth grade they were a local item, best friends, and childhood sweethearts. Pelican was a small pool from which to discover a mate, but Chooky and Woosh were so well-matched they might have found each other in a city of millions. But their paths would eventually diverge, and it would be many years before their love and the beauty of Southeast Alaska would draw them back together.

Because they lived in a largely white town, Chooky and Woosh's parents made every effort to ground them in their Tlingit identity and heritage. They regularly sent them by boat to spend weeks at a time with their grandparents in the all-Tlingit village of Hoonah on the other side of Chichagof Island. Tlingit is widely spoken in Hoonah, and so Chooky and Woosh were pretty much forced to learn their native language.

Their grandmothers taught them the Tlingit myths and stories, including the Tlingit creation story centered on the Raven-Creator mythology. They also wove the Russian Orthodox Christian teaching they grew up with into the Tlingit beliefs and traditions, fabricating a resilient and colorful rainbow coat of belief for their grandchildren to wear as they emerged into the wider world.

Their school was a thirty-student K-12 public school housed in a low-slung, modern brick building, one of the few brick structures in Pelican. It was situated on the back bay on the outskirts of town where silver salmon spawned in their thousands from late summer through the end of the first semester. Woosh was a bright, but indifferent student, more interested in fishing and hunting with his father or roaming the woods. Chooky loved school and showed a remarkable aptitude for science and mathematics.

One of her teachers, Kalle Raatikainen Jr, a descendant of one of the early Finnish settlers in Pelican, spotted Chooky's giftedness very early in grade school. He encouraged her math and science interest all the way through Grade 12. After graduation, he helped Chooky get a scholarship to the Marine Biology program at Boston University. Woosh stayed in Pelican working on his father's boat. He loved the life of an Alaskan fisherman too much to say yes when Chooky pleaded with him to go with her to Boston. Eventually, Woosh was able to save enough to buy his own boat, and went into business for himself with his own small crew of young Tlingit men.

This separation after high school was very difficult for Chooky and Woosh to navigate. Their relationship became a roller-coaster. When Chooky was away in Boston they would grow distant, and sometimes even break up. They would rekindle their relationship when she came home during the summers. Only then to break up again when Chooky left Pelican for the rest of the year. Woosh could not imagine dating anyone besides Chooky, although several local girls from Pelican and Hoonah certainly expressed an interest, and so he always waited for Chooky's return.

In contrast, Chooky dated a great deal and had several boyfriends during her years in Boston. She got fairly close to a couple of them, but then she would start to compare them to Woosh, find them wanting, and suddenly break it off, leaving the men bruised and confused. Despite their ups and downs, the spark between Chooky and Woosh sometimes flickered and dimmed, but never completely went out.

Their worst years came after she finished her doctorate in marine biology at BU and decided to study linguistics with Dr. Mario Gutierrez at Washington University in St. Louis. Woosh was devastated. He thought she would return to Alaska after her doctorate, and they could finally build a life together. When he found out she was not returning anytime soon, he ended their on-and-off relationship, and stopped talking to Chooky completely. He began spending almost all of his time on the water on his fishing boat, often alone, unsuccessfully trying to forget her.

Chooky went to Washington University—or as some St. Louisans pronounced it "Warsh U"—to further her research on humpback whale songs. In her doctoral dissertation she posited the theory that the songs constituted a language, and that there may be ways to decipher it. She adored Dr. Mario and enjoyed her studies at the university, but she found St. Louis a difficult adjustment.

Boston was a much larger, louder world than she was used to, but it was at least on the ocean. She could sometimes escape the noise of the big city and find solace and some sense of home at the beach or out on the ocean doing research. The two great rivers that come together at St. Louis, the Mississippi and the Missouri, were meager substitutes. She felt claustrophobic and homesick in this Midwest city in the center of the continent.

The university itself was a very cosmopolitan, diverse, and welcoming place. But she found native St. Louisans to be cordial and outwardly friendly, yet clubby, tribal, and difficult to really get close to. She could never understand St. Louisans' obsession with where you went to high school, and—despite St. Louis' French history—why they could not properly pronounce any of the many local French place names.

She also could not comprehend how a place so distant from any major bodies of water could be so oppressively humid. The only marine biology to be studied in St. Louis was swimming in the air. On some especially oppressive days she thought the 2020 climate change forecast of "truly dangerous heat and humidity" in the Mississippi river valley by 2040 had already come to pass. St. Louis looked like Cincinnati or Milwaukee, but it felt like a Louisiana bayou. She never felt at home or at ease in St. Louis.

As she finished her studies with Dr. Mario, she began to increasingly long for Southeast Alaska. Even more, she realized how much she missed Woosh, and decided to reach out to him. They began talking again long distance, and started to discuss a reunion, and how they might build a life together in Alaska. They dreamed about how Chooky could do her research aboard Woosh's trawler in between his fishing trips. They could merge their lives, Woosh helping Chooky pursue her research, and Chooky working as crew for Woosh's seasonal fishing ventures. Both would pursue their passions in an environment which they loved, Southeast Alaska, in the heart of the Tlingit homeland.

This became their plan. Both of them were anxious to start. It remained unsaid that they were also anxious it might not work. That they would discover their dreams were not compatible, and they would break up yet again. They wondered whether they had been separated too long. Or perhaps Chooky had been changed too much by her years in the white man's world of the Lower 48 and by her scientific and academic training.

Woosh also struggled with jealousy and insecurity about the boyfriends Chooky had in Boston and in St. Louis. Could a small-town Indian boy, a fisherman—not a high-powered academic—compete with them, and win Chooky back? He was doubtful.

Chooky had no doubt about her love for Woosh, and that he was superior to any man she had met in the Lower

48, but she had a hard time convincing Woosh about this. Chooky's own struggle was her uncertainty that she could accept a life in a world where Nature was much more expansive, but the human world was so much smaller. She had come to love the excitement and diversity of a large city like Boston, despite her need to periodically escape its busyness and noise pollution.

Now she wondered whether she could readjust to living in an area of very small towns, most of which—including the state capital and largest city of the Southeast, Juneau (population 32,000)—were only accessible by boat or by air.

They both felt they had recaptured their deep bond from when they were young and carefree back in Pelican, but they also had a great deal of fear, largely unspoken, that these issues could yet pull them apart again.

They were a passionate couple. As with many such couples, their passion would not infrequently lead to heated arguments. Then their history of break-ups, Woosh's insecurity, and Chooky's struggle to return to Tlingit life would flare up.

In the worst fights, Woosh would accuse Chooky of becoming "way too white" for him and for her family, and of abandoning her Tlingit culture. Chooky would rage back, call Woosh "narrow-minded and provincial" and mockingly sing the line, "There's a world out there, Barnaby!" from *Hello Dolly.*

At such times, Woosh thought the old Tlingit tradition of arranged marriage might make better sense than a Western relational system based on attraction, passion, and unpredictable emotions. But then their old bond of friendship and their renewed passion for each other would help them weather the latest storm, and they would continue to dream of a future together.

Chapter Nine

On the day Clare and Aavani arrive in St. Louis, Chooky and Woosh are searching for humpbacks on the broad, open waters of Prince Frederick Sound, surrounded by coastal mountains, forests, glaciers, and vast snowfields. It is an incredibly rich marine environment and one of the favorite feeding grounds for hundreds of humpbacks.

Chooky is listening to humpbacks singing to each other through the hydrophones she deployed, and is watching the sound patterns or spectrograms on her computer, trying to discern some sort of systematic, linguistic pattern. As she explained to Woosh, she is looking for the Rosetta Stone of humpback language.

She listens all day long to the haunting moans, grunts, blasts, and shrieks of the songs, some at very high frequency, some at ultra-low frequency. The same song, with minor variations, is sung over and over by all of the humpback males in the area.

There are several active singing whales Chooky is following, but in the late afternoon one's vocalizations seem especially loud and frequent, almost frantic. The whale sounds in distress, but Chooky cannot discern what it might be saying.

As she listens and watches her computer screen, a humpback whale surfaces right beside the boat. It is entangled in a web of crab traps and attached lines. Weighted down by several hundred pounds of these traps and ropes, the whale struggles to swim properly or even stay afloat. Hundreds of yards of line are wrapped around its tail and torso, and thick rope is coiled tightly around its snout, making it impossible for it to feed.

Chooky and Woosh immediately see that the humpback is in serious distress.

They quickly assemble their gear and jump into their Zodiac, racing over to the humpback. Diving into the water with the whale, they begin painstakingly cutting the heavy lines with their fishing knives. While they work to free it, the whale stops its struggle, and lies placidly on top of the water, breathing slowly, obviously exhausted from the struggle to swim entrapped in the nets and ropes.

The humpback focuses its left eye on Chooky and seems to plead for help. Chooky feels as if the whale is looking deep into her soul, and she is looking deep into its soul. She senses a deep connection with the whale that startles her. She has been studying whales for years, yet has never before felt a personal bond with her objects of study.

Chooky and the whale lock eyes for several minutes. She is mesmerized and feels as if in a pleasant trance, a feeling she has not felt since childhood when she took part in Tlingit dance and prayer ceremonies.

It takes hours for Chooky and Woosh to cut the fishing gear slowly, delicately off the whale's giant body. They have to be very careful not to cut into its skin. As they are untangling and cutting, Chooky notices the whale is a male, probably one of her singers. A few times it looks like the whale is not going to make it.

When his breathing becomes slow and labored, Chooky talks softly to the humpback, encouraging him and pleading with him to hang on. She even sings to him, hoping that chanting Tlingit ceremonial songs will soothe and calm him. He seems to respond, especially to the songs, and his breathing becomes more even and relaxed. The humpback's eyes follow every move they make as they cut the lines and traps off his body.

Eventually, they succeed in freeing the whale. Once free, the humpback swims in what seems like joyous circles around the trawler for several minutes. He swims back to Chooky and Woosh, who are still in the water, gently nudging them with his snout, as if thanking them. Then the whale slowly swims away and dives underwater, leaving Chooky and Woosh awestruck.

The exhausted couple return to their boat. Chooky checks her computer and sees there is one humpback vocalizing very close to the boat. She assumes this is the humpback she has just rescued. At first, her computer registers his song in the usual indecipherable waves, peaks, and valleys on the screen. The Artificial Intelligence (AI) software kicks in, attempting to discern some linguistic pattern as programmed. However, once again, it cannot produce any language sequences from the humpback's singing. Chooky is frustrated, sensing another dead-end in her research.

Then something new and startling happens. Her computer, with the aid of the AI component, begins turning the sound patterns into words. These words appear on her computer screen, like the hidden lyrics of a mysterious song:

> "Thank you for freeing me from those ropes. I was close to giving up. I am very grateful. Now I am going to do you a favor, because I can see some of your kind are good. You have stopped hunting us, and you try to rescue us when we are in trouble. Mother Gaia has told us not to reveal to any humans what I am about to tell you. So, you must speak to no one, except for the one whom Mother has chosen, concerning what I am about to reveal to you.

Mother has spoken to my people and to all of her creatures in all of our languages and ways of knowing. Mother tells us she loves her human children, but her human children have greatly saddened her by their careless actions and are threatening the end of too many of her other creatures, even threatening Mother herself. So, with great sadness and increasing anger, Mother is turning against her human children, and is contemplating extinguishing them from the face of the Earth.

She would do this only to save her other children and herself. She has commanded us and all creatures, and all of the forces of Nature, to prepare for battle against you. Some creatures have even agreed to fight to their own death, offering their lives for Mother. If she chooses to do this, Mother will turn all of her might against you. There will be a mass human extinction. You will be wiped off the face of the Earth. Mother will save a remnant of all of her other creatures, except for you humans.

It is nearly too late, but I offer this warning to you, because I felt your love today as you gently freed me. Go in peace."

The words are repeated three times on Chooky's computer screen, each time accompanied by the haunting sound of the humpback singing to her. Then her instruments and computer go completely silent and dark. Chooky sits stunned and speechless, unable to comprehend what has just happened. She does not know what to think of the message.

It is likely that it is just some bizarre, random computer glitch, or even some clown pranking my program, that created these words, she tells herself. *It likely has nothing to do with the humpback's song. But where could such an explicit message have come from? How could it have been produced from her programming? Did the AI go nuts on her? But there was nothing random about the message. It was crazy, yet very specific—and ominous.*

Chooky saves and prints the message. Then, leaving her below-deck science station, she climbs up to the deck to look at the mountains and the sea, and breathes in the pure air of Alaska, trying to clear her mind and sort out scientifically what just happened.

She had sometimes joked with fellow marine biologists that if she did discern a language in the humpback song, since male whales did most of the singing, it would probably simply translate to something like, "Hey, guys, did you catch that hot, fertile whale babe over in Icy Strait?" Or maybe, "Whoah! Did you fellows see Sam miss that shoal of cod in the last bubble feed? He was clowning around as usual. Just you wait. He'll be hungry when we don't eat for a few months in Hawaii. Then he'll start whining and complaining. Guard your krill, boys, Sam'll be trying to steal it."

She thought that most likely the whale songs would translate into mating arias, love songs, the males crooning over and over to the females to win their attention. Or maybe the songs were a form of humpback karaoke, all the males singing to each other the same song, just for the fun and socialization it brought. It seemed to serve some communal bonding function, but what exactly?

It was certainly some expression of humpback culture, as she described it, like all of the males performing a sing-along rock concert or opera with the females listening attentively in the audience.

There were a lot of theories about the songs, but she had never expected anything like this. She believed humpbacks were quite intelligent and had some kind of rudimentary language, yet she had never conceived that they could structure language into concepts, paragraphs, and sentences, much less deliver such a specific message.

So, this message can't be real, she thought, *It must be an artifact of some glitch in my AI program. Can you imagine if I reported this to my fellow marine biologists? I would be laughed right out of the profession!*

Woosh is at the helm on the bridge deck above her. Chooky is undecided whether to go up and show the message to him. There has to be a rational explanation. All her scientific training tells her so. But her Tlingit upbringing and culture makes her wonder. Weren't there stories from the ancestors that humpbacks and other creatures sometimes spoke to the shamans of her tribe? But she wasn't a shaman. She was a scientist and had long ago decided these stories were just entertaining fables from the past. She decides not to tell Woosh.

He won't be able to understand all of the scientific ramifications, and will probably jump to hasty conclusions, based on his love for the old Tlingit stories. I'm not ready for that, she thinks to herself.

As planned, they turn south, leaving Prince Frederick Sound, and begin cruising back to their home port of Petersburg, Alaska. When they arrive the next morning, Chooky can finally access the internet, and starts to catch up on the news of the world. She is flabbergasted by what she learns. As she reads the startling news reports, she sees the first plumes of smoke blowing down the coast from the Sitka volcano.

Miami Herald: "There have been simultaneous outbreaks of toxic algae in several places around the globe. Scientists are alarmed and puzzled. The red tide algae bloom has returned to the Southwest coast of Florida, this time in an even more toxic form. Hundreds are sickened; dozens have died from its toxic fumes. It's now reported to be heading up the coast toward Tampa.

Blue-green algae has quickly spread over the whole of Lake Erie. The water supplies of Toledo, Cleveland, and Buffalo have had to be shut down. Hundreds are sickened and dozens have died. Dozens of dogs have also been sickened or died from swimming in the lake. An immense algae bloom has also invaded most of the Baltic Sea, impacting Russia, Finland, Sweden, Norway, and Denmark, threatening their fisheries and coastal populations. A similar bloom of toxic algae covers the whole southwest coastline of South Africa and Namibia."

BBC World News: "Huge clouds of voracious locusts have suddenly appeared, as if from nowhere, and are devouring vital grain crops in several spots on the globe at the same time. The Midwest and Plain states of the U.S; Kenya, Uganda, Sudan, and Somalia in Africa; as well as Argentina, Brazil, and China are all reporting the sudden invasion of huge, dark clouds of locusts descending on their croplands. The U.N.'s World Food Programme is warning that a widespread, maybe even worldwide, famine is a likely result of these unprecedented locust swarms.

Scientists interviewed by the BBC report that it is only in the last few years that science has understood how individual, usually solitary, grasshoppers are driven by environmental factors to transform into these all-devouring hordes of millions of locusts. It is now widely believed that global warming is contributing to the more frequent development of these extraordinary, devastating locust swarms.

Dr. Otis Jack Cunningham, professor of entomology at Oxford University, commented, "It is truly amazing, even to us bugologists, how these lowly, lonely grasshoppers transform, seemingly overnight and out of sight, into such ferocious monsters capable of such rapid mass destruction of our food supplies. It is the insect equivalent of Frankenstein; except that in this case, millions of

Frankensteins are let loose on the world at once. I shiver to think that this will be happening more often in the future."

Miami Herald: "On the same day the toxic algae bloom reappeared on the Gulf Coast, there are more than 100 reports of fatal shark attacks on swimmers, surfers, and fishermen in the Bahamas, up and down the East and West coasts of the U.S., and the beaches of Australia, South Africa, Tahiti, and Hawaii. This one-day total of over a hundred fatal shark attacks is shocking, since the global average is only four per year.

The attacks are not by solo sharks, which is the usual pattern, but by sharks that appear to be actually hunting humans in packs of three to ten, sometimes with several different species of sharks involved in the same attacks. Shark experts are saying the large number of worldwide attacks and fatalities in one day, and the involvement of several sharks at once, are both highly unusual and unprecedented. Dr. Michael P. Eaton, a marine biologist from the Woods Hole Oceanographic Institution in Massachusetts, had this comment:

> "I am shocked at the very high number of fatal shark attacks reported in one day around the world. I am at a complete loss at this time to explain it. This is extremely unusual. Unprecedented. It is also highly unusual that groups of sharks, which we call a "shiver" of sharks, are doing the attacking. Almost all attacks on humans in the past have been done by solo sharks. My research team and I will do our utmost to figure out what might have caused this incredible outbreak of attacks."

In one such multi-shark attack, a young American woman, Victoria Robbins, 21, of Point Richmond, California, was savagely attacked and killed by three sharks while snorkeling with her family in Half-Moon Bay. The sharks bit Victoria on the arms, legs, and buttocks, detaching her right arm. Victoria was brought to shore and pronounced dead at a local hospital. Ms. Robbins was a communication studies major at Santa Clara University in Santa Clara, CA. Her family described her as "An amazing daughter who threw herself into life with great passion. She was a devoted animal lover and climate change advocate, who had just recently gotten involved with environmental activism. We will greatly miss her joyous and infectious spirit."

NPR News: "In a recently published peer-reviewed study, U.S. volcanologists studying the Yellowstone Caldera, a supervolcano located in the world-famous Yellowstone National Park, report that there are increasing signs the massive supervolcano under the park is waking up. They cite evidence of frequent swarms of minor earthquakes, increased geyser activity, especially the recent revival of Mammoth Geyser, and bulging and swelling in the ground below the geo-thermals and in other areas of the park.

The scientists warn that past explosive eruptions of Yellowstone have caused incredible destruction throughout much of the North American continent, especially downwind of the park.

Based on data about past eruptions, scientists estimate as many as 100,000 deaths could be expected along with a massive die-out of many species and vital crops downwind of a possible explosion of Yellowstone's supervolcano. The eruption would very quickly spread a layer of ash 3 to 10 feet thick as far as 1,000 miles from the park.

Explosions from volcanic super-eruptions have been some of the most extreme events in the Earth's history, ejecting enormous volumes of material—at least 1,000 times more than the 1980 eruption of Mount St. Helens— with the potential to cause massive destruction and death, and even alter the planet's climate.

Dr. Richard Kerckhoff, the lead volcanologist of the Yellowstone research team, reports that the last major eruption was 630,000 years ago.

"Since the eruptions seem to occur once every 1.5 million years, we thought we had up to 900,000 years before another super-eruption would occur. However, this recent recorded activity suggests the pattern may be changing, and another super-eruption may come much sooner, although we cannot forecast when that might occur."

KOMO 4 News – Seattle: "The mystery of the deaths of 51 beekeepers in the Seattle area in the past week may now have been solved. A spokesperson for the Washington State Department of Agriculture has announced the discovery of Asian Giant Hornets, so-called "Murder Hornets," in several areas in the state. This invasive species is responsible for 30-50 human deaths a year in Japan. Its sting carries far more toxin than any native bees, hornets, or wasps.

The spokeswoman said she did not know how the hornets arrived in Washington but speculated they may have "hitchhiked" on ships or planes from Asia. Previously, law enforcement authorities were completely stymied in explaining the large number of deaths. They had theorized that either there was a serial killer obsessed with beekeepers, or that the bees of their own hives had turned against them and attacked them. There was no evidence for either theory. Now they are saying the culprit is most likely the Murder Hornets. Autopsies are now being performed on some of the deceased beekeepers to see whether their bodies show signs of fatal levels of Murder Hornet venom."

The Guardian: "Scientists are baffled by incidents of orcas ramming sailing boats along the Spanish and Portuguese coasts. In the last two months, from southern to northern Spain, sailors have sent distress calls after worrying encounters. Two boats lost part of their rudders, at least one crew member suffered bruising from the impact of the ramming, and several boats sustained serious damage.

The latest incident occurred on Friday afternoon just off A Coruña on the northern coast of Spain. Halcyon yachts were ferrying a 36-foot sailboat to the U.K. when an orca rammed its stern at least 15 times, according to Pete Green, the company's managing director. The boat lost steering and was towed into port to assess its damage.

On August 30th, a French-flagged vessel radioed the coastguard to say it was "under attack" from killer whales. Later that day, a Spanish naval yacht, *Mirfak*, lost part of its rudder after an encounter with orcas ramming them under the stern of the boat.

Nick Giles was motor-sailing alone when he heard a horrific bang "like a sledgehammer," saw his wheel "turning with incredible force," disabling the steering as his 34-foot Moody yacht spun 180 degrees. He felt the boat lift up, and said he was pushed around without steering for 15 minutes by a pod of orcas.

The Spanish maritime authorities warned vessels to "keep a distance" from pods of orcas. But reports from sailors around the strait throughout July and August suggest this may be difficult—at least one pod appears to be pursuing boats in behavior that scientists agree is "highly unusual" and "concerning."

It is too early to understand what is going on, but it might indicate stress in a population that is endangered.

On July 29th, off Cape Trafalgar, Victoria Morris was crewing a 46-foot delivery boat that was surrounded by nine orcas. The cetaceans rammed the hull for over an hour, spinning the boat 180 degrees, disabling the engine, and breaking the rudder, as they communicated with loud whistling. It felt, she said, "totally orchestrated."

Earlier that week, another boat in the area reported a 50-minute encounter; the skipper said the force of the ramming "nearly dislocated the helmsman's shoulder."

After her last experience, Morris is a little jumpy, but, as a science graduate with plans to study marine biology, she is concerned for this vulnerable population of orcas and interested to learn more. She'd just prefer not to get too close a view next time."

As a marine biologist, Chooky is astonished by the reported incidents of orcas attacking boats off the coast of Spain and the multi-shark attacks in so many places around the world. She realizes these events happening all together are highly unlikely. It doesn't make sense scientifically for these disconnected, widespread incidents to occur almost simultaneously in multiple places around the world. Rationally, she believes all of these events must be random and unrelated.

Or are they really random, she wonders?

She turns on her computer and reads the message from the humpback again. She immediately leaves her science station below deck, and rushes to the top deck with her laptop, barging breathlessly through the door to the bridge to show Woosh the message from the humpback, as well as all of the strange, ominous news stories.

Chapter Ten

Sr. Clare and Aavani are staying at the Provincial House of the Madames of the Sacred Heart with Clare's old friend, Sr. Helen McLaughlin, in the trendy Central West End neighborhood of St. Louis. The Provincial House is an old, three-story red brick mansion built in 1904, at the time of the St. Louis World's Fair—an event St. Louisans still recall in nostalgic detail as the last time St. Louis was considered a great city.

Sr. Helen has been holding court in one of the elegant old parlors, entertaining Clare and Aavani with hilarious stories of her dual ministry with St. Louis sex workers on odd days, and children as a grade-school counselor on even days. Sometimes she would forget which day she was on and use very inappropriate language, learned from the prostitutes, in the middle of a teachers' meeting.

It has been raining almost nonstop for three days by the time they are able to schedule a meeting with Pastor Mark. The Missouri-Mississippi Meramec River basins are being inundated. Pastor Mark agrees to see them, although the women sounded a little mysterious and evasive about the purpose of the meeting. He did not meet either of them in Crestone but assents to meet with them out of professional courtesy.

He thinks the woman from the ashram will be alright with his being gay and a pastor. But he wonders about the Catholic nun, given what the Catholic Church teaches about homosexuality. He feels strangely apprehensive about meeting with them, almost a feeling of dread, but he chalks it up to his uncertainty about the Catholic nun. He doesn't know they are aware of his meditation meltdown, as he now calls it.

Mark is still unsure what to make of his visionary experience. He is in the midst of discerning its meaning with his psychotherapist. Their working theory is that it was some kind of hallucinatory flashback related to the shooting at his church. He knows he has PTSD and has had direct flashbacks of the mass shooting before, but he wonders how his Crestone experience could be connected to that. Both are similarly horrendous, yet somehow what happened in Crestone feels different. Mark thinks to himself, *Maybe I have just seen too many horror and disaster movies? Or maybe the trauma of my childhood and my coming out is coming back to haunt me?*

Mark Krummanocker grew up in a strict German farm family in Southwest Illinois, the second of three children. His parents had abandoned their traditional Lutheran faith, and joined a small fundamentalist, evangelical Church just before Mark was born. The bible, as their church interpreted it, became their parenting manual.

Mark became aware around the age of seven that he was different. He wasn't interested in sports like the other boys or like his older brother, Greg, who at ten was already becoming a local sports phenom. He wasn't interested in girls either. He started to notice, even at seven years old, that he was attracted to other boys.

Mark was horrified, confused, and deeply ashamed to discover this. He already knew what his parents would think. Eventually, he learned what his church and the Bible taught—or at least what he was told it taught—about this sort of "abomination" as well.

He kept his feelings well hidden, sometimes even from himself. He fought the feelings whenever he developed a crush on a boy in his class or at church, but he could never make them go away. He knew God knew he was different, and that God disapproved, and must hate him for it.

His father clearly favored his brother, Greg, and was less than happy with how Mark was turning out. Uncomfortable with Mark's demeanor and interests, his father pushed Mark into sports, at which Mark failed miserably. He told him he should be more like his older brother. He lectured him on being a man and scolded him that he was not more masculine.

Mark got the message: his father hated him for who he was, just like God. Mark tried to live up to his father's expectations, sometimes harshly delivered, but he always felt he failed the test for masculinity. He concluded there was something deeply screwed-up about himself, and that he could not change it. It, he, was hopeless. He grew deeply ashamed of himself and lived in constant fear that his secret would come out, and he would be discovered for the defective, sinful miscreant he must be.

Over and over, Mark tried to force himself to be straight. When the attraction for men intensified at the onset of puberty, he purposely started to make friends with the girls in his class. In high school and college, he episodically dated girls he met, but nothing romantic ever developed. He even had sex with a few of them, but the only way it worked was if he fantasized that his female partner was a man. This made him feel even more ashamed and left him with the sense that he was somehow being unfaithful to the girls he slept with. He made a lot of good friends among these young women, but no girlfriends.

His parents, especially his father, worried about there being no girlfriend in sight, and would frequently suggest this or that local girl as a potential partner. This just intensified the pressure and the shame Mark already felt. When he felt his worst, and he was old enough to drive, he would secretly act on his homosexual attraction with anonymous encounters in a public park or a gay bathhouse over in St. Louis, a hundred miles away.

For a brief time, he would feel better, and sense that this life was closer to being right for him, but the shame would quickly return. He would end up feeling even more depressed than when he started. Then, he would shut down his emotions and suppress his sexual desires once again. The circle would close and he would be left even more desperate and alienated from himself.

During his freshman year of college at the University of Missouri–St. Louis, his occasional forays for anonymous sex in the park and at bathhouses became more frequent. He would try desperately to stop, and at first he could for a couple of weeks. He would binge on sex for a couple of weeks, and then totally white-knuckle abstain for a couple more. Only to repeat this binge-purge cycle again. By his junior year, his secret sex life was completely out of control. He was vaguely aware that he might have a sex addiction but was terrified to admit it to himself or to seek help.

Like a slow-growing cancerous tumor, his sexual compulsion had been growing deep inside him since he was a child, fed by the secrecy and shame he felt about his sexuality. Now it was erupting into his consciousness after it had had already metastasized into many areas of his life, affecting even his studies—and he was now powerless to stop it.

Mark's solution to this conundrum was to begin studies after college to become a minister, a decision that arose from both a spiritual sense of being called and as an unconscious plan of escape. His parents were enormously pleased and relieved. Now, they believed, Mark would not fall into the pit of perversion they had secretly feared. Now, he would be saved.

Mark attended New Covenant Seminary, a conservative Christian seminary in the tony St. Louis suburb of Frontenac, not so affectionately known by the black maids who worked in its numerous mini-mansions as "Front 'n Back."

He excelled at his studies and became absorbed in his biblical and theological courses. He became kind of a star at the seminary, admired and respected by both his professors and fellow students. This affirmation and his academic success provided him some modicum of inner peace. He had found his niche. He believed he had finally found his life's purpose and a genuine source of personal worth.

He still did not know how to reconcile his homosexual attraction with all of this, particularly with the biblical interpretations he was learning from his professors. But the intensity of his feelings subsided for a time, and he acted on them less often. Although deep inside he knew better, he hoped this was a sign that maybe God would rescue him, and somehow make him straight—or at least a little less gay.

He kept this all under lock and key in his inner vault of shameful secrets. He enjoyed being looked up to and well-liked at Covenant Seminary. However, he knew that would all change, and his ordination would be blocked, if his secret ever came out. He lived with constant dread of being discovered for who he really was.

After ordination Mark joined the ministry staff of a St. Louis mega-church, New Destiny, a non-denominational evangelical church similar to his parents', but much larger. He was a gifted preacher, and rapidly advanced to become the youngest member of the preaching team. He kept his secret well-hidden from the church, although some wondered why he was not married or even dating. A few suggested that perhaps he had been graced with a special call to celibacy "for the sake of the Kingdom" as scripture refers to it.

Mark himself came to think that celibacy was the key to controlling his sexuality, and that celibacy was what God was asking of him. So, he worked even harder to ignore and suppress his sexual feelings and attractions. At times he was successful. And then his sexual feelings and desire for a partner would become so intense he could not stop himself, and he would compulsively seek out another anonymous sexual encounter, now usually in the woods or public restrooms of Forest Park, the expansive central park of St. Louis.

Mark returned home from these desperate forays with deep remorse and intensified shame. He got down on his knees, pleading with God to forgive him and remove this "thorn of the flesh" and change him. Sometimes, he felt forgiven, but never changed. He was still gay. His sex addiction was resurrecting again and dragging him back to his old binge-purge cycle.

For a time, he would be highly promiscuous; then, he would revert to being shame-filled, emotionally shutdown, and sexually anorexic, desperately attempting to completely deny and avoid anything sexual. He could only manage this purge phase for a few weeks, and then he would swing back to sexually binging again.

He hated himself more than ever, and believed, despite his success at his ministry, that God must hate him more too. His own homophobia had turned into homo-self-hate and an intense terror of God's judgement.

This pattern continued for the first three years of his ministry. It began to change one day when he met Simon at Herbie's in the Central West End of St. Louis, a high-end restaurant which morphed into a gay bar after the diners left for the evening. Mark was eating alone, as he often did, finishing up his Beef Wellington as the restaurant began its nightly transformation.

He was getting ready to leave when he spotted Simon at the bar. There was an instant attraction. Simon was tall, blonde, and blue-eyed; his lean, muscled body, obviously gym-hewn beneath his tight-fitting shirt. Their eyes met and, to Mark's surprise—because he couldn't imagine such a gorgeous man being attracted to him—Simon came over to Mark's table and sat down.

They talked into the wee hours. They soon found out they were very dissimilar, and yet somehow their different pieces seemed to fit into one remarkable puzzle. Mark was out of shape and a bit lumpy; Simon was as athletic as Mark's brother, Greg. Mark's mind was well-wired for literature, the humanities, and especially biblical studies and theology; Simon was left-brained logical, mathematical, and scientific. Mark was a Christian pastor. Simon was an agnostic research physician at the nearby Washington University School of Medicine. Somehow, they quickly felt a bond that defied these differences.

That night Simon invited Mark to his condo in the Park Plaza tower just a few blocks away from Herbie's, and they had sex. For the first time in his life Mark felt whole. Lying in Simon's arms, he felt he had come home to a house which he had vaguely imagined, but never believed really existed. The next day he had some guilt, but did not ask God's forgiveness. Mark and Simon began seeing each other as frequently as their full schedules would allow. They were in love.

This was simply marvelous for Simon, and equally marvelous—but not so simple—for Mark. He didn't know how to reconcile what he was feeling for Simon with what he believed as a Christian. He certainly couldn't square it with his role at his Church and with the ministry he loved.

Their love would have to remain a secret and be kept in a hidden compartment of his now-even-more-divided life. He sometimes thought he had to end the relationship with Simon, but he could never bring himself to do it. He felt too good and too much in love to pull the plug.

He increasingly thought, *How can anything that feels so good, supposedly be so bad? How can God, who is supposed to be love, not want me to have the wondrous love I experience with Simon?*

About six months into the relationship, Mark's compartmentalized life was blown wide open.

David, one of the other ministers from his Church, was cycling in Forest Park when he spotted Mark and Simon together holding hands as they walked down the hill alongside the cascading fountain below the 1904 World's Fair Pavilion. He stopped and stared to make sure it was Mark.

David had always wondered about Mark and had also long been jealous of Mark's gifts for preaching, being himself significantly less than eloquent. He reported what he saw to the head pastor, Reverend Peter Davis, who authorized an investigator to look into Mark's private life.

When the investigator reported to Rev. Davis that it appeared Mark was in a homosexual relationship with an openly gay man, Dr. Simon LeClerc, the pastor called a meeting of the board of elders. The elders were scandalized and incensed. It was decided that the pastor would publicly expose Mark's sin from the pulpit during the next Sunday service.

It was Mark's turn to preach. His parents were in attendance that Sunday to hear their son's message. As Mark started to walk across the sanctuary toward his usual preaching spot on the top step at the head of the main aisle, Rev. Davis walked up from a pew in the congregation and blocked his path. The pastor then turned around and addressed the congregation in a grave voice.

"Every sin is grievous and offends God. But when a pastor sins it is especially grievous, and when that sin is a perversion of God's plan for mankind, it greatly offends the Lord. Such sins must be called out and condemned so that the flock may not be led astray."

Turning to face Mark, he directs his preaching to him, "Pastor Mark, you are living in the sin of homosexuality, an abomination against the Lord and a heinous aberration of God's plan for sexuality and family life. The bible condemns these acts. In the name of the Lord Jesus, I condemn these acts. But, as scripture says, 'God is slow to anger and rich in mercy.' Mark, I implore you! Repent and renounce your sin, and you will be forgiven. If you do not repent, and disown your homosexual life, I must remove you from the pastoral team, and expel you at once from this church."

Walking closer and facing him head-on, Pastor Davis continues, "Mark, we need your answer now. Will you repent, and allow us to pray over you for deliverance from this evil?"

Stunned by this surprise intervention, Mark looks at Pastor Davis and then turns to look at his parents' shocked faces. Tears begin to well in his eyes, and yet they appear steely and resolute behind the tears. He takes a couple of deep breaths, looks up as if in prayer, and in a voice trembling with grief and fury, begins to speak, "Peter, I know your love for the Lord and for this congregation. I know your devotion to the Word. I know you are doing what you think God wants of you. But the only thing I can renounce is your narrowmindedness and ignorance. I cannot renounce the love I have come to experience with my partner, Simon.

This is the love I have asked God for my whole life. I believe now it is God who has given me this love, and that he blesses it. It says in First John: 'God is love, and he who abides in love, abides in God and God in him.' God abides in this love I have been gifted with. How can I repent of what I believe is of God? If I renounce this, I would be renouncing the Lord himself and disowning who, I now realize, I truly am. This is who God has created me to be. So, no, Peter, I will not repent loving someone wonderful like Simon."

Mark turns to the congregation and silently bows to them. He looks at his parents. His mother is sobbing while his father glares at him. Mark begins to walk down to them, and then thinks better of it, instead pivoting and walking out of the sanctuary to the parking lot—never to return.

Despite his brave words in church, Mark is devastated by this public outing. He is quickly defrocked and excommunicated by the church's leadership council. He loses the ministry he so loves and the church community he cherishes. Most of the church, even his friends, now shuns him. His parents refuse to see him and stop talking to him. Only his youngest sister, Andrea—and, of course, Simon—continue to support him.

Stripped of almost all that he holds dear, Mark once again fights against being consumed by shame or paralyzed with fear. Something deep inside tells him that what he said from the sanctuary that day is the truth. *This is who I am, and who the Lord has made me to be. How can I be anything other?* These thoughts sustain him in the midst of his grief. He grows more determined to never be false to himself or abandon himself ever again.

Simon encourages Mark to get professional help to deal with the trauma and grief of being forcibly outed by the church. Mark admits to Simon that despite his love and their wonderful sex, he still struggles with a compulsion to act out with anonymous sex.

Simon's professional network surfaces the name of Fr. Patrick Phelan, a Jesuit priest psychologist at St. Louis University, one of the few therapists in town who is a CSAT, a Certified Sexual Addiction Therapist, specializing in both trauma and sex addiction. Mark readily agrees to begin therapy with him and starts to attend SCA—Sexual Compulsives Anonymous, a 12-Step group for sex addiction—which meets at a midtown Episcopal church. He is amazed and relieved to discover there are so many others suffering from the same compulsions as he.

Accustomed to being part of a Christian community, Mark seeks solace in a congregation he had heard about but had always been afraid to attend. He joins the Metropolitan Church, housed in an old neo-Gothic, formerly Catholic Church in South St. Louis. Metro is an inclusive, affirming Christian church noted for its outreach to the LGTBQ community, and led by pastors who are open and public about their own sexual orientations.

Mark feels he has found his spiritual home. He loved his ministry at New Destiny, but the church itself had never felt like a true dwelling place for his soul. Metropolitan is a spiritual sanctuary where he is accepted, and can worship God in congruence and truth. After a year there, he is invited to join the ministry team, and begins preaching again. He is overjoyed to once again be proclaiming the Gospel of Jesus, now in the Spirit of Jesus' love for all humanity.

Two years later, he is invited to become the head pastor of Metropolitan.

When the Supreme Court makes same-sex marriage legal, Mark and Simon are married at Metropolitan by a close lesbian friend of Mark's on the ministry team. For the first time, Mark feels whole and at peace with himself and with God. He believes he is finally free and safe from the homophobia and homo-hatred he had directed against himself, and had received from his family and his former church.

Until the day of the shooting.

Chapter Eleven

In Petersburg, Alaska, aboard the *Raven*, Chooky shows the humpback's message to Woosh.

He silently reads it over and over.

"Oh, my God!" he finally blurts out, "What do you think of this?"

Chooky looks away for a moment, then back toward Woosh.

"At first, I thought it was just some bizarre computer anomaly, but then I started reading all of these news stories and wondered if something strange—but real—is going on here."

Chooky then shows the news stories to Woosh. He quickly reads the accounts of strange, unexpected events all over the world, "I see what you mean. These events could be related to the humpback's message."

Chooky responds, "But I think that there must be a scientific explanation for all of this. We don't even have proof yet that whales have a language, much less that they are delivering messages to humans from Mother Earth. Something must have happened to my computer program. Maybe a virus? Maybe I was hacked by some weird nerd somewhere with a strange sense of humor? And these news events have to be just random. There can't be any logical, scientific connection between them."

Woosh is more inclined than Chooky to believe the whale's message is real. He reminds her of the many stories told by the Tlingit elders about messages and visions from humpback whales, killer whales, ravens, and bears. Tlingit shamans frequently reported such encounters. These were often the source of the shamans' spiritual power.

Chooky is still skeptical, torn between her scientific training and her Tlingit heritage. They get into a familiar argument about their culture and its ways versus science and western rationality. It's an old point of contention between them which on occasion has gotten pretty heated.

Woosh tries to uphold the wisdom of their culture and their spiritual teachers. Chooky counters with the rationality and evidence-based explanations of the worldview she has learned from her scientific training.

In exasperation, feeling beaten down by Chooky's superior reasoning abilities and her onslaught of words, Woosh finally repeats his fallback argument, "Sometimes, Chooky, I am afraid that you have let your science steal your Tlingit soul."

Woosh instantly regrets saying this. He can see the fire rise in Chooky's eyes. They both realize this argument has gone too far and threatens to escalate into one of the destructive fights they occasionally have. They both stop talking.

After several moments of silence, Woosh apologizes for his last comment.

"I'm sorry. That was not fair. You know how much I believe in you as a scientist and as a Tlingit."

"Thank you, Babe. I know how much you support me. I am just so thrown by this message, or whatever it is. I don't know what to make of it. I think we need an outside opinion. How about if I call Dr. Gutierrez?"

They agree they should go see her mentor and teacher, Dr. Mario Gutierrez, a distinguished professor of linguistics at Washington University in St. Louis. Chooky calls him and simply says she has had a surprising and puzzling result in her research project and needs his expertise to figure it out. Could she come and meet with him? Dr. Gutierrez readily agrees.

Chooky and Woosh get on the next Alaska Airlines flight from Petersburg to Juneau, to Seattle, and then—after four plane changes and a five-hour weather delay—finally on to St. Louis. As they descend, they experience extreme turbulence from a band of thunderstorms moving into eastern Missouri. It feels like the plane might crash.

Chooky and Woosh hold hands, whispering their love to each other in case this is the end.

While they deplane, shaken but grateful to be back on the ground alive, another very heavy downpour hits the terminal. Large hailstones bombard the roof of the jetway filling the tunnel with an ear-splitting roar.

When Chooky and Woosh emerge into the gate area, they stop to watch the TV monitor. The meteorologist warns St. Louis may be heading for another major flood event, "Perhaps even worse than 1993, 2015, 2017, and 2019. If this happens, it would be the fifth "once-in-100-year flood" in the St. Louis region in the past thirty-two years. Go figure! Maybe we need to recalculate this whole century flood thing, if these monster floods keep happening this often."

Chapter Twelve

On the way to their late-morning appointment with Pastor Mark, Clare and Aavani stop at an overlook to watch the nearby swollen Mississippi, its waters rising rapidly. They arrive at the Metropolitan Community Church in the old Carondelet neighborhood of South St. Louis under glum, leaden skies with even darker clouds and distant thunder approaching from the West.

Carondelet, once an independent city of its own, is a very old neighborhood of St. Louis close to the Mississippi River. It's an area of St. Louis with red-brick houses of different sizes in various states of disrepair and rehabilitation.

The church office is a beautifully rehabbed red-brick former rectory next to the large, matching red-brick church, capped by twin steeples towering above the narrow street. The church has also been renovated, having been converted from an old German Catholic parish, St. Wenceslaus, to be the new home of Metropolitan Church, a predominantly gay church community, drawing parishioners from all over the St. Louis region.

The two women ascend the stairs to the office and give Pastor Mark a big hug when he greets them on the landing in front of the house. Clare is particularly warm in her embrace, easing Mark's concern about her. He shows them around his church, and then brings them into his office. They chat for a time about the beauty and unique spiritual environment of the Crestone area.

Mark finally gets around to asking the two women what brought them to St. Louis. He says he assumes other business must have occasioned their trip, and that he is just a secondary part of their visit to St. Louis.

"But I'm puzzled you have even heard about me. How did you get my name and how did you know I was at the Zen Center?"

Aavani replies, "Well, Crestone is a small community. Everybody knows everything that happens in town and at the spiritual centers. We actually got your name from the Village Witch, Cassandra."

"Well, I've never been outed by a witch before!"

Mark and the two women share a laugh about Cassandra, and discuss for a few minutes what kind of town has its own witch.

Mark continues, "I'm glad you paid me a visit, but what else brings you to St. Louis? Sr. Clare, you mentioned you have a friend here in town."

Clare answers, "Yes, Sr. Helen over in the Central West End. But, actually, you are the reason we drove all this way."

Mark looks surprised. "Why? Did I offend someone in Crestone?"

At that point the next round of thunderstorms hits. The sky turns the eerie, sickly green that often presages a tornado. The old house shakes from the thunder and the sudden gusts of wind. A wind-driven rain pelts the windows of Mark's office sounding like small pebbles being thrown against the glass. Mark jumps in his chair, startled by the sudden sound and fury of the latest storm.

He fights a flashback of the shooting trying to invade his mind.

There is a long silence, then the two women look at each other, noticing Mark's sudden change in demeanor. Both of them are unsure how to ask him about his meditation experience. Finally, Aavani says, "No you didn't offend anyone. We heard from Cassandra, who heard from Gisella at the Zen Center, that you had a very powerful and disturbing experience while you were sitting in meditation at the Zen Center."

Mark becomes agitated and confused. He tries to hide his reaction.

"Yes, I did have a strange experience and I'm working on it with my therapist. He thinks it was probably a part of my PTSD from the hate crime and mass shooting at Sunday services here six months ago. But I'm puzzled that what happened to me during my meditation would be of interest to you."

The two women say they read about the awful shooting, and were very sorry it happened to his church community.

Clare chimes in, "Well, the real reason we have come to see you is to tell you we both experienced a profound and frightening spiritual experience at the same time as your own experience in the Zen meditation room. It happened to me in my Nada chapel and to Aavani in her temple of the divine mother goddess. All three of our experiences happened at exactly the same time and had a similar effect on each of us. And so, we have come to ask if your vision was in any way similar to ours. Mark, what did you see?"

Mark turns pale and blurts out, "Oh my God! What happened to you? What did you two see? What happened to you when this thing hit you?"

So, Clare and Aavani both describe what happened to them in their meditation time, relating just a few details of the actual vision.

Clare asks, "Is this anything like what you saw? It's just so unbelievable that all three of us saw something so frightening, and then all three of us passed out at the same time in a similar fashion."

Mark starts to feel another anxiety attack coming on. He can't talk and feels a tightness in his chest and throat. He focuses on slowing his breathing and calming his amygdala like his therapist taught him. The two women see he is distraught and stay silent, reluctant to push him any further about his vision.

Finally, when he feels the panic starting to pass, he says, "As you can see, this whole situation is very upsetting to me. I have been in great turmoil since the shooting. Now this. I don't think I can talk about what happened to me in Crestone here. If I can get an appointment, would you be willing to meet with me and my therapist? I think I would handle this better and be able to talk about it, if he were with us. Would that be okay?"

Clare and Aavani readily agree. Mark calls his therapist, Fr. Patrick Phelan, S.J. at St. Louis University, who says he has a free hour in the late afternoon after his last therapy client of the day.

Chapter Thirteen

The previous night Fr. Phelan meets with Dr. Mario Gutierrez, the Washington University linguistics professor, over heaping plates of *linguini tutto mare* and a bottle of Super Tuscan at Cunetto House of Pasta on the Hill, an old Italian neighborhood in St. Louis. They are old friends, having gone to high school together at DeSmet Jesuit High School in Creve Coeur, a St. Louis suburb near the seminary Mark attended.

After a couple glasses of wine, and the retelling of well-worn high school stories they both feature in, Mario mentions to his priest friend the phone call from his former student, Chooky. He describes her research into humpback whale songs in Alaska, and then relates the strange results she got one day with one particular humpback she rescued.

"She claims it appears she received some kind of actual message from the whale. In English, no less! Of course, this is absurd, or at least highly unlikely. It has to be some kind of computer glitch, or an AI program gone off the rails. Or maybe even an ingenious, mischievous hack of some kind. In any event, I'm going to meet with her to figure this out. It is certainly a strange story though, to say the least."

Mario paraphrases the humpback's stunning message for Fr. Phelan. "What do you think, Patrick?"

Fr. Phelan is stunned and grows quiet. He realizes this is very similar to the message his minister client heard as part of his Zen meditation experience. Both because of client confidentiality and because he is at a loss for words, he doesn't say anything at first. He thinks to himself, *What does this mean that both the marine scientist and my counseling client got parallel messages? Maybe my diagnosis of Mark is wrong. Maybe this isn't PTSD?*

Finally Fr. Phelan regains his composure and tries to make a joke of it, "Well that's quite a wild fish story, Mario. Let me know if Jonah shows up too and has something to say. I'll warn Nineveh."

They both laugh.

Fr. Phelan grows quiet again, and they focus on finishing their pasta. He makes some excuse for his silence. They finish their dinner, and hug goodbye. The Jesuit says in parting that he would like to hear what they figure out scientifically about the message, "Keep me posted would you, Mario, it certainly is an interesting story."

Chapter Fourteen

At 4pm the next day, when Fr. Phelan, Pastor Mark, Aavani, and Sr. Clare meet, the rain has gotten even heavier and is now an almost constant downpour. Fr. Phelan's office is in the rectory next door to the College

Church on the campus of St. Louis University on Grand Avenue in the heart of the city.

They hear the dull roar as frequent gusts of wind pound the rain onto the windows of the office. At times, they almost have to shout to hear each other. The women take charge of the meeting, describing to the two men a small portion of what they saw and heard during their ecstatic experiences. Mark goes pale and silent.

After listening for several minutes, Fr. Phelan blurts out, "Oh my God!"

He turns to Mark and says, "That's almost exactly what you described happened to you at the Zen Center. I don't know what this is, but it's not PTSD. This is something beyond psychology."

He goes on to reveal what his professor friend told him about the message from the humpback whale given to his marine biologist protégé. Now all four sit in stunned silence. The incessant drumming of the rain is the only sound in the room.

"What does this all mean?" they finally ask, almost in unison.

"I don't know," Fr. Phelan replies, "But there is something powerful and unusual here. Maybe even sacred. We must listen to what you three have been given—and, I guess, to the message from the whale—and carefully discern what it all means. Also, with your permission, I would like to speak to my friend, Dr. Gutierrez, and find out more about the message the marine biologist received. Is that alright with the three of you?"

They all agree.

Sr. Clare adds, "Please remember not to reveal very much about our visions. We were told not to reveal the whole vision. I know you will respect that, but I just needed to say it. I have a sense that there could be severe consequences if we don't do as we were told."

At that moment the wind and rain intensify even more, and the power suddenly goes out with a flicker of the office lamps. They continue to talk in the semi-darkness as the wind howls outside their window. The women say they have one more thing to discuss. Clare speaks for them both, "In our visions we were directed to take certain actions. We are to find a certain young woman and share the vision and message with her and with no one else. When we do this, more will be revealed."

Mark says this is what he was told to do as well.

"But who is this young woman? Where is she? Why her? What role does she play in all of this? And how do we find her, for God's sake?"

No one has an answer.

That evening, Fr. Phelan calls his professor friend and says, "Mario, we have to talk, it's urgent." They agree to meet for lunch again the next day at Cunetto's.

Patrick won't tell him what the urgency is about.

What kind of trouble could my Jesuit friend be in? Mario wonders, *Priests seem to be always getting into trouble these days. God, I hope Patrick isn't one of those priest pedophiles who are in the news all the time! Have sexual allegations been made against him? I would be totally shocked. Perhaps he's just met a woman and fallen in love? That would be a whole hell of a lot better.*

Chapter Fifteen

The next morning, Dr. Gutierrez once again meets with Chooky at his office at Washington University to review their findings about her humpback research. He has invited a colleague in the Computer Science department, Dr. Pawel Pozinski, to examine the validity of the computer program that received the message. Dr. Pozinski is widely known for his application of computer science to the petrochemical industry. He built his tenured professorship on numerous research grants, some disguised as environmental studies, that he received through the years from oil and gas companies. He is secretly double-dipping, working for the university and covertly for the oil industry. At times, he has even acted as a mole, spying on environmentalist groups, and reporting his findings to the oil companies.

Pozinski says he cannot find any error in the functioning of the computer or in the AI program, but there must be something technically wrong somewhere in Chooky's system.

"It is highly unlikely, of course, that the program translated an actual, worded message from a whale. It has to be a technical anomaly. I will keep examining the programs and the hardware. Let's meet again in a week. I'm sure I will have some explanation for you by then."

Everyone agrees.

When the meeting is over, Dr. Pozinski goes to a secluded spot in the back of Graham chapel, the English Gothic, non-denominational campus chapel, variously used for everything from alumni weddings to porn film festivals. He immediately calls the CEO of Moxxon Oil and Energy Co, Sam Burroughs. He talks to him for 20 minutes and then makes a call to his contact at the National Security Council in the White House, Admiral James Childs.

He tells both parties something potentially explosive and dangerous to the oil and gas industry and U.S. national economic interests has surfaced. He tells them it might be a hoax, but the data appears valid, and he fears what the tree-huggers might do with it if it becomes public. He asks both of them what he should do with this information.

Chapter Sixteen

Dr. Gutierrez and Fr. Phelan meet for lunch. They both order the *linguine tutto mare* again, but the Jesuit declines any wine, saying he needs to stay stone-cold sober to tell this story to his friend. Without identifying the three people, he tells Gutierrez they all received the same message as Chooky, along with an accompanying vision and directive. All three said it was from Mother Gaia. Furthermore, this happened at exactly the same time, in exactly the same way, just a few miles from each other at three different spiritual centers in Crestone, Colorado.

Mario is stunned. He is a scientist but was also taught by the Jesuits that science and spirituality are alternate ways to perceive and understand reality, each with its own authenticity. *Could it be that something real, some entity, is trying to send a message through both scientific data and spiritual experience?*

The two of them decide they need the bottle of wine after all to help them absorb what they just learned. Sharing another bottle of Super Tuscan Italian red, they discuss what all of these revelations could mean.

They both believe in global warming by human action. They both have read the scientific literature and prophetic warnings. Both have studied Pope Francis' ecological encyclical, *Laudato Si*. How did this phenomenon fit in? Were the messages and visions real? Or were they just a combination of a weird computer blooper and overactive or even delusional imaginations?

But how could it be random coincidence if all four people received the same message? Why was this message given to these four people? And if it is real, what should they do about it? They decide they should have all four of the message recipients meet with them at Patrick's counseling office at the College Church the next day.

While Mario and Patrick are eating their *tutto mare* and debating the meaning of these events, the mid-day news reports include several new stories.

St. Louis Post-Dispatch: "The St. Louis Zoo reports that many of their animals were very restless and aggressive last night. There were several unsuccessful attempts to escape. Five zookeepers were attacked and bitten by animals they care for. Three had to be hospitalized. The attacks involved several big cats, lions, tigers, jaguars, and grizzly bears, along with several species of venomous snakes. This has never happened before at the St. Louis Zoo, especially all at once.

A zoo spokesperson is quoted as saying, "It was like the whole animal kingdom went berserk. So many of our animal groups were highly agitated all night, the Bird and Reptile Houses, Big Cat Country, all the chimps, orangutans, and gorillas in the Ape House, and the elephants in River's Edge. Even the sea lions barked all night long. The keepers report that everything is quiet now, but they sense a tension in many of their animals."

NBC News: "The Taal volcano in the Philippines, located just 31 miles south of the capital city, Manila, has begun a major eruption. 30,000 people have been ordered to evacuate. Volcanologists say this might be the precursor to an even more destructive eruption by the supervolcano that lies under Taal and the lake in which it sits.

There are also reports that a volcano on the Kamchatka Peninsula and one near Anchorage, Alaska, have blown their tops at the same time. Volcanologists have expressed surprise that all three eruptions would occur almost simultaneously, and so closely following the devastating eruption of Mt. Edgecumbe in Sitka, Alaska, but they deny there could be any connection between the eruptions beyond an unfortunate coincidence."

BBC Breaking News: "These reports just in: Several prides of lions appear to have joined together to form a large super-pride of an estimated twenty-five lions, and invaded the town of Maun in the Okavango Delta region of northern Botswana, mauling and killing dozens of locals and tourists. The same sort of incident is reported to have just happened at a village in the Maasai region of Kenya. There are no details at this time about the Maasai attacks."

Los Angeles Times: "Swarms of moderate earthquakes occurred this morning along the San Andreas fault in California and the Juan de Fuca Plate off the Washington and Oregon coasts. Seismologists warn this could be a harbinger of the "Big One" that has long been feared. A USC seismologist is quoted as saying, "It is highly unusual for these swarms to happen on two different fault systems at the same time. Although it is highly unlikely, it makes me wonder whether a major earthquake could happen along the whole West Coast, from LA to Seattle."

Volcanologists have also reported seismic activity that may be signs of impending eruptions along the whole line of the Cascade Volcanoes from British Columbia to

Northern California, including Mt. Rainier, Mt. St. Helens, Mt. Hood, and Lassen Peak.

"If even a few of these thirteen volcanoes were to erupt simultaneously, it would be totally unprecedented—and an incredible catastrophe for the Pacific Northwest and the rest of North America," one expert is quoted as saying.

USA Today: "There are strange reports from global news outlets that large numbers of domestic cats have suddenly escaped overnight from their human owners and from their houses, and seemingly disappeared into the darkness without a trace. One prominent veterinarian, Amanda Sapanski, remarked, "I doubt if these news reports are accurate. However, with cats you never know what they are up to. Give me a loyal, dependable dog any day over an unpredictable and inscrutable cat."

BBC World News: Breaking News: A devastating flash river flood in India's northern state of Uttarakhand killed at least 64 people. More than 340 people are missing—including workers on a dam construction project, presumed trapped in underground tunnels. 24 workers were pulled out alive from one tunnel after being trapped for 20 hours in the freezing dark. Indian authorities continue to be in rescue mode, although they are cautioning that the conditions are so dire the hope of live rescues is diminishing rapidly.

A team of Indian scientists, flying in a helicopter over the rugged, mountainous area may have discovered the cause of the massive flood. The scientists believe a large "hanging glacier" appears to have broken loose from the side of Mt. Raunthi (5600 m or 18,372 feet) due to increased glacial melting caused by climate change. The falling glacier hurtled down a steep mountain slope into a narrow canyon, forming a temporary dam in the river.

When the water built up to a critical volume, this glacial dam then broke, sending a sudden tsunami of water downstream. The scientists maintain global warming is the "main factor" in this disaster. Local villagers have been warning and protesting for at least six years about the growing dangers in their mountains from out-of-control deforestation of mountainsides and unregulated, ill-designed dam construction.

Coincidentally, the magazine *Popular Science*, on the same day, published a scientific report about a similar looming disaster in Peru. Scientists have issued a warning that Lake Palcacocha, perched above the Peruvian city of Huaraz high in the Andes, is vulnerable to a glacial avalanche bursting its banks.

"You have a very precarious situation," says Gerald Bromschweiger, a glaciologist from the University of Wisconsin, "Were an avalanche or landslide to land in this lake it would create a tsunami-like wave that would breach its banks and send a torrent of water down the valley. The last time such a flood occurred in 1941, 1,800 people died. A similar incident in the present-day city could kill 6,000."

"Recent research finds that the risk to all of those lives is directly attributable to climate change. That research is the latest step in the growing field of climate change attribution science, which connects day-to-day events like heatwaves, floods, and superstorms to human-caused warming of the climate. Among the most surprising results of the research is that human-induced climate change not only has elevated the risk of future floods from Lake Palcacocha; it was also responsible for the flood of 1941.

"Humans have been warming the planet since at least the 1850s," said Dr. Bromschweiger, "And melting glaciers—like the one that caused the 1941 flood—end up being purer signals of climate change than even thermometers or pressure gauges."

Chapter Seventeen

Dr. Gutierrez, Chooky and Woosh, Pastor Mark, Sr. Clare, Aavani, and Fr. Phelan all meet at Phelan's office at St. Louis University College Church. The professor and priest reveal to the group that all four—the marine biologist, the Catholic nun, the Protestant minister, and the Hindu devotee—received the same message, and that the Crestone trio saw the same horrific vision.

Everyone gasps.

Chooky is the first to chime in and express the doubts of the whole group, "How can this be? It doesn't seem possible. I'm not saying I don't believe each of you. It just is too unlikely and too wild to be true. And most of all, if it *is* true, what does it mean?"

Sr. Clare takes over leadership of the meeting. She says none of this can be mere coincidence. There is too much of a common pattern. It must be a message from something or somebody beyond them, perhaps from the Great Mystery, from God, or the Universe itself.

She also thinks she knows who the young woman might be that they have been directed to speak to. Unlike the others, she received a name in her vision.

"The name I was given is Grainne. I think this might be Grainne O'Malley, an Irish teenager who is involved in climate activism. She was Iona McCleod's close friend and assistant in the climate resistance movement before Iona was assassinated. She has also been in the leadership of the Extinction Rebellion Group. But she disappeared when her life was also threatened. No one seems to know where she is."

The group discusses all of this. Chooky is very skeptical. None of this makes sense to her scientifically. Both Patrick and Mario are cautious and say they don't know what to make of it.

Woosh responds, "I believe the humpback's message is real. It is so much like the stories our Tlingit elders and ancestors would speak about. They often told stories of the humpbacks or the orcas appearing to deliver a message to the people. If the humpback's message is real, the visions the three of you received must be real too."

Mark speaks up and says, "I no longer think my vision was from PTSD. I thought I was going crazy, but now…" Looking at his Crestone companions he continues, "I see I am not alone. Either all three of us went crazy together and the humpback or some hacker is putting you on, Chooky, or this is truly a divine revelation of some kind that we have to listen to and do something about. I think it's real, and I think we have to find this Grainne."

The discussion devolves into a heated discussion with Chooky and Mario on one side, and Woosh and the Crestone trio on the other side. Patrick, always the therapist, tries to stay neutral, facilitate, and calm everybody down.

Then, suddenly the ground beneath the rectory shakes violently, the room sways sickeningly, the bell tower of the College Church crashes and falls onto the street outside their window. All of them rush outside to the street, fleeing the brick rectory just before it starts crumbling behind them. The ground is still moving out on the street, now in long waves that make it feel like they are standing on the undulating waters of a stormy ocean.

Clare and Mario are knocked off their feet. The rest of them cling to each other, both for safety and comfort. They look east down Grand Avenue toward downtown and see that even the Arch appears to be swaying. The earthquake lasts unusually long, just under six minutes, although it seems to the group to last an eternity.

Aavani swears in Sanskrit and shouts, "Dear Devi, Dear Mother, save us!"

Patrick, finally losing his cool, exclaims, "Holy Mary! Sweet Jesus!"

They get on their cellphones and iPads as news reports and alerts begin to flood the internet. They learn that the

New Madrid Fault in South East Missouri has just let go with an 8.8 earthquake. They can see several buildings on Grand Ave and on the university campus which have collapsed. Watching live feeds on their cellphone screens, they see in horror that a river tsunami is sweeping up the Mississippi toward St. Louis. Live-streaming cameras from the Arch grounds show the massive wave approaching the Arch, climbing about 40 feet up both legs of the Arch, and then sweeping into downtown, racing at incredible speed up Market Street, the central artery of downtown St. Louis.

The tourists in the long, narrow observation room inside the top of the Arch are first terrified by the violent swaying of the Arch. Then, they are reassured that the Arch has not fallen, only to be terrified again upon finding that the Arch train system has shut down, and they are trapped.

They can only watch as a disaster movie rapidly unfolds beneath them. Inside the stainless-steel legs of the Arch, the people in the tiny, claustrophobic train capsules, in both the ascending and descending legs of the Arch, are also trapped after their capsules jerk to a halt, and swing sickeningly side-to-side along with the whole Arch structure.

The people in the claustrophobic observation deck watch in horror as the river tsunami sweeps up the Mississippi from the south, and begins to climb the legs of the Arch. Below them, they can see also that the tsunami has shattered the large glass ceiling of the main entrance to the underground museum and visitor center. Hundreds of tourists, enjoying the museum or waiting in line for their ride up the Arch, are immediately submerged and drowned. A few survivors manage to swim to the surface, only to be swept along with the massive wave into downtown St. Louis.

At the historic Old Cathedral on the Arch grounds, the stone steeple is toppled and the whole stone front wall collapses. A special pre-baseball game Mass is being celebrated with a packed church. The priest is just lifting up the host and the chalice at the doxology when the quake hits.

> "Through Him, with Him, and in Him,
> in the unity of the Holy Spirit,
> all glory and honor are yours,
> almighty Father, forever and ever."

The people do not even have time to answer "Amen" before the church shakes violently, and the ceiling begins to rain down on their heads. The surviving worshippers able to climb out of the rubble are met by an enormous wall of water and are also swept into downtown.

The enormous wave roars over the landscaped lid of the depressed lanes of the I-44, flowing down into the narrow concrete canyon, turning it into an instant lake and a watery grave for a couple dozen truckers and motorists who have no time to escape.

It then surrounds the Old Courthouse, where the infamous Dred Scott decision was issued, like an enormous moat. The stairs from which thousands of black slaves were auctioned to their white owners are ripped off the front and back of the Old Courthouse, leaving a white stone island of precarious safety. There are large cracks in the sides of the old building from the severe shaking that threatens to widen, and topple, the historic courthouse into the rising water.

It is a Cardinal baseball day in St. Louis and the Cards are playing their archrival, the Chicago Cubs, in an afternoon game, so the streets of downtown are flooded with people. Thousands of fans dressed in their team colors of red and blue are immediately swept away, and drowned, by the towering tsunami.

At a large fan rally around the central fountain in Kiener Plaza, the fountain is quickly swamped and snuffed out. The red-and-blue-clad bodies of hundreds of fans are swept down Market Street on the rampaging crest of the Mississippi-brown tidal wave.

A few blocks south, the tsunami sweeps into Busch Stadium and Ballpark Village. The water flows through Gates 4 and 5, over the left-center field wall through the Cardinal's bullpen, and onto the field. Dozens of players from both teams drown either on the field or in the inundated dugouts. The water fills the bowl of the stadium and rises into the field boxes. Most fans are able to flee up into the cheaper seats, but some are caught by the water and pulled back onto the flooded field.

As the tsunami surges up Market Street, it inundates the City Park Sculpture Garden, toppling most of the sculptures and drowning several art lovers and families picnicking on the grounds. The massive steel panels of the Richard Serra sculpture, Twain—maligned by many St. Louisans—are not damaged. But the ground beneath two of the panels is scooped out. The panels fall over. Three people, who had been contemplating the meaning of the sculpture, and climbed on top of the rusty iron slabs to escape the onrushing water, are thrown into the maw of the tsunami.

The water surges past the collapsed remains of St. Louis City Hall, its faux French exterior now just a jumble of pink granite, pink-orange brick and buff-colored sandstone. On the opposite side of Market Street, the classical columns of the Soldiers Memorial and Military Museum have been toppled. The water rushes through the broken front wall, stripping away the military exhibits memorializing America's great wars. The tents of the periodic homeless encampment in the park between the two buildings are swallowed by the watery monster along with all of its hapless inhabitants.

The Message Bearers hear the roar of the massive wave as it comes closer to them. It inundates Union Station—the renovated train station—bursting open the already cracked giant fish tanks in the new aquarium, releasing thousands of fish and sharks onto the streets of St. Louis. The wave swamps Aloe Plaza, across Market Street from Union Station, toppling the Milles statues of water gods in the Meeting of the Waters sculpture fountain. The tsunami finally stops about ten blocks east of them and begins to recede, dragging the released fish, sharks, and thousands of bodies with it back toward the Mississippi, which begins to flow south again.

Later, the group learns the sudden earthquake raised the bed of the already swollen, flooding Mississippi, just south of St. Louis, causing the river to flow backwards as it did in the great earthquake of 1812. As in 1812, the tremor is felt over an incredibly wide area, as far away as Atlanta, New Orleans, New York City, Chicago, Boston, Montreal, and Washington D.C.

Church bells in Boston are rung by the shaking, and the President and First Lady feel the old White House walls shuddering as the earthquake wave passes through D.C. There is widespread, catastrophic damage and loss of life across parts of Alabama, Arkansas, Illinois, Indiana, Kentucky, Mississippi, Missouri, and Tennessee. Tens of thousands have died in Southeast Missouri and Southern Illinois, and Northern and Western Tennessee, with thousands also killed in St. Louis. Many more are missing.

The group gathers in a circle amidst the rubble in the middle of now-traffic-free Lindell Blvd. They are shocked by what they have just witnessed. They again discuss what all of this could mean, and whether there is a connection between the disaster that just occurred, their visions, and the humpback's message.

Chooky, silent till now, chips in, "Well, I'm convinced. Call me Doubting Chooky, but now I have seen and touched the wounds. Now I have all the evidence I need. None of my science can explain all of this, so the only explanation can be that the humpback's message to me and the three visions given to you must be founded in some reality that is beyond my comprehension."

Together they agree that the earthquake and river tsunami is a confirming sign. What has been revealed to them is real, and they must act on it. They all concur that the Message Bearers—the scientist, nun, minister, and devotee—have been commissioned to carry the message as directed. They must find Grainne as soon as possible. Woosh offers to accompany them. Fr. Phelan and Dr. Gutierrez are in agreement with the plan. The Jesuit priest silently blesses the four Message Bearers and Woosh, still seated in a circle in the middle of the empty street, with the sign of the Cross.

Chapter Eighteen

The group doesn't notice that Dr. Pozinski—the computer scientist from Washington University—is watching them from down the street, standing in front of the now-collapsed Scottish Rite Temple. As the group walks off, he signals to three men, former CIA operatives, standing further west on Lindell, who begin to follow them discreetly.

The group spends several days helping in the rescue and recovery efforts after the earthquake and river tsunami, except for Sr. Clare. She finds a small undamaged chapel on the university campus, and spends hours in prayer, asking for further guidance. Outside the rain continues to pour down on devastated St. Louis in stormy waves.

While praying in the chapel, it finally comes to Clare: Grainne must be in Ircland, probably hiding somewhere along the wild west coast she grew up in. Her Carmelite community has a house and a retreat center in Sligo. She leaves the chapel and immediately calls them by cellphone. She finds out from the superior of the community, Fr. Liam, that they heard rumors Grainne had returned to Ireland. He was certain she was somewhere in the West of Ireland, but he is not sure where. He heard she was being protected and hidden by the Guardia, the Irish Army, a band of Tinkers, and a small international group of young environmentalists.

Sr. Clare goes to the rest of the group and tells them what she found out.

"I believe we are being called to go to Ireland and find Grainne and deliver our message. It is urgent. All of humanity is at risk. If we don't, the next extinction will be us, our whole human species."

They debate the best way to proceed. They make plans to fly to Ireland to begin the search for Grainne. But then, Woosh bursts into the meeting, and tells the group he has noticed three men who have been following them. He thinks they are being watched.

"Someone else must know. And their interest may not be exactly benign. From now on, I think we have to be very careful."

Woosh calls his friend, George Gustafson—a climate-aware oil CEO—to get his advice and seek his help. They became friends when they both worked on an oil spill off the coast of Copper River Country in Alaska. Without revealing the whole story of the message and the visions, Woosh tells Gustafson he is leading a small group to Ireland to join an environmental movement fighting global warming.

Gustafson says he has already heard about the group. He also heard they have some sort of special message for the world, information he received from his contacts in the energy industry. He has also been told by his informants that climate deniers in the White House and in the oil, gas, and coal industries have learned of the group's mission, and will try to stop them.

Gustafson tells Woosh, "Stout and Burroughs know something is up, and they cannot let the climate people get the upper hand with American public opinion. They are ruthless and will do everything within their power to keep any climate information or message suppressed."

"Let me tell you what happened to me a few days ago in California. I think it may be connected somehow to your group. I attended my nephew, Timothy's wedding in Napa Valley last weekend. He's my favorite nephew, and it was important I be there. He's like a son to me, since my ex, Danielle, and I never had any children. The wedding and reception were held at a gorgeous winery, Castello di Amoroso, built to resemble a Tuscan castle in the hills to the east of Calistoga, halfway between Calistoga and Santa Rosa.

The morning of the wedding, I was awakened at dawn by the thump-thump of a heavy helicopter flying over the resort where I was staying, Indian Hot Springs in Calistoga. I was a little alarmed, but didn't think much about it, because it was April, and the fire season had long been over. But, when I went out to my car about an hour later, there was a towering gray, brown, and black cloud of smoke looming over the resort. There were already lines of fire-fighting aircraft in the sky circling to dive into the fire and release their load of fire-retardant on the rapidly spreading flames.

I called Timothy, who knows Napa like the back of his hand. He said the fire had started around 4am in the foothills east of the Silverado Trail. It was spreading quickly. Already at 8am it had consumed 8,000 acres. The fire was a surprise in April, but it had been a very dry winter, and had suddenly gotten hot the day before. Global warming is changing everything, extending the fire season throughout the year by increasing the frequency of extreme conditions like drought, high temperatures, and high winds.

That day it was a record 94 degrees with very low humidity. Timothy thought everything would be fine for the wedding, since the fire was to the southeast of Calistoga, and the wedding venue was some distance to the northwest. The only wild card was the wind, expected to pick up that afternoon out of the east-southeast and might gust to 40-50 mph.

The wedding ceremony was held at 4pm outside in the shade of a massive spreading walnut tree which must have been hundreds of years old. The ceremony was beautiful. But throughout the ceremony, plane after plane flew over us heading for the fire: 747s, DC-10s, MD-87 jets, Grumman S-2Ts, Lockheed P-3s twin- and four-engine turboprops, and heavy-duty helicopters outfitted with giant red buckets of water slung by cables below their fuselages.

I joked with the minister that I had never before seen a wedding ceremony with an accompanying airshow. This aerial display continued during the reception, held outdoors in an open piazza next to the winery, a scene reminiscent of a Tuscan wedding feast. Because both Timothy and his new wife, Marie, work in the Napa wine industry, they have access to the best chefs and, of course, the best wines available.

The four-course dinner they planned was sumptuous and elegant. The atmosphere was peaceful and celebratory despite the unseen fire off in the distance. The sunset during the reception was spectacular, but a little ominous, the sun and clouds turned fire-red by the smoke. After dark, the sky must have cleared, because a nearly full, brilliantly white moon hung over the reception, flanked by the planets, brilliant white Jupiter and Saturn to the right, and red-hued Mars to the left.

Everything seemed in propitious alignment for the bride and groom. I was very happy for my nephew and for his new bride.

The first discordant note came halfway through the reception banquet when I noticed two men in dark suits hovering in the shadows on the edges of the reception. They looked vaguely familiar. I thought I had seen them before, but I couldn't remember where. I asked Timothy about them, and he told me they were security guards recently hired by the winery, because a few previous weddings had gotten very rowdy. I dismissed them from my mind and rose to toast the bride and groom.

Around the time of the cheese course, about 10pm, I noticed the air had changed. It was noticeably hotter, and there was a distinct odor of smoke. I looked up and noticed the moon had turned orange-red, and was illuminating a large cloud of billowing smoke just below it. The line of planets had disappeared, blotted out by the smoke cloud.

A few minutes later, during the dessert course, while the last toast was being delivered, dozens of cellphones went off with blaring Nixle alerts from the Napa County Sheriff's Office. The Napa fire on the east side of the valley had spotted, and suddenly expanded to the westside mountains near us. This new fire was growing fast, pushed toward us by the rising wind. We were in a danger zone and were being ordered to evacuate immediately.

I was just about to ask the very hot, blonde server whom I had flirted with all evening what she was doing after the reception, when Timothy got up to announce we would all need to leave as soon as possible. No time even to finish our Citrus Buttermilk Panna Cotta. Orgasmically delicious, by the way! We had to pack up our belongings, gather in the parking lot, and convoy in our cars to the southern end of Napa Valley where Timothy and Marie lived, some distance from the fire. The plan was for everyone to retreat to their house and continue the celebration in safety. He thanked everyone for coming and reassured us we would all be safe. However, he ended with a note of urgency, "Okay, everybody, we're out of here. Now!"

I quickly tossed all of my clothes into my suitcase and rushed to the parking lot. I decided to stay behind for a while to help Timothy and Marie organize the escape convoy. After all of the other cars left, I got in my car to follow Timothy and Marie in their red Tesla. I felt like James Bond, still dressed in my black Tux, and driving my rented gun metal Maserati Ghibli S Q4.

You know, I have to confess, I still like my fast gas-guzzlers. It all felt very surreal, like we were really in a Bond movie, fleeing an inferno started by a hidden enemy intent on killing us. I thought we were the last to leave, but then I noticed the two security guards getting into a black Suburban and pulling in behind me.

We drove out of the parking lot of the winery and turned east toward Calistoga onto the hilly, winding Petrified Forest Road. As I rounded a curve about halfway down the mountain, a huge flare of flames erupted out of the dark on the hillside a few miles away above Calistoga. It looked like a grove of trees or some structure had exploded. Then, I could see several lines of high, red and orange flames trailing down the mountain toward the town. It looked like the whole world had caught fire.

The usual route, the Silverado Trail highway on the east side of Napa Valley, had already been closed by the encroaching fire. So, we turned south onto Highway 128 on the west side of the valley, the only road south still open. The fires were now on my left only one to two miles to the east of the highway. I wondered how long it would take for the flames to reach our side and close 128, trapping us in the fire zone. It was a nightmarish scene, driving through the dark with flames behind and to the left of me, trying to keep the Tesla's rear lights in sight.

To make matters worse, more piercing Nixle alerts sounded on my cellphone notifying me the fire was spreading even further, and more areas had to evacuate. Then my GPS voice, Siri or some other obnoxious chick, came on to tell me to leave 128, and turn left onto a side road. But left was the fire. I shouted back at her, "Siri, you, stupid bitch, are you trying to kill me?" All she would answer was, "Back to route. Back to route."

This happened several times. I had left the winery feeling pretty calm, but now my nerves were getting really frazzled. I gripped the steering wheel tighter, concentrating on following the beacon of Timothy's taillights.

Then a thick bank of smoke blew in from the left, and I could no longer see the Tesla. I instinctively slowed down. I think Timothy sped up. When I came out of the smoke, his Tesla was out of sight. I was on my own, except for the Suburban behind me with the security guards. They had been following me very closely, practically on my back bumper. I figured they were just trying to stay close for safety. Then it hit me. I remembered where I had seen them before. At a meeting of the Petroleum Council. They were some of the hired hands, ex-Special Forces types, recruited into Stout and Burrough's secret oil militia. What were they doing here? Their presence hanging on my bumper certainly didn't make me feel safer.

With Timothy gone, the Suburban began to drive more aggressively. They tried several times to pass me on the left, as if they might try to run me off the road. I floored the Maserati and was able to speed away from them. But each time they caught up with me, and would try to cut me off again. Now I knew they were out to either kill or kidnap me. Siri's voice came back on and commanded, "In a quarter of a mile, turn left on Zinfandel Lane."

I made the split-second decision to follow her command this time, even though it meant I was turning right into the fire. I hoped if I could do this maneuver quickly, I would lose the Suburban. I executed a high-speed, four-wheel power-drift turn onto Zinfandel Lane, getting smoke and loud squeals from all four tires. The Suburban sped by, missing the turn, coming to a screeching halt a quarter mile down 128. They turned around and onto Zinfandel Lane, but I had gained a few seconds on them.

I was now driving through an area of vineyards directly into the fire. I scanned my brain for a plan. A wall of flame was coming right down Zinfandel Lane driven by the gusty wind. A line of trees along either side of the road were exploding in the approaching inferno. Winery buildings were burning on my left. I saw the sign for Raymond Vineyards, one of Timothy's, and remembered Timothy had said that in a fire vineyards sometimes provide a natural firebreak. I pulled off the road, counting on the AWD to power me through an open, grassy field toward the vineyard. I drove till the low-slung Maserati bottomed out a few yards short of the long rows of vines. I heard the Suburban driving through the same field toward me. They wouldn't bottom out.

I jumped out of the Maserati and ran for the vineyard. I could feel the scorching heat of the approaching fire. I reached the vineyard and raced toward the center where I hoped to be safe, at least from the flames. The two men jumped out of their Suburban and began to run toward the vineyard after me.

Just as they approached the edge of the first line of grapevines, a wall of flames surged over my head—pushed by a sudden gust of wind—and enveloped the field outside of the vineyard, consuming the dry grass and super-dry brush on which it was feeding. As I flattened myself into the ground between the rows of vines, I heard the two oil militiamen screaming. They had not made it to the sanctuary of the vineyard and were being incinerated.

I lay there for a couple of hours until I could see the fire had moved on. Then I began to walk back toward Highway

128. The charred bodies of the two men lay only a few feet from the edge of the vineyard. Both the Maserati and Suburban were completely burnt-out skeletons of metal. A Napa County Sheriff picked me up on 128 and brought me to my nephew's house. I told no one, other than Timothy, the full story of what happened that night.

Hey, Woosh, I'm sorry I got so long-winded here with you. But you know me, I'm a Texas storyteller at heart. I needed to tell the story to someone. Besides, I wanted you to get a clear picture of what you are up against. The oil bosses know something is stirring. They don't know what it is yet, but they are very fearful of being exposed, and will try to silence anyone in the environmental movement that could make them look bad and threaten their profits. They know I am dangerous because these days I am an environmentally enlightened petroleum executive. Sounds like they think your group is potentially dangerous too.

That's why I urge you to be very cautious, Woosh. I strongly recommend you and your friends not fly to Ireland, because that way you would be too easy to track. You could be stopped, and arrested on some kinda trumped-up charges. Or something worse could happen."

Gustafson suggests instead that the group go by sea to Ireland, and he offers the use of his sailboat, *Ruach,* which features a new technology that makes it invisible to radar and satellite surveillance. The boat is docked close to Northeast Harbor, Maine, just outside Acadia National Park.

After he gets off his cellphone, Woosh brings the news and Gustafson's suggestions back to the group meeting in Fr. Phelan's office. Everyone agrees to the plan. They will travel to Maine by car as secretly as they can, then sail to Ireland on Gustafson's boat, and deliver their message to Grainne O'Malley.

Clare comments at the end of their meeting, "I never imagined we would be put in personal danger. Or that someone like me would be called to such an important mission. Or, for that matter, that anyone would feel threatened by a little, old contemplative nun."

Everyone laughs.

"But now I'm like one of those "Nun-on-a-bus" sisters. We've been given a mission to deliver a message the world desperately needs to hear. It's turned into a dangerous mission, I guess, but I, for one, am willing to do whatever it takes no matter the risk. Gaia, and maybe God as well, has called us to this mission. So, I'm on the bus. Are you with me?"

Aavani, Mark, Chooky, and Woosh, each in turn, responds to Clare, "I'm on the bus with you, Clare." "I'm on the bus." "I'm on the bus." "I'm on the bus." Woosh finishes the litany, "Clare, I'm not only *on* the bus, I'll *drive* it for you."

The whole group joins hands in a circle and begin to pray.

Chapter Nineteen

Like Donald Trump before him, American President Rex Stout is a tweeter. In the Spring of 2025, in a string of tweets, he hints that there is a conspiracy brewing among extreme environmentalists. "Eco-terrorists" is what he calls them. They are making ridiculous claims about the recent worldwide disasters to further their radical agenda to ruin the U.S. economy and make America into a "socialist nation." He assures his followers that he won't let that happen. He vows to stop the extremists and the "fake news" they are spreading.

He also tweets that he is praying for the people of St. Louis killed or impacted by the floods, the earthquake, and the Mississippi tsunami. He promises, "The best disaster aid response ever. We arc here for you." He quotes scientists who are saying the St. Louis disaster, as well as several others around the world, are just tragic coincidences. President Stout retweets one scientist's opinion, "Global warming cannot cause earthquakes or tsunamis."

At the same time, he secretly calls Sam Burroughs, the CEO of Anthrakas Energy—who Stout handpicked to replace him at Anthrakas—and orders him to do whatever it takes to stop the Message Bearers. President Stout instructs Burroughs to call up the secret militia he created when he was CEO of Anthrakas and deploy them against the group.

Over the years Stout's militia, recruited from retired U.S. Special Forces soldiers of various services, was used to covertly harass and sabotage alternative energy projects, climate researchers, and environmental groups. Stout had even considered emulating his friend Kiril Sokolov and poisoning his opponents with military grade biochemical nerve agents, but decided it would be harder to cover up in the U.S. than in Sokolov's Russia.

He tells Burroughs, "I can't directly go after this group because the fucking Dems might get wind of it and try to impeach me like they did Trump."

President Stout fears Nancy Pelosi, still Speaker of the House at 85, like Captain Hook feared his crocodile. Stout orders Sam Burroughs to issue the command to the operatives of the militia, "Employ whatever means is necessary to stop the Message Bearers group and bury their message. You and your actions are commissioned at the highest levels, and you will be protected no matter what you have to do. These eco-terrorists must be stopped at all costs."

The Republicans, to no one's surprise, had nominated and then elected Rex Stout to the U.S. Presidency in 2024. He was another business leader without any previous government experience, but he possessed a lot of political clout, especially in his electorally crucial home state of Texas.

At sixty, he is a younger, more polished version of President Trump. He is seemingly kind, empathetic, and open-minded, and publicly displays a charming, self-deprecating humility and sense of humor, accentuated by his distinctive Texas drawl.

Privately, he is known to be ruthless, steely, shameless, opinionated, egotistical, and driven by a deeply seated need to be admired, even adored. His parents both idolized him.

He was the family hero who helped distract from his father's alcoholism and his resultant business failure as a small-time oil equipment supplier in the great Permian Basin of West Texas, one of the world's largest oilfields. His two younger sisters sarcastically, and somewhat jealously, called him the "Prince of Midland" in their high school where he was the star quarterback and prom king in the Texas world of "Friday Night Lights." This nickname stuck.

He rose to become the best-known public spokesperson for the oil industry, preaching the virtues and necessity of petroleum, often employing religious language and biblical metaphors. He became known among other oil executives as the "Prince-Archbishop" of the petroleum industry. Or sometimes the "Prince of Darkness."

Within the upper echelons of his own company, he was secretly called the "Ayatollah of Anthrakas." He was widely liked by the average employee and the larger public, because of his outward sincerity and feigned compassion. But the insiders who saw how he actually operated, both feared and secretly mocked him.

Psychiatrists would diagnose Rex Stout with closet narcissistic personality disorder. This is a person who displays an external persona of kindness, concern, and stability, but with a hidden core personality of egoism, complete self-focus, chronic resentment, and a fragile ego. Or as Jesus would characterize him, "A whitened sepulcher."

Part of what is in his closet, carefully screened from the public, is that he is a climate change denier. As CEO of Anthrakas, he appeared to speak the politically correct climate change language, and even promoted and funded some alternative energy projects. Secretly, he worked to undermine scientists and research that supported the global warming forecasts, doing everything he could to ensure a future of continued expansion of fossil fuel production.

He used his evangelical faith, adopted at college, to impress and win a girl—now his wife—to rationalize his actions.

He fervently believed the End Times were near. So, he thought, *Why not exploit the Earth as much as we want till Jesus comes? Furthermore, didn't God tell Adam in the book of Genesis that humans are commanded by God to have "dominion" over all other lesser creatures of the Earth?*

When Stout was President and CEO of Anthrakas, some of the company's scientists developed a computer program that modeled what would happen if the world continued to burn fossil fuels at its current rate. The computer models forecasted there would be progressively increased global warming that would alter the world's climate in calamitous—eventually catastrophic—ways, adversely impacting all of humanity.

Anthrakas' own product, and the source of its profit and wealth, would cause this. Stout could not admit this, even to himself. He certainly wouldn't allow the public to see this information, like a brewery or a distillery cannot admit its product can be misused and contribute to alcoholism, drunken rages, or violence.

He was an engineer himself, and fully understood the science behind his researchers' findings. He also saw the threat to the company's bottom line and eventually to its very existence. He quickly moved to suppress the scientists' report, firing the offending truth-telling scientists who had produced the findings.

Soon afterward, Stout organized the other chief oil executives to develop a secret program of systematic disinformation about climate change. Their strategy was to sow doubt and confusion in the public's mind about the validity of global warming, its predictions, and even the growing scientific evidence emerging, confirming the computer models.

This strategy was the same one Big Tobacco had employed for years to undermine the scientific evidence, which definitively showed smoking led to lung cancer, heart disease, and death. This strategy worked for several decades, until the truth finally caught up to Big Tobacco, and their cynical ploy was unmasked. Like Big Tobacco, Big Oil began to secretly pay various scientists who were willing to publicly question global warming or dismiss it as "just a theory."

That they were on Anthrakas' payroll, and were experts in scientific fields other than climatology was kept well hidden.

Stout believed he could succeed at his climate cover-up where Big Tobacco had eventually failed. Even when the petroleum industry began admitting the reality of global warming, promising to achieve net-zero carbon emissions, oil companies were actually continuing to expand its oil and gas production.

Rex Stout's explanation was that they would invest in tree planting and carbon capture technologies to counteract the continued oil and gas production. Some experts described this as simply moving from denial to delusion. One commentator likened this ploy by Stout, Burroughs, and other captains of the carbon industry, to a nicotine addict going from one pack a day to two packs a day, and then claiming they are cutting back or quitting smoking, because they switched to filtered cigarettes.

Chapter Twenty

At the last minute, Mark's spouse, Simon LeClerc—a research physician at Washington University Medical School—asks to join the group. Mark and Simon have been together for eleven years and got married as soon as it became legal in 2015. They live together in a magnificent old mansion they rehabbed on Portland Place, a leafy private street in the Central West End near Simon's work at the medical school.

Mark and Simon couldn't have been more dissimilar in appearance. Mark is significantly overweight and readily admits he is gym- and exercise-phobic. Simon has the long, lean physique of a swimmer, having been the goalie for his high school and college water polo teams. He went to the pool and gym at the university almost every day. He once described himself to his grandmother as "a science nerd in a cool guy's body."

The group readily accepts Simon's request to join them in their mission. Woosh even suggests it might be handy to have a doctor travel with them, just in case. The group decides to leave under the cover of darkness. Fr. Phelan and Dr. Gutierrez create a diversion to throw off the men who have been following the group.

They put out a press release announcing a major statement from unnamed experts about a new scientific explanation for the recent worldwide spate of natural calamities. It is to be held at Washington University's Graham Chapel. The ex-CIA agents take the bait and show up along with several members of the media. But no one is there and the chapel is dark.

While this diversion is occurring, just a few miles to the east the Message Bearers—now numbering six—pile into two white Chevy Malibu borrowed by Fr. Phelan from his Jesuit community. They hope using these vanilla cars, registered to the Jesuits, will make it more difficult for them to be tracked. They will drive at night and stay off the interstates, traveling on backroad, blue highways wherever they can. It takes them three days to make the 1,900-mile trip, with two daytime rest stops at Jesuit houses along the way, all arranged by Fr. Phelan.

The leader of the CIA operatives had left one agent behind to shadow the Message Bearers as they leave for Washington University and the feigned press conference. Woosh spots him sitting in a car on Lindell Boulevard across the street from Jesuit Hall. Woosh approaches the car and speaks to him. "I know who you are and what you are doing. But don't worry I'm on your side. In fact, I'm going to show you where the Message Bearers will try to make their escape."

When the agent gets out of the car to follow Woosh, Woosh uses one of his black belt karate moves learned as a youth back in Pelican to knock the man out. He drags him behind a bush and rejoins the group.

Just as the Message Bearers are sneaking out of town, a contingent of the oil militia arrives surreptitiously in St. Louis in five unmarked black Humvees. The oil militia mercenaries, secretly organized by President Stout when he was the CEO of Moxxon, was drawn from several different Special Forces services—CIA, Navy Seals, Delta Forces, Blackwater USA, and BORTAC, the infamous Border Patrol Tactical Unit.

Along with the ex-CIA agents, the militia searches frantically for the Message Bearers once they realize—two days late—they have left St. Louis. They monitor the roads, airports, train and bus stations, but can find no trace of the group or even where they are heading.

Just before dawn of the third day the Message Bearers arrive in Northeast Harbor unnoticed. Posing as tourists, they catch the local mail boat out to Little Cranberry Island, a few miles off the Maine coast near Acadia National Park where Gustafson has his estate and sailing yacht. The next night under the cover of darkness, the group quietly sneaks away from *Ruach*'s slip on Little Cranberry Island using only their sails to get underway and sets sail for Ireland. Woosh and Gustafson share the helm. An old couple from the village, out for their nightly walk, are the only ones to see them go.

At sea, in the peaceful rhythm of wind and wave, they have long discussions about climate change, science versus religion, the meaning of the visions, and where all of this is leading. If they can get the message to Grainne O'Malley, they have no idea what will happen next. They theorize over and over about what might occur, and even about what the purpose of the message is. No one has any clear answers. They only know they have to find Grainne and tell her of their visions and the humpback's warning. That is their mission. Perhaps then their mission will be accomplished, and the next step will be up to Grainne.

Despite her earlier declaration of faith after the earthquake in St. Louis, Chooky is still struggling with believing the message, or even the idea that there is such a thing as Gaia or Mother Earth. The scientist in her sees the Earth as just a physical planet that randomly, and through the process of natural selection, was able to evolve life in its oceans and later on land. Her Tlingit spirit is at war with her scientist mind, and she can't resolve her inner conflict.

She sometimes wishes she had the faith the others seemed to possess, but even with Woosh's encouragement she can't get there. Mark's spouse, Simon, despite being married to a Christian minister, also holds on tightly to his scientific viewpoint and agnostic philosophy. And yet, he too is at a loss to explain some of the things that have been occurring around the globe.

Simon and Chooky are often on one side of the friendly debates, seeking scientific explanations. Clare, Aavani, Mark, and Woosh don't dispute the reality and importance of scientific evidence. However, they insist spiritual phenomena are also real—albeit unseen and unquantifiable—and are another important source of truth about the universe. They express the belief that there has to be a spiritual explanation for the unusual things they have experienced and that are happening around the world. They admit they don't know exactly what that explanation might be either.

Clare, Aavani, and Mark are still wary of sharing any details about their visions, despite gentle prompting from the other members of the group. Mark has come to believe that what he experienced is real, and not some sort of PTSD-induced hallucination. George Gustafson, an engineer with a spiritual side and a recent convert to the reality of climate change, is usually somewhere in the middle of the two sides.

On the fourth day at sea, an especially placid day on the North Atlantic, everyone is gathered below deck for morning coffee in the cozy, mid-ship salon. Having set the autopilot, Gustafson is able to join the group. After some general morning chatter, Clare, back in her nun-teacher mode, poses a question to continue what had become a daily informal colloquium.

"What is needed for humanity to resolve the climate crisis and stop global warming? I know there will have to be a lot of technical advances and societal changes and a lot of sacrifices. We have to trust the scientific evidence and look to science for many of our solutions. However, I don't think we will really be able to make the necessary changes unless science and religion join forces and end their long-standing enmity. Scientific facts are vital. But people are not moved to action by dry data. They need a spiritual vision, which includes the data, to inspire them to change, especially when the change required is so drastic and urgent."

Clare pauses and then continues, "The Book of Proverbs says, 'Where there is no vision, the people perish.' We are all going to perish, the whole planet and all its creatures, if we don't get a vision soon. Science alone can't produce the vision we need. Only religion—or rather spirituality—working together with science can produce a vision powerful enough to inspire humanity to truly change. You might say humanity needs a massive ecological metanoia, a total change of heart and mind that leads to action. Only science and religion working *together* can bring us to this sort of conversion."

Scanning the group, Clare asks, "What do you all think?"

Mark is the first to respond, "I agree with you, Clare. In my own life, science has confirmed over and over that my homosexuality is a normal human variation, not a deviant disease, and that it is programmed either in utero or in very early childhood. It happens way before we are able to choose. It is not a choice. It's just who we are. And it's a glorious part of humanity's diversity. But for people to accept this—and not all have, especially religious types— the gay community and others had to promote a vision of our full humanity, backed by science.

I once asked my psychotherapist, Fr. Patrick Phelan— most of you have met him, of course—'What really gets people to change?' He immediately answered, 'From my clinical experience, 75% of people only change when their fear and pain, or the negative consequences of their behaviors, gets so intense they are more or less forced to change. In other words, pain makes them change. But 25% change because they see something better they want for themselves, and become determined to create it.'"

Mark pauses to let Fr. Phelan's word sink in then continues, "The problem I see with climate change is that most people will only be willing to change when the consequences of global warming get so severe and painful they are forced by the suffering global warming will inflict, to face the facts and change. We know then it will be too late. Our dependence on carbon is like a nicotine addiction. Most smokers now know cigarettes will likely shorten their life and kill them. But that is 20-40 years in the future. Meanwhile, the current effects of smoking aren't too bad, and nicotine makes them feel good. So, it's easy to put off quitting, and act as if lung cancer won't get them in the end. It's the same with global warming. The scientific evidence clearly tells us what will happen in ten, twenty, or fifty years, and that what will occur is really bad. But it's not so bad right now. So why quit smoking now? Why give up the comforts and convenience of carbon now?

We humans are masters of self-deception. We can be very skilled at telling ourselves a lie so convincingly we believe it. Then we bend the truth, search for false, self-confirming evidence or bizarre conspiracy theories. All to support our lie. Some people even become so convinced about their personal lie that they promote it publicly, trying to convince other people to believe it. This category of people, by the way, are called politicians."

Mark pauses to get a laugh from this comment and continues.

"Our incredible ability to self-deceive and remain in denial or even delusion is why so many people find it hard to accept the inconvenient truth of global warming. We are like a frog in a pot of slowly heating water, which convinces itself the increasing warmth is nice and comfortable—so need to jump out, until it's too late, and it becomes a frog-leg supper.

As I understand it, evolution primed the human brain to focus on survival and keeping things simple, so it's very easy to fool. And, I hate to admit it, but I'm a perfect case study in human self-deception. Despite all the evidence to the contrary, I refused to face the truth, convincing myself for years that I shouldn't be, couldn't be, gay. So, look at me now. Gay as can be, and finally happily living in the truth—and in love."

Mark reaches out and takes Simon's hand. They look deeply into each other's eyes for a few moments. Mark's eyes start to overflow with tears. Several others in the group tear up watching them. Finally, Mark lets go of Simon's hand and turns to Clare.

"So, Clare, you are right. Science and religion have to join up soon, and develop a spiritual vision backed by scientific data. Only this will inspire and motivate the reluctant 75%, those not yet in pain, to change now—and not wait for the horrible consequences of global warming to hit them, by which time it will be way too late."

Clare interjects, "Perhaps that's why spiritual contemplatives like Aavani and me, and a religious leader like Mark, have been called together with scientists like Chooky and Simon, to be the Message Bearers. We need each other's perspectives to accomplish whatever this mission is."

Chooky, who has been getting agitated as Clare and Mark have been speaking, blurts out, "But religion really has been the enemy of science and scientific truth. Look at how the Catholic church attacked and attempted to suppress Galileo and his discoveries. What about the many religious people who still oppose the proven theory of Evolution? Or the Christians who are still climate change deniers, despite overwhelming scientific evidence of global warming? Some of these religious types are so focused on saving unborn children they don't give a damn about saving the planet these children are going to have to live on."

Simon speaks up and adds to Chooky's objections, "And what about all the people throughout history and in our own time that use religion to justify hate, prejudice, and even violence? There is nothing worse than when someone uses God or the Bible to vindicate their violence against some other group. Like the 9-11 terrorists and their damned jihad. Or ISIS beheading people who are, by their definition, infidels? All of them claim God wanted them to do these awful acts, and they will even be rewarded by God for performing this violence."

Getting more heated and raising his voice, Simon continues, "Clare, what about your church, the Roman Catholics? It doesn't have the best record either. How about the Crusades, the Inquisition, or the extermination of millions of native people in the name of converting them to Christ? How many Catholics—including the Pope and the bishops—spoke up against the Nazis and tried to stop the Holocaust? And what about all the other wars and genocides perpetrated in the name of religion? Or how about the extreme-right Christian white nationalists, who promote racist ideas and violence, claiming God is on their side, and prefers people of their color? The left-wing extremists can be just as bad, and equally violent, but— since they are mostly atheists and agnostics like me—they at least don't claim God is somehow behind their violence."

Directing his words now to his spouse, Simon lowers his tone and a gentleness returns to his voice, "Mark, I love you and I respect the work you do as a minister. You do wonderful work with people, but I have a hard time stomaching the religion and God part of your work."

Mark turns toward Simon, reaches over and takes his hand, and smiles. "I love you too, Babe, I know some of my work is hard for you to fathom. I can't stomach the ways people misuse religion either. The homophobes have certainly used God against people like us for many centuries."

Responding to Chooky and Simon, Clare says, "I sometimes think religion can be like sex."

This turns everyone's heads—a nun talking about sex— but Aavani, who knows Clare well, just smiles.

"It is beautiful, wondrous, ecstatic, powerful, and yet potentially abusive and even dangerous. I believe both religion and sex are to be deeply enjoyed and yet closely watched. Religion can be a powerful force for good in the world—think of the Dalai Lama, Pope Francis, or Mother Theresa —or it can be misused to rationalize the awful things you are talking about. All you are referring to is an abuse of religion and even an abuse of God. It is not true religion. I have fantasized sometimes that we need to set up a God Abuse Hotline and also a Bible Abuse Hotline to report and investigate when people abuse religion in these ways. It reminds me of a bumper sticker I saw several years back that read, "Lord, save me from your followers!"

A ripple of laughter spreads through the gently rocking salon.

Woosh enters the conversation. "We Tlingits never had a tradition of what you call science, but we always lived close to Nature, and are keen observers of what we see around us. We know the ways of the creatures in the sea and the animals on the land. We see them as our brothers and sisters and know that there is a Great Spirit within them and within all of Nature. It is all one, in the One. Maybe this is the vision we need, Clare. Maybe this is what we indigenous native people must teach the rest of the world, if we are going to save it."

Clare responds, "Woosh, that is what I think too. That's exactly what we need. We have to rediscover the sacredness and unity of Nature and draw closer to her again. One of the reasons I live in Crestone is that it is there in the mountains that I experience God most intimately. It is a "thin place" as the Irish call it. The veil between the world of matter and the world of spirit is thinner there, and I sense her Presence in every mountain peak, every crystalline stream, every little mountain bluebird or mighty elk. Crestone is where I pray best and feel closest to our Creator."

Aavani interjects, "Amen, sister, me too! The Divine Mother Goddess definitely lives among those Sangre de Cristos. The curtain between us is very thin there. I see her, and feel her all around us, and within me, all the time. That is what our guru, Baba Ji, taught us."

Clare continues, "For some people modern science threatens to take away the awe and sacredness of Nature. It has done the opposite for me. The new cosmology of the origins of the universe, the Big Bang Theory, the possibility of multiple universes, the amazing, life-affirming story of Evolution, the information systems transmitting life that we call DNA and epi-genetics, the intricacies and even bizarreness of the Quantum Physics at the hidden core of Nature. If all of this does not inspire awe, what can?

This wondrous science just deepens my spiritual sense that Nature is sacred, and that it is infused with the very Presence of God and is somehow the expression of God's love and His inner life. I still believe that in some fashion God is Creator. That the universe emanates from her love. That God desired to breathe forth a self-creating world that evolved into us. We don't have a story yet to fully express this great mystery, and I believe someday we will. One way I imagine it poetically is that Nature is God's great work of art, while evolution, the Big Bang, and all the complexities of physics and biology are God's palette and brushes. These are the tools and God is the artist."

Clare pauses to take a deep breath as she always does before quoting someone.

"The biologist J.B.S Haldane is quoted as saying, "The universe is not only queerer than we suppose; it is queerer than we *can* suppose. After reading the new cosmology theories, or some of the stranger aspects of Quantum Physics, Nature reveals to me a God who is weirder and queerer than we ever thought. Yet also greater and more awesome than we can suppose."

Mark interrupts, "Really, Clare, God is queer and weird? That's wild. I can hear the new church hymn now (Mark sings an old hymn from 1 John, changing the words), "God is weird, and he who is weird too, abides in God, and God in him."

Clare laughs and goes on, "In short, science hasn't made me question my faith; it's deepened it. And I don't see any real contradiction between science and faith. They are simply two different ways of coming to know the truth of the universe. I have come to believe science without spirituality is empty, and spirituality and religion without science is blind. We need both kinds of truth to save our planet."

Chooky applauds, "Holy cow! A nun who talks about sex and understands science. Who would have thought? I always believed you gals lived in a cloistered world very removed and different from us. You're nothing like the nuns I remember."

Aavani interjects, "Not this old gal. She's really with it. And most of her nun friends I have met are the same. That's part of the reason I really love Clare."

Clare blushes a little, and then Mark speaks again.

"I consider myself a science-enlightened Christian. There are some stories in the Old Testament, like Noah and the Flood and the destruction by God of Sodom and Gomorrah—that's where we gays get our nasty label, Sodomite—which seem to teach that God at times punishes the sins of humankind by unleashing his wrath on us through destructive natural disasters, like the Great Flood. I always refused to take this biblical teaching literally, but in the last few years, as global warming worsens, and especially because of what we all have witnessed in the last few weeks, I have started to change my mind. Maybe there is a kernel of wisdom and truth in these biblical stories.

But it's not God's wrath that brings on natural disasters to punish us. It's our own environmental sins against Nature that causes ecological consequences which "punish" (Mark makes air quotes) us for our—let's call them—eco-sins. Our pollution, our chemicals, our spewing of so much carbon into the atmosphere and into the ocean. Our selfishness and small-mindedness, and our failure to treat

Nature as sacred. These are the sins that bring on "punishment." But not directly from God, rather as natural consequences of our actions against our planet.

The events of the past few weeks, though, make me think something even more might be happening. Some of the disasters we have seen, I guess are just the growing effects of global warming which you scientists (he looks at Simon and Chooky) have been warning us would come.

But some of what is happening around the globe, what we have seen in our visions, and in the message given to you, Chooky, makes it look like Nature herself is turning against us, and is now out to get us. Maybe the sixth extinction scientists have been telling us is unfolding around the world is our *own* extinction. Is the extermination of so many species, which we are causing, going to include the human species? Maybe that's what our visions and the whale's message is warning us about. Is that how it looks to the rest of you?"

This leads to a heated discussion with Chooky and Simon maintaining that Nature turning against humans is scientifically impossible. Clare, Aavani, Mark, and Woosh argue that it seems to them something beyond normal science is going on, perhaps something—who knows what—that is spiritual and beyond science.

Chooky interjects, "I guess I'm growing skeptical again. It just doesn't fit with everything I have learned scientifically. I really don't know what to do with all of this, or where to put it in my mind. But my scientific training tells me to refrain from making conclusions until there is evidence to support a theory."

George Gustafson, fifty and with the weathered good looks of a Robert Redford doppelganger, has been listening in silence to this discussion. He breaks into the debate with a booming baritone and West Texas accent, "Hi, you all, I'm George and I'm a gratefully recovering fossil fuel addict."

Everyone laughs, and responds in unison, "Hi, George!"

"I used to love my carbon. I'm an oil engineer and oil executive. I drilled into Mother Nature and drained out her juices all over the world. I refined and sold all that dinosaur juice to all my fellow carbon junkies for years, and I was proud of it. Couldn't get enough fossil fuel. I even worked with my fellow oilies, like Sam Burroughs over at Moxxon and Rex Stout before he became president, to try to stop climate scientists and question their conclusions. This has been a secret, but I'm confessing to you now that I also helped organize and fund what you could call an oil militia. We did this in case we needed to use force to protect our businesses and our profits. I'm ashamed of all of that now.

To show you how insane and perverse things have gotten with the fossil fuel industry, listen to this: Did you know that for the past several years oil companies have actually been using cooling technologies to freeze and preserve the permafrost that has been melting underneath their oil drilling rigs on the north slope of Alaska? Here they are pumping more oil than ever in the arctic, causing more global warming, which is leading to massive changes up North including the melting of their permafrost foundations. Instead of considering not drilling, and working faster on alternatives to oil, they simply drill more, and use more energy to freeze the very permafrost which they themselves are thawing. How crazy is that? Sounds like something that Kafka fella would have made up, doesn't it? Denial isn't just a river in Egypt, as the AA saying goes; it's also an oil rig in the Arctic National Wildlife Refuge in Alaska.

And talking about insane and perverse denial, do you remember the great freeze of 2021, when the polar vortex flipped out and invaded Texas? All those millions of my fellow Texans who were without heat, power, and water for days, or weeks on end, some of whom quite literally froze to death. Remember that?

Do you remember too what the Texas politicians and some of the petro-people tried to blame it on? Frozen wind-turbines! When it was really their damned natural gas plants and pipelines that froze up, leading to the massive power outages. The very natural gas systems which created the climate warming that led to the great freeze in the first place. I think these people's minds—or maybe their consciences—froze first. Or maybe because, in America, we don't listen to our prophets, only to profits – the latter word spelled with a $ sign. Which is why America, and many other wealthy nations, probably won't listen to us either. But, we have to try don't we?"

George pauses to let these stories sink in.

Chooky and Woosh interject and describe to the group the changes they have observed in Alaska due to global warming. Chooky speaks for them both, "It's affecting us up North more quickly and more severely than almost anyplace else on the planet. We are seeing the changes from the warming of the planet in real-time, almost on a daily basis. Our way of life in the North is in danger. The hunting, the fishing, many of our traditional ways of sustaining ourselves and our culture, all of it is disappearing, literally melting away."

George continues, "Yeah. I hear the same stories from some of my buddies up on Prudhoe Bay, at least when they think no one else is listening." He nods toward Chooky and Woosh.

"Back to my sad story. About eight years ago, I went diving on the Great Barrier Reef, one of my favorite places in the whole world. I had dived the Great Barrier a few times before and marveled at its beauty. So many different colors of coral and fish. Such an incredible variety of ocean wildlife. When I dove in 2015, the ocean had warmed and there had been a widespread devastating coral bleaching event. For miles and miles along the reef, the coral had turned white and was dying. All the incredible color was gone, along with many of the fish, turtles, and such. Man, that was awful to see!

This woke me up. To lose something like that I loved. To lose such beauty. To see such death and devastation finally opened my eyes and my deluded brain to see that the scientists and climate activists were right.

It was like an alcoholic—which, by the way, I'm one of those too; fifteen years of sobriety now—waking up one morning, and finally getting what the booze had been doing to them. Denial and self-delusion are bitches, people, and incredibly strong. You become semi-blind. My sponsor calls it "macular degeneration of the soul." You can't see the center of things, only the periphery.

Anyway, I started to research all of the climate science I had been ignoring and denying. My God, I was stunned! It was like I was knocked to the ground like St. Paul, and my eyes were finally opened to what was actually going on. And here I was one of the worst contributors to global warming with all my oil pumping. I vowed to do what I could to change things as fast as I could.

My board of directors was none too happy, but I set a plan in motion to shift our business to alternative energy and reduce our carbon footprint. Surprisingly, it's turning out that we can still make a decent profit with a plan like this. I lobbied my friends in the oil business and politicians I knew. Mixed success with the oil execs, although many of them do see the writing on the wall and know the future of their business has to change. No luck at all with the politicians. Surprise, right?

So, that's my story. That's how I got here. I consider myself a recovering carbon addict and a born-again environmentalist. That's why I'm here with you and support you all one hundred percent. But I'm not any kind of philosopher, much less a theologian, so I don't know what to think about it all, especially the God thing. I'm an engineer. We design and fix things. So, I'm here to help you fix global warming, no matter what it takes.

By the way, besides all the carbon dioxide we are pumping into our atmosphere by burning oil, let's not forgot plastics. As you know they're petrochemicals, derived from oil, and we are putting enormous amounts of these plastics into our environment. The bodies of fish in the sea, animals on land, the bodies of our own babies and children, you and I, are being filled with minute plastic fibers. Who knows what this is doing to us? Some scientists think the widespread exposure to plastics is behind the pervasive drop in men's sperm count. Some of these chemicals are actually shrinking our penises. Now that's getting personal! Worldwide, human fertility rates are steadily declining as well. That's an oncoming train which should wake us up. All from plastics and other chemicals we're spewing everywhere. Pretty soon, I think, we will all be pooping plastics!"

Everyone laughs.

George waits for the laughter to subside and continues, "Sorry for the sick, scatological joke, but if we don't laugh at some of this stuff, we will all die of depression and despair. I'm not sure where this little adventure of ours is leading us. I just got the feeling it's the right thing to do, and that we're heading in the right direction, even though we don't know our ultimate destination or outcome. It's like building a bridge from one side without seeing the opposite shore, but that's what we got to do."

George pauses, looks out the hatch, and watches the sails for a few moments. Then he turns back to the gathering in the salon, "Speaking of destination, folks, I'm noticing the wind is shifting and we might be getting off course. I better check the autopilot. We don't want to miss Ireland, do we?"

"Woosh, would you come on deck and help me adjust the sails?"

"As for the rest of you, I think it's time to end today's little colloquium. Get topside and get some sun. You never know on the North Atlantic how long good weather will last. Ya gotta enjoy Mother Nature even while you try to save her. Ya can't just sit around all day and talk about her. Enough philosophizing for now, get up on deck and enjoy what our Mother is offering today."

Everyone files up the gangway and spreads out to various favorite spots on the deck and in the cockpit. Chooky, Woosh, Mark, and Simon continue talking about the questions raised in the morning discussion. Clare and Aavani find private spots on the deck to meditate and pray about what was said. Aavani closes her eyes and softly chants her mantra, her voice blending with the wind coursing past the sails, lifting the boat forward through the waves. Clare keeps her eyes open as she meditates, watching the gentle, rolling ocean swells, and looking to the empty horizon, searching for answers, but finding only the emptiness of the great ocean.

Chapter Twenty-One

Later the same day, Gustafson maneuvers to be alone with Aavani back in the main salon. He has done this several times during the voyage, flirting with her each time. Aavani is quite deft at handling men like George from her years living in Kolkata and New York City. So, each time Aavani ignores the flirtation, tries to deflect the conversation to a safer topic, and gets away as quickly as she can politely do so. She does not want to offend George, since he is their patron and the owner of their vessel, and they are in the middle of the North Atlantic.

This time George decides to push his luck and comes on more directly, if also more creatively.

"Aavani, you are so beautiful. You are one of those hot, dark beauties I find so irresistible. And you meditate and are so deeply spiritually. I've read in Redbook or somewhere that people who meditate and pray make the best lovers. Something about being in tune with the Spirit putting you in sync with the pleasures of the flesh. Almost makes me want to pray more myself. You're Indian too. You must have studied the Kama Sutra. I bet there are some great moves from that book you could teach me. I'd be glad to be your student."

George pauses and moves closer, hoping his words have had their desired effect.

"So, what do you say? Would you come with me now, or some other time, to my captain's cabin, and make some lovely meditation and Kama Sutra together?"

Aavani has a brief flashback to the incidents in Kolkata when the sex traffickers tried to entice her and force her into the sex trade. She feels the old fear and helplessness growing inside her. But she quickly recenters herself and—using the tools of emotional alchemy she learned from Mother Teresa's sisters—turns her fear into what the sisters called "holy anger."

By the time she speaks, Aavani is incensed.

"Well, that's a unique pick-up line! Look, George, you're pretty cute, and I am grateful for all you are doing for us to support our crazy mission. But I'm not in the least interested. I would appreciate it if you would stop coming on to me like you've been doing. It has to stop now! Has your AA sponsor ever suggested to you that you might be a sex addict as well as an alcoholic?"

George looks a little taken aback, and replies. "Well, yes, but he thinks everything is an addiction. How could something as beautiful and natural as sex be an addiction?"

"George, for your information, I have a serious boyfriend: a Buddhist monk, back in Colorado. We have a marvelous relationship and are totally faithful to each other.

Besides, how can you even think of sex when we are on such a crucial, possibly dangerous mission? Are you taking this seriously? Or is this just another adventure, and I'm just another conquest for a playboy millionaire?"

George looks away for a minute then turns back toward Aavani and continues, "You know how the Bible says, 'Eat, drink, and be merry. For tomorrow we die.'? Well, my translation of "be merry" is to have as much spectacular sex as possible. Like I know we would have together."

He pauses, hoping his words elicit some interest from Aavani. He sees only disdain in her eyes, but presses on regardless.

"Yes, I do take our mission seriously. But if we are heading to the end of the world, or we are going to get killed on the way there, why not go out with great sex? We might as well enjoy ourselves as we sail on outta here."

Aavani, getting angrier by the moment, raises her voice and responds, "I can't believe how some of you Westerners use your Bible to justify everything and anything! I don't think Sr. Clare would agree with your interpretation of that verse. And she's no prude. By the way, Clare has been warning me about you. I do hope you work on your prayer life, George. Not to have better sex, but to finally grow up. Because it's time to grow up, George, and stop acting like a testosterone-driven teenager. In fact, it's time for the whole human race to grow up, leave its adolescence behind, and become spiritually mature. That's what Clare was talking about this morning. We need a new spiritual vision to save the planet. We won't ever have such a vision until there is a widespread spiritual transformation and maturity of soul that spreads all across the planet—including you, George."

Aavani pauses, working to keep her intense anger from getting out of control. Taking a few deep breaths, she continues in a lower, yet equally outraged, voice, "So, no, I will not have sex with you no matter what the future holds. Do you get the #MeToo movement at all? Women aren't putting up with this sort of crap anymore, no matter who you are. I'm certainly not. So, back off, George, and stop harassing me! If you don't I will have to speak to the rest of the group and out you, George. Go away, little boy, and leave me alone. Most of all, grow up!"

Aavani gives George one last fierce look, pivots on the balls of her feet, and with great poise and confidence strides out of the salon and up the gangway to the fresh air of the top-deck.

George is left speechless and shamefaced. He is not used to being turned down, much less lectured to. He knows inside that Aavani is right. He plops down on the couch, stares out the companionway to the blue mid-ocean sky, and starts to think about what Aavani has just said to him.

Yeah, okay. It is time for me to grow up. Maybe helping with this mission might get me to finally take life seriously. Maybe instead of trying to lure Aavani into bed with me, I should ask her to teach me how to meditate. Well, I guess Clare would be safer. I would probably just keep hitting on Aavani, instead of meditating. Yeah, George, my friend, it is high-time you grew up—before it's too late.

Chapter Twenty-Two

Two days after the Message Bearers leave the Maine coast, the oil militia operatives finally receive word from a spy in Gustafson's office that Gustafson had recently spoken to them. And immediately after that he had traveled to his estate on Little Cranberry Island off the coast of Maine. Perhaps the Message Bearers were also headed there.

The militiamen hurry to Northeast Harbor. They rent a boat and invade Little Cranberry Island. When they find Gustafson's mansion empty and his sailboat not in its slip, they begin questioning the residents of the island. They pressure the old couple who witnessed the sailboat's departure to reveal what they saw. The militia conclude that the whole Message Bearers group must be with Gustafson on his sailboat. But heading where? They can't determine that. The operatives report their findings to Sam Burroughs and to President Stout at the White House.

President Stout tries to get the Navy to pursue the Message Bearers, claiming they are terrorists. The admirals and the Secretary of the Navy refuse, noting that everyone involved is an American citizen, citing the law prohibiting the military from getting involved in domestic or civilian affairs. They suggest that President Stout call the FBI. But Stout has alienated the FBI, and doubts they would pursue the group without evidence of some criminal action.

Frustrated with his own government and its unwillingness to do his bidding, President Stout calls Sam Burroughs at Anthrakas, and orders the oil militia to pursue the Message Bearers at sea. Burroughs calls around among his billionaire buddies, and finds a fellow oil tycoon and climate denier who has a large, luxury ocean-going power cruiser, a Selene 128, named *Crude*, berthed in Bar Harbor, Maine, not too far from Little Cranberry Island. He convinces his friend to lend his boat to the cause. The militia force arrives in Bar Harbor, commandeers the yacht, and heads out to sea in pursuit of the Message Bearers.

Early May in the North Atlantic is usually, depending on the route you choose, one of the best times to make the crossing. The weather is generally calmer and the winds more agreeable, although a storm can brew at any time.

Gustafson has made the passage several times and knows the usual routes. He chooses the less-frequented northern Great Circle Route over the easier, less risky, more popular southern route via the Azores. He knows the northern route is likely to be stormier and very foggy. There is also a greater possibility of encountering icebergs drifting away from the coast of Greenland. However, he hopes the northern route will get them to Ireland quicker.

And, more importantly, it will make them less detectable. In case someone is following them, he reasons they are more likely to guess that he would take the southern route. He navigates away from any shipping channels and bypasses the usual ports of call in Nova Scotia and Newfoundland.

The intelligence the oil group has obtained only tells them the Message Bearers are heading somewhere in Europe or the British Isles. It could be Portugal, Spain, France, Britain, Ireland, or even one of the Scandinavian countries. This means the best they can do is make an educated guess and take the most likely route.

Tom Heatherstone, the captain of the *Crude* and a veteran charter captain with many years at sea, guesses—as Gustafson suspected—that the Message Bearers will choose the usual southern route. He believes that with his much faster boat he should catch up with them in three or four days.

After five days with no sign of the *Ruach*, President Stout gets information from the spy in Gustafson's office that he usually takes the more challenging northern route to transit the Atlantic. When this is passed on to the militia, they order Captain Heatherstone to change course in the mid-Atlantic, east of the Azores, and head north. The intelligence also suggests that, on that course, the Message Bearers are likely heading to either England, Ireland, the northern coast of France, or through the English Channel to one of the northern European countries.

Chapter Twenty-Three

The North Atlantic is strangely quiet. The Message Bearers spot few other ships, and sail away from any that they see. The weather has been surprisingly gentle, and the sleek Beneteau is making good time.

On the tenth day of the passage, the Message Bearers awake at dawn to find they are becalmed and surrounded by huge icebergs peeking through a grey shroud of thick fog, like the giant white and blue fortresses of a Disney Ice Queen. The unexpected ice has drifted east from the swiftly deteriorating Greenland Ice Cap. They sit for several hours waiting for the wind to return and for a passageway through the bergs to open up.

They are peacefully contemplating the eerie beauty of this scene when they suddenly notice some disturbance in the water around them. Woosh is the first to spot them, *"Ke'eet, "Ke'eet!"* he shouts in Tlingit, "Oh my God, orcas, dozens of them!" Chooky says in an awed whisper.

The whole group comes up to the top-deck and stares in wonder at the sight of so many killer whales with their tall, dark dorsal fins piercing the water's surface, arcing with flashes of black and white in and out of the water, as they swim toward the *Ruach*. They are approaching the boat from four sides in four different pods.

"That's strange," Chooky comments, "It's very unusual for this many different pods to be in the same territory together. I wonder what's going on?"

At that point, an especially large orca in one pod spy-hops to get a better look at the sailboat.

"She must be the leader," Chooky says, "Orcas are a matriarchal society like us Tlingits."

The four pods then merge, as if obeying a signal from the matriarch and form a moving circle around the *Ruach*.

Chooky, with noticeable awe in her voice, speaks again, "I have never seen anything like this. This is spectacular!"

Woosh, with a tremor of fear in his voice responds, "I think it's ominous."

Sr. Clare, who has been completely silent since she emerged on deck from her cabin, finally says, "I don't know anything about killer whales, but this feels very ominous to me too. I have a bad feeling in my spirit."

Suddenly the Message Bearers see a second ring forming, outside the orca circle. Dozens of shark fins surface, and the sharks organize into another ring, rotating counterclockwise in the opposite direction of the orcas.

"Sweet Jesus!" Chooky exclaims, using an epithet she had not voiced since her childhood catechism days, "This is even stranger. Orcas and sharks don't usually congregate or hunt together. And it looks like there are several different species of sharks out there. I can't tell for sure, but it looks like Great Whites, Tiger sharks, Bull sharks, and maybe others. This does look ominous, but most likely there are some unusually large schools of prey fish below the surface which we can't see. They are probably the reason for this strange behavior. These predators are all just here hunting."

The *Ruach* is now totally encircled by sharks and killer whales. The group watches mesmerized in silence, some awed, some with a growing sense of dread. Woosh, Clare, Aavani, and Mark are especially agitated. Finally, Aavani can't contain herself any longer and screams, "What the fuck is going on? Devi, please protect us!"

At that moment, they see that the circles have stopped moving and a gap has opened to port in both the orca and shark rings. Immediately, a huge blue whale, the largest animal on the planet, swims at high speed through both openings and is heading straight toward the portside of the sailboat. Woosh finally gets the whole picture, "The big blue is going to ram us and capsize us. Then the sharks and orcas will devour us. Get ready for impact. Find your life vests and put them on now! Get the lifeboats ready."

Their trance is broken, and everyone scrambles about the boat to prepare for being capsized.

Before the group can pile into the two Zodiacs, a ring of eight huge humpback whales bursts out of the water, as they do for one of their feeding circles. They are so close to the boat they splash a large volume of water onto the deck. The Message Bearers are all drenched.

The humpback circle blocks the blue whale. It stops out of respect to its smaller cousins, and dives beneath *Ruach*, slapping its huge tail on the surface of the water as it descends, splashing the Message Bearers a second time. The humpbacks form another circle around the sailboat as if providing a safe escort. The sharks and orcas also break out of their circles and back away.

Aavani spits some water out of her mouth and shouts, "Holy shit! Devi heard our prayer. Praise you, Devi. Thank you, Devi!"

Simon responds, "I don't know who or what saved us, except for these humpbacks, but I'm grateful too. Let's get the hell out of here before the orcas and sharks change their mind and attack again!"

Chooky, with a mixture of wonder and perplexity, adds, "That was awesome! That was the humpbacks' feeding circle. It's something I have studied a lot. The humpbacks work as a team to surround and entrap their prey fish. But this...this...what was this? This kind of humpback behavior has never been reported before. What motivated them to rescue us? Could the humpback who spoke to me in Alaska somehow be connected to this? I can't see how. But who knows? I'm not certain of anything anymore."

The wind finally picks up a little and the group, who have learned from Gustafson and Woosh how to manage the innumerable sheets, cleats, and other paraphernalia of an ocean-going sailboat, together host the mainsail and set the genoa.

The *Ruach* slowly sails through an opening forming between two icebergs. The Message Bearers are underway once more, now encircled by the protective sentry force of humpbacks, who swim alongside them, port and starboard, bow and stern. Gustafson sets the autopilot for the west coast of Ireland.

At this moment, before the *Ruach* can fully get underway, the *Crude* arrives on the scene. An advance, secret spy satellite had penetrated the stealth defenses of the *Ruach* and captured a fuzzy image of the sailboat. It was clear enough that U.S. intelligence was able to discern the sleek lines of the Beneteau and pass the information on to President Stout. He radioed the oil militia aboard the

Crude. Captain Heatherstone is ordered to change course to the coordinates provided by the satellite. The Message Bearers are much farther north than anyone expected.

When Heatherstone spots the sailboat, he speeds up to intercept her. The oil militia gather their weapons and prepare to board the sailboat.

Mark is sitting in the stern of the *Ruach*, still in shock about their narrow escape, and wondering what it means. As he watches the icebergs slowly disappear into the fog behind them, he spots the *Crude* swiftly bearing down on them and sounds an alarm.

The Message Bearers once again assemble again on deck, watching in horror as the fast yacht quickly narrows the gap with the much slower sailboat. They all sense that the boat has evil intentions and is there to stop them. They are unarmed and would not have the desire to fight even if they were armed. They watch helplessly as the oil boat slows to begin its attack.

Clare speaks for them all, "Is this how our mission is going to end, Lord? We thought you were going to protect us, so we could deliver the message we believed was from you."

Quoting St. Teresa of Avila, she adds, "If this is how you treat your friends, Lord, no wonder you have so few."

The matriarch of the orcas spy-hops again and sees the power boat has slowed. She signals to the whale and shark attack groups to turn their fury on the oil boat. Her orders from Gaia are to begin attacking humans. She figures one group of humans is as good as another and realizes the other group is being protected for some reason by the humpbacks.

The blue whale resurfaces and with great force rams and capsizes the *Crude*, its luxury boat hull no match for the power of the whale. Most of the militia, on deck to attack and board the *Ruach*, are thrown overboard where the sharks and the orcas go into a feeding frenzy. The water boils crimson red all around the overturned hull. The few crewmembers who are not thrown into the water are trapped under the hull and drown.

Captain Heatherstone watches all of this in horror from the bridge of the *Crude*.

He has only a few seconds to wonder: *What the hell is happening here? I don't believe what I'm seeing. Why is this happening to me? I'm just following orders. I don't even like these oil people.*

He jumps into the water from his post on the bridge as the ship capsizes, and is quickly devoured by a waiting great white. There are no survivors.

Everyone aboard *Ruach* has been watching these events. A horrified, reverent silence comes over them. They are safe after all. There is a palpable feeling of relief. However, they are also aware of the appalling loss of human life which just happened in front of them. Chooky and Simon are especially stunned and speechless. None of their scientific training can explain what they just witnessed.

Finally, Mark breaks the silence, "Whoever you are, God bless each and every one of your souls."

Clare silently makes the sign of the Cross over the blood-drenched water. Then everyone, even George, either kneels or bows their head in prayer for several minutes before rising to reset the sails and the autopilot, as *Ruach*—under a freshening wind—surges forward over the rising swells toward Ireland.

Chapter Twenty-Four

Just before the *Crude* sinks, Captain Heatherstone is able to radio a Mayday message. In his last communication he describes the attack that capsized his ship, reports that they found the *Ruach,* and reads out their last position coordinates. This is picked up by the NSC and reported to the White House. President Stout immediately calls Sam Burroughs at Anthrakas. They agree on a new plan.

President Stout calls President Sokolov, who is almost as good a friend to Stout as President Putin was to Trump. He requests that the Russian Navy find, and capture, the sailboat and the Message Bearers. Sokolov agrees.

Russia's economy, and Sokolov's power, are almost totally dependent on maintaining the hegemony of oil as the primary source of world energy. The Russian Navy begins its search for the *Ruach*. The last coordinates given suggest that the sailboat is either heading to northern France, Britain, or Ireland. They can only rule out southern Europe. The Russians guess Britain, but they begin to patrol all possible routes. Because of the stealth features of the sailboat, the Russians know they have to get close enough for a visual confirmation.

A lone Russian ship, an Admiral Gorshkov-class frigate, the *Admiral Gorshkov*, without yet knowing it, is getting close to spotting the sailboat when Gaia suddenly stirs her molten iron core. In response, Earth's magnetic field weakens and its magnetic pole switches rapidly and unpredictably from north to south and back again for three terrifying days, causing a massive disruption in electronic systems all over the planet.

As a result of the magnetic havoc, the whole Russian fleet loses their navigational instruments including the *Admiral Gorshkov*. The frigate gets turned around by the magnetic pole fluctuations, and begins to head south away from the sailboat, thinking they are going north. The *Gorshkov* had gotten within four miles of the sailboat, just short of when it would have become visible on the ocean's horizon.

The northern and southern lights intensify and can be seen over most of the planet. People around the world are both awed and terrorized by the amazingly colorful and brilliant auroras shining in shimmering veils and sheets across the night sky. To some, it signifies the end of the world.

Massive disruptions and chaos develop with GPS, GPS navigation satellites, power grids, and navigation systems all over the planet. There are widespread power outages. The great majority of people in the world are in the dark. Everyone on the planet who is traveling and relying on their cellphone GPS gets terribly lost, confused, and disoriented. Fundamentalist Christians who believe in the Rapture think this is it, and wait to be snatched up into heaven on the spot.

Instead, they merely get lost like the rest of GPS-dependent humanity.

Geophysicists around the world are stunned by these events. They had been noting for several years that the location of the magnetic north pole had been shifting more rapidly than in the past. They also knew the Earth's magnetic shield had weakened by 9% over the past 170 years. But they are at a loss to explain how the magnetic poles could have switched back and forth so rapidly.

"This shouldn't be physically possible," one scientist is quoted as saying, "The last time in the Earth's history that this polar switch happened it took a thousand years to switch back. I don't know what caused this, but perhaps it is some kind of warning?"

Other scientists reference a 2021 study that demonstrates that the last polar flip—42,000 years ago—caused cataclysmic changes in the planet's climate, which led to massive extinctions of a number of species; including, it is theorized, the extirpation of our "cousins," the Neanderthals.

A co-author of the 2021 study, geoscientist Terence Turnkey, comments, "To the Neanderthals and to the Homo Sapiens alive at the time, it must have seemed like the end of days. For the Neanderthals it was."

On the *Ruach*, Gustafson also becomes disoriented, having lost all of his navigational aids. The autopilot and GPS are now worthless. Woosh takes over the helm, employing his nature-based ancient Tlingit sea skills to continue on course toward Galway, Ireland. While this is happening, Sr. Clare is able to talk by radio to her Irish contact, Fr. Liam O'Reilly. He says he has now heard that Grainne has fled to Inishmore Island, one of the Aran Islands off the west coast of Ireland in Galway Bay. Clare rushes to the bridge to tell Woosh. The *Ruach* adjusts her course and heads to Inishmore.

The priest also tells Clare about all of the apocalyptic events happening around the world which the media are reporting. In the U.S. and Canada, huge flocks of Canadian Geese are gathering around airports, and systematically attacking airliners taking off, purposely flying into the intake of the jet engines and stalling them. Three airliners have crashed, killing all aboard.

The Thwaites Glacier, also known as the Doomsday Glacier, in a remote part of Antarctica, has suddenly collapsed, as scientists have been warning for several years. It slides rapidly into the sea, raising global ocean levels three to four feet. In some places King Tides and local storms exacerbate the flooding, which suddenly inundates hundreds of coastal cities and towns. There is significant loss of life and property. Many beachside hotels and condo towers are now islands in the sea. A massive rescue effort in coastal areas all over the world is necessary.

There is also a report of another ominous swarm of earthquakes on both the San Andreas and Juan de Fuca faults on the U.S. West Coast. Seismologists warn again that two "Big Ones" might be coming. A seismologist in Seattle warns that these swarms of tremors might be precursors of the 9.0 one they have been expecting.

A very lethal new Coronavirus—again spread by bats and another unidentified animal at a Chinese wild meat market—has infected thousands in Shanghai, China. It threatens to become another worldwide pandemic, perhaps worse than the Coronavirus of 2020, even more deadly and infectious than Covid-19.

Chapter Twenty-Five

In the middle of a cloudy, moonless night, the *Ruach* silently glides into the small harbor of Kilronan on the east side of Inishmore facing the Galway coast. The Message Bearers are all awake, having been awakened and brought topside when their humpback escorts noisily leave them—all eight breaching at once—just off the coast of Inishmore. They all wave to the humpbacks and silently thank them. Chooky whispers to the dark waters, "Thank you, my friends."

At 9:30am the next morning the Irish harbormaster, Fergus Connelly—whose speech alternates between Gaelic and English—motors out to meet them in his slightly modernized curragh. He inquires who they are, and what their business is on Inishmore in the usual wryly humorous and indirect Irish fashion.

"Welcome to Inishmore, *mo cara*! You have a mighty fine-looking sloop there. *Ruach*? Almost sounds Gaelic." Then he mentions a few Gaelic words that do sound much like the sailboat's name.

"You all look to be Americans. All different colors, like America. Except for one color is missing, if you don't mind my saying so. We Irish love Americans, except for your president; well, and the last fellow too."

Gathering himself up in a mock official demeanor, Fergus continues, "So, the government, way off in Dublin, requires me to ask—I wouldn't be wanting to know myself—what might be bringing you to Inishmore, all the way by sail from America? By the bye, I didn't hear your engine when you came into the harbor last night. Nice bit of sailing that'd require, if you don't mind my saying so. A lost art—and a fine way of sneaking into a harbor. That is, if you needed to."

Gustafson, reluctant to reveal their purpose for coming to Ireland, takes charge of the conversation. "Fergus, my friend, we are just tourists, cruising your beautiful west coast of Ireland. Just wanting to stay a few days to see the sights of the Aran Isles, and get refreshed by the peace and quiet of Inishmore after our long trip across the Atlantic."

Offhandedly he adds, "We've heard though that there might be some kind of environmental gathering on one of the Aran Islands. Have you heard anything about this? We might want to visit with them. We are kind of environmentalists too, back in the States."

Fergus immediately grows suspicious and wary, but, like an Irishman dealing with the British occupiers of the past, he hides his true feelings behind a screen of words. "I might have heard of such a thing. Now I'm an environmentalist, so to speak, myself. But I don't go for all those extremists you read about, burning gasoline autos, oil pumps, coalmines, and all that. Everyone here on the Arans are true environmentalists. We love our rocky land and take good care of it. We respect the ocean that surrounds us. We are part of the ocean, as much as the whales and the dolphins.

That's why we originally fished from our curraghs, only powered by our oars and Aran muscles, as some still do. You can see a few offshore a bit just now. They're as natural a boat as you ever will see. Lays so lightly on the water, the fish can't even feel them coming. They think the curragh is just one of them; another large, black species of fish. You won't find many places as pristine and wild as here. So, for sure, there are environmentalists all around here."

Fergus pauses to scan the *Ruach* more closely. Then looks away, toward the distant Galway coastline. "But, you know, sometimes the answer to a question depends on who's doing the asking."

Pausing again, he purposely feints to a different tangent. "Did you know there's no word in Gaelic for "Yes" or "No." Fine language, Gaelic. Many things make better sense in Gaelic than in English. English can be such a harsh language. Everything is yes or no, either or, this or that, black or white. No room for the thousand shades of grey or the thousand shades of green we have here in Ireland. No room for mystery either, even for the Great Mystery of God. It's a shame Irish is not spoken much outside the Gaeltacht.

We Celts have a great knack for mystery and mysticism with all of the knots, spirals, and rings on our sacred stones. We kept the knack even after we became Christians—God bless, St. Patrick—we put the same sacred circles on our High Crosses. Then Rome—not saying anything against the good Pope—came and tried to take it away. Tried to turn us Irish into Romans. Then the English came and tried to make us English…when they weren't trying to starve us into submission. Almost worked too, but we Celts have endured, especially in places like here in the wild west of Ireland."

Clare decides it might help to identify herself as a Catholic nun. When the harbormaster hears this, he lights up and drops his caution.

"Ah, sister, now why didn't you say so? My own dear sister is a nun down in Dingle. Much like yourself."

Finally answering Gustafson's question, Fergus decides to tell them a little bit of the truth.

"Now, some people say there is one of those eco-groups camping behind the walls of old Dún Aonghasa, way on the top of the island, just a few miles from here. The only way to get there is by horse-drawn Irish jaunty carts. You know there is no carbon pollution from those beauties. Only a little methane here and there.

One of my cousins, he owns a few of the carts to haul around the tourists. The tourists love 'em. Think they've really discovered the ol' sod. I prefer electric golf carts myself. I could see if my cousin is free today to bring you up to the fort and see what there is to see. That way you could look like you really are the tourists you say you are."

With that, Fergus winks knowingly at Sr. Clare, boards his curragh, and rows slowly back to the landing in front of his little white-washed cottage office. About an hour later, everyone piles into *Ruach*'s two Zodiacs and motors to shore, where they meet Fergus at the quay. Fergus has arranged two jaunting carts for the group and introduces them to his cousin.

"This is my cousin, Columbkille. He'll be your jarvey and guide. He's a fine lad from the next island over, Inishmaan. He's also been to New York and Boston, and just returned. So, he speaks American too. We're glad to have him back here in the Arans. He'll take fine care of you."

Columbkille is a tall, striking young man with the classic Black Irish look of dark hair and piercing blue eyes. He arranges the group into the two jaunty carts: Clare, Aavani, and Gustafson in the first, and Mark, Simon, Chooky, and Woosh in the second.

They ride briskly up the hill on the Killeany Road past the whitewashed thatched roof cottages of Lower Kilronan, then Kilronan proper, and finally Upper Kilronan, all three tiny villages. The window frames and doorways are painted a riot of vivid colors in contrast to the whitewashed walls of the cottages and the grey rock of the barren landscape. Many of the cottages sport traditional thatched roofs.

Leaving the villages, they climb through the rocky, treeless countryside of Inishmore toward Dún Aonghasa. The rugged karst landscape is dominated by vast pavements of grey limestone, fissured and crumbling, outlined in places by intricate networks of dry-stone walls, dark grey containers for tiny brilliant green pastures. The cart path itself is lined by the grey rock walls.

They pass a number of these small, vibrant green fields, delineated by limestone rock walls meticulously fitted together stone upon stone by local farmers. Even the gates to the tiny fields are piled rock, since there are no trees for wood on the island to fashion a gate.

It's a clear, blue-sky day, and they can see the grey-blue and green mountains of Connemara in the distance on the mainland, rising above the waters of Galway Bay—now grey, now green, now blue, depending on the ever-changing light.

They bounce and roll in the jaunty carts up a gradual incline toward Dún Aonghasa. The outlines of the ancient prehistoric stone fort gradually take shape as they approach. Before them rises a massive lump of dark grey limestone rock brooding atop a gently sloping hill, encircled by four concentric circles of dry-stone constructed walls and jumbles of rocks.

The original layout of Dún Aonghasa in the Bronze and Iron Ages was either oval or D-shaped. But parts of the cliff and fort have subsequently collapsed into the ocean, leaving the Dún more of a semi-circle spreading over fourteen acres, protecting the inner semi-circular flat courtyard that falls away down the high cliff into the sea.

It looks to have been built by its ancient architects as a last-ditch defense against some unknown, yet dreadful and overwhelmingly formidable enemy. An aura of simultaneous awe and intense fear emanates from the dark stones. The Dún was obviously intended to intimidate, yet also bespeaks the terror instilled in its builders by the enemy it was built to protect them against.

Clare feels a chill run through her, a wave of foreboding similar to what she felt in her vision.

Trying to shake it off, she leans over to Aavani and whispers, "It looks like a movie set for *The Lord of the*

Rings, don't you think? If it had a tower, it would be Lord Sauron's fortress. In fact, except for the kind people and the bright green fields scattered all about, the whole island reminds me of Mordor."

Aavani nods and adds, "I keep waiting to see Sauron's all-seeing Eye rotating toward us."

She feels a similar sense of dread as Clare but doesn't want to voice it out loud.

Columbkille, having been briefed by Fergus to act as if they are just another group of tourists, goes into his guidebook spiel as the carts roll toward the Dún.

"Ah, now you're seeing Dún Aonghasa. That's its name in the Irish. It's also known as Dún Aengus in English. This is an actual prehistoric stone fort with a very thick semi-circle, inner stone wall backed by a 1000-meter, or almost 400-foot, cliff that falls straight into the North Atlantic.

This thick wall is four meters wide—that's nearly 14 feet to you Americans—and built of dry-stone construction, one stone at a time; fitted so finely that even if St. Patrick hadn't driven the snakes out of Ireland, they still couldn't have slithered through these walls. This final fortification is a semi-circle that encloses about one acre of flat land. Of course, the next stop after the wall and the enclosure is your America.

In front of this great wall, as you see, are three concentric circles of various types of stone; these are defensive perimeters. Outside of the third wall is a classic *cheval de frise* with sharpened rocks planted upright into the ground to better deter the invaders. These concentric bulwarks were built to provide outer defenses to slow the enemy, with the last, stout wall as the final fallback fortification.

Dún Aonghasa was built in various stages during the Bronze and Iron Ages. Excavations indicate that the first construction goes back to 1100 B.C. The traditional story is that it was built by the Fir Bolg, one of the early Irish

peoples, and named after one of their kings, Aonghus mac
Úmhór.

Or maybe it was named after the pre-Christian god,
Aengus, one of the Tuatha Dé Danann pantheon of early
Irish gods. Aengus was the god of youth, love, and poetic
inspiration. I think maybe we Irish still secretly worship
Aengus with our love of language and our romantic souls."

Columbkille pauses to laugh at his own comment, then
continues his tour guide patter, "Whoever built the Dún,
they had some powerful enemies for them to build such a
place. Imagine a big battle here. The Fir Bolg, with their
Stone or Iron Age weapons, fiercely resisting along each
line of defense, and pulling back behind their thick stout
wall if they needed to. They were probably pretty safe
there.

If the invaders—and we don't know who they might
have been—breached the final wall, perhaps the plan was
to lure them to the cliff's edge, and push them down onto
the rocks and into the sea far below. Or maybe the Fir Bolg
would jump themselves rather than be captured. In a sense,
Dún Aonghasa might be our Irish Masada.

But I like to imagine that when the invaders streamed
over the final wall, the Fir Bolg and the invaders
recognized that they were Celtic cousins, stopped fighting,
and broke out their kegs of prehistoric beer—an ancestor,
to be sure, to our eighth holy sacrament, Guinness. Now
have you ever seen our publican's sacred ritual when he
pours a pint? So, I imagine that the two sides, they make up
with each other. They turn the Dún into a monster pub,
don't you think? Imagine the craic going on behind these
walls."

Columbkille pauses again to laugh at his own joke. The
Message Bearers join in to be polite.

"You know, we Irish have always been better at
fighting each other than fighting our enemies. Some say
that's why the English were able to capture Ireland and

occupy her so long. Our Irish Chieftains were too busy fighting each other to unite, and together push the English out of Ireland."

Columbkille pulls back the reins on the horse, bringing both carts to a stop. A new seriousness enters his voice. "You'll notice we have some guests camping among the stones of Dún Aonghasa right now. They are here, they say, to do restoration work on the fort. Most times, Dún Aonghasa is a mighty lonely, foreboding place, perched with its dark rock on top of that hill falling into the ocean. So, we're happy to have all of these fine young people visiting and fixing things up."

The Message Bearers can see a couple hundred young people camped among the stone circles surrounding the main walls. Backpack tents of all shapes and colors and strings of Buddhist prayer flags brighten the dark rock circles. They hear a cacophonous mix of music from various people's playlists clashing with each other. There is also an encampment of small, weathered caravans and tents set up just outside the main wall with several families mingling amongst them, as well as several units of Irish Guardia and Irish Army personnel appearing to stand guard at various spots around the fort.

Gustafson asks Columbkille, "What about the Guardia and the Army? What are they doing up there? And who are those families in the caravans?"

Before he answers, Columbkille says something in Gaelic to the other driver, then turns to answer Gustafson. "Well, don't you know that wherever there is a group of young people, there's bound to be a little mischief. The Guardia were called in to keep the peace. And, ah, the Army just so happens to be here on regular training maneuvers. Great place to practice for battle, don't you think?"

Columbkille stops to point to the row of rusty, dented caravans.

"Those people in the caravans are the *lucht siuil*, "the walking people," who most people call the Travelers. Irish Gypsies you might say. But they're not Roma, like on the continent. They're as Irish as I am. They've been wandering around Ireland since Oliver Cromwell—his name be cursed—drove them from their land during his genocide of the Irish people in 1649. The Travelers say they are here to help the young people restore the Dún. Many people in Ireland traditionally shun the Travelers, calling them "Pikey" or "Tinkers," but I'm happy they are here to help. Their leader is an incredible woman named Shelta. She has become a bit of an *anam cara*, a soul friend, to me in the months that they have been here. Perhaps you will meet her later on."

When the two jaunty carts approach the first wall of the Dún, a couple of Guardia stop them at a makeshift gate set up in a gap in the first circle of stone revetments. They tell the group the fort is closed today for tourists, because of the army maneuvers and the ongoing restoration work.

"Maybe you want to go back to town and find a snug pub with a cozy peat fire. God knows, it will probably rain soon," one of the Guardia tentatively suggests.

Gustafson tells them they are not tourists; they have a special message for Grainne O'Malley. The Guardia pretend not to know who Grainne is, or where she might be.

Clare speaks up and identifies herself as a nun, hoping this will open some doors, as it did with the harbormaster. "Hello, officers, I'm Sr. Clare McCulloch. We have an urgent message for Grainne and those young people. I was told by a priest friend that Grainne was here at Dún Aonghasa. We would appreciate it if you would help us find her, or at least let us into the fort so we can look for her ourselves."

The Guardia looks a little flustered, as if flooded with memories about getting his knuckles wrapped with a metal ruler wielded by his eighth-grade nun-teacher.

"Ah, sister, I didn't realize without your habit. But now I see your Cross. We'd love to help you, of course, but we have our orders. You know what that's like. And it might be too dangerous for you up there with the Army fellas roaming about."

Clare introduces the group, pointing out the other Message Bearers: Aavani, Mark, and Chooky. Then she adopts her authoritative schoolteacher voice, and directs her attention to the two Guardia.

"Do you believe in Our Lady of Knock, and in her apparitions and message over there in Mayo? We Message Bearers have been graced with something like that. We each had a vision and have been told to share this with Grainne. It's urgent. You may remember from Knock that the parish priest refused to leave his rectory and missed seeing the apparition. You wouldn't want to be like that priest, now would you, and ignore or stand in the way of a vision?"

"Ah, no, sister, we wouldn't," the Guardia answers very quickly, not pausing now to measure his words, "We'll call our captain, and see what he says. He's just up the hill, if you don't mind a little wait here."

One of the Guardia gets on his handheld radio and asks the captain to come down to the security gate. While they wait, the Guardia chat up the group, talking about the weather, their favorite pub in Kilronan (there are only two), and American politics, a constant source of conversation for the Irish.

"Now, who do you think is worse?" the Guardia who remained at the gate asks, "Donald Trump or your man in the White House now, President Stout? Not meaning to offend anybody, but I think they run neck and neck. If you believe in global warming, they both want to turn the world into a pressure cooker, I'd say. Of course, some would love to see Ireland heat up. You could finally use our beautiful, cold beaches for sunbathing. Tourists would come here for beach vacations. Can you feature that? Ah, here comes the Superintendent now."

The group is surprised to see a tall, African man—built like an American football running back—dressed in a Guardia uniform approaching the security gate. They are even more surprised when he opens his mouth and begins to speak in a heavy Irish accent.

"Good day to ya! I'm Superintendent Seamus O'Dowd." He notices the surprised look on their faces, a reaction he is used to, "Sure, you've heard of the "Dark Irish," haven't you? I'm what you might call, the "Very Dark Irish." He laughs to set everyone at ease.

"I hear one of you is a Catholic sister."

Clare introduces herself.

"Sister, do you remember when Catholic school students would "buy" a pagan baby? Well, that's me." He laughs again. "I was rescued from an orphanage in Nigeria, brought to Dublin, and raised by a Catholic priest, Fr. Diarmuid O'Dowd. A fine man, like a true father to me. Not a hint of anything like those priests who took advantage of the young ones. Nothing but love and kindness. He's been gone ten years now—God bless him— and I still miss him every day. Anyway, that's me, by way of explanation. Now, what can I do for you?"

Sr. Clare speaks for the group, "We are here with an urgent message for Grainne O'Malley. We have been told she is here with this group of young environmentalists. I'm assuming you are here, Captain, to protect her. Since the assassination of Iona McCleod, I imagine she has been threatened too. We know her presence here is supposed to be secret, but we are no threat to her. We support her cause and have come to help her. We must see her as soon as possible, and deliver the message we have been given for her."

The superintendent turns away and looks up toward Dún Aonghasa thinking about how to answer.

"Well, Sister, I cannot confirm or deny, as they say, that anyone named Grainne O'Malley is here or not here. We Guardia have to keep our confidences about some things, much like the Seal of Confession for a priest. I'm sure you can understand, Sister. As to why we are here, some of the young folk reported that some of their things got nicked. So, we are here to supervise a bit just to keep everything peaceful."

Pointing to his two Guardia comrades, he continues, "My two mates here told me your message for Grainne came by way of some visions. I'm a devotee of Our Lady of Knock myself, so I respect such things, but I need to hear more about your visions and your message before I know whether I can help you."

Clare pulls the superintendent aside, and in a low voice tells him what she can about the visions.

"Superintendent O'Dowd, we were told in the vision not to share its contents with anyone, except Grainne. But this is the gist of what we saw, and what we were told." She whispers an abbreviated version of the visions into the superintendent's ear. He looks stunned.

"There is more, and some things we do not yet know. We were told even more would be revealed after we speak to Grainne. Can you see now how urgent it is that we speak to her?"

O'Dowd turns and looks back up to the dark massif of Dún Aonghasa looming above them.

He thinks for a few minutes, then walks back to the others along with Sr. Clare and addresses the entire group, "I don't know what to think about what Sr. Clare just told me, but I can feel something holy about it. Something *scafar*, something very fearsome. I don't know if it's my

African or my Irish spirit—probably both—that tells me you are on a sacred mission. But I can't take you to Grainne, or even tell you if she is here or not. I have my orders. But what I can do, if it is agreeable to you, is introduce you to the Council, the elected leaders of the environmental group up there. Tell them your story, and we'll see what they have to say."

Superintendent O'Dowd borrows one of the Guardia's radios, calls up to the Dún, and sets up a meeting with the leaders of the Council. The carts proceed up the hill, letting the group out at the base of the massive inner stone wall. The wall towers about 40 feet above them and is fourteen feet thick. Noticing how the ancients had very carefully fit the stones together without any mortar, they walk silently through a dark stone passageway, the only way through the wall.

They are amazed at what they see when they emerge on the other side. The tunnel through the wall opens into a large semi-circular, flat field of vibrantly green grass and dark grey stone, almost like a park or the commons of a small Irish village. All within the confines of the massive stone wall. It would make an excellent, dramatic venue for a rock concert or a setting for a grand opera. On one side of the clearing, there is a mysterious rock table, five feet high and ten feet in diameter, that could be used as either a stage for the concert or an altar for Mass.

The enclosure is filled with more mountaineer and backpack tents. Tibetan prayer flags and various environmental banners blow in the stiff breeze coming off the ocean. Small groups of youthful environmentalists and a band of Irish Travelers are clustered around campfires, animatedly debating the finer points of climate change. In the background they can faintly hear the crash of ocean waves against the rocks almost 400 feet below the high cliff, which constitutes the final defensive feature of Dún Aonghasa.

O'Dowd leads the group to a small cluster of tents and introduces the Message Bearers to the Council: four young women and two young men in their late teens and twenties, hailing from several different nationalities and ethnicities.

Sr. Clare is once again the spokesperson for the Message Bearers. Revealing only a little of their visions, she lays out their reason for needing to see Grainne. The young people are skeptical, wary, and very closed mouthed. They have a private conversation among themselves, and finally, one of the young women—an American named Zoe—says, "Why should we believe you are anything, but a group of delusional, religious—ah, well—nuts?"

Clare responds with a laugh, "Well, we probably are a bit nuts to come all this way with such a wild story. But our message for Grainne is real and it's very urgent."

She shares a little more of their message, but repeats that they have been directed to only tell the whole story to Grainne. The young leaders continue to be skeptical and ask how the group can prove who they are, and why their message is so important.

Chooky takes over as the Message Bearers' spokesperson. "Hi. My name is Chooky. I am a Tlingit Indian from Southeast Alaska. I am also a scientist, a marine biologist, and a linguistics expert. I understand your skepticism. I still have a hard time accepting that what we are describing to you is real. But let me tell you about an experience I had in the course of my marine research that opened my mind to something mysterious that might be happening on our planet."

Chooky then tells the young leaders about her experience with the humpback whale in Alaska. She pulls her laptop out of its bag. She first plays the haunting music of the humpback's song, and then reads the translation of the whale's message to them. The young people are awed. They pull away from the Message Bearers and gather in a circle on the other side of their line of tents to discuss Chooky's revelation.

After several minutes of animated—at times heated—discussion, the Council come back to the meeting place. Zoe speaks for them. "We have reached a consensus. You are right. Grainne must hear about this. We will bring you to her immediately."

Chapter Twenty-Six

The Message Bearers, escorted by the Council and Superintendent O'Dowd, are brought to a small red tent in the center of the clearing. A twenty-year-old woman emerges from the tent and greets them. She is rather ethereal in appearance, tall and lithe, a dark Irish beauty with black hair, intensely blue eyes, and a pale Irish complexion. She is dressed in rainbow leggings, hiking boots, and an oversized green hoodie with the logo of Trinity College Dublin on the front.

The Message Bearers greet her and explain they have an urgent message for her, but they must meet with her alone. Grainne agrees to listen to them and directs them to a large Plains Indians Teepee Council Tent. Inside, they sit in a circle around a smoldering, fragrant peat firepit, which makes the teepee smell like a pub or an old thatched cottage.

Each Message Bearer tells their story, describes their vision, and gives their message to Grainne. For the first time Clare, Aavani, and Mark describe in full the horrors they saw in their visions, of Nature attacking the human race and threatening human extinction. Chooky again reads from her computer the message from the humpback. The Message Bearers also mention that, from what the news has been reporting, some of these events have actually been happening recently around the world. Sr. Clare is the final one to speak, adding that she was told in her vision that something more would be revealed once the message was delivered to Grainne.

The three visionaries are not surprised to hear the contents of each other's visions, but it is shocking for each to hear that the others saw the exact same thing. They had only sensed this. Now it was confirmed. Chooky is even more shocked because she had only received the verbal message from the whale, and had not heard any of the details of the visual images. Woosh, Simon, and Gustafson remain silent, but look horrified. Simon and Gustafson in particular have gone very pale, all the blood drained from their faces.

Grainne sits still throughout, listening silently, her eyes closed and her head down, betraying no emotion—exuding a centered presence far beyond her years. After the Message Bearers have spoken, there is a prolonged silence; the only sound is the wind blowing over the partially open top of the tepee, along with some muted camp sounds from the young people in the enclosure.

Grainne keeps her eyes closed and appears to be praying.

After taking a deep breath, Grainne finally breaks her silence, "Ever since Iona's death..." Her words catch in her throat, and she pauses to let the emotions pass, "Ever since Iona's death, I have been waiting for some inspiration to help guide me about what the next step in the climate change movement ought to be. But I have been completely immobilized by the loss of Iona and her leadership. She was the visionary and the energy of the movement, not me. I was just her friend and assistant. Some people want me to replace her. But I can't. I'm not Iona. I can't speak or inspire like Iona. I'm just a simple girl from the small town of Lisdoonvarna, in County Clare back there on the mainland, who fell in love with Iona's message.

I have believed for some time that Gaia is angry at the human race. Now the message I am hearing from you Message Bearers leads me to think she is so angry at us it is too late to save the planet. Gaia is right to be angry at us. We have harmed her and her creatures so badly. Perhaps she does have to destroy us to save the planet. Maybe we should just disband, go home to our families, and prepare for the end?"

She begins to sob. The Message Bearers gather around her and embrace her, some of them breaking down in tears as well. Sr. Clare stands away from the group, praying and watching with tears in her eyes.

Then, Clare once again summons her old classroom-commanding, nun-teacher voice and loudly says, "Children, pay attention! We have to pull ourselves together. There must be some reason Gaia has granted us this message and vision. Perhaps there is still hope. Perhaps, there is still something we can do. Remember what we were told. Now that we have gotten the message to Grainne something else will be revealed. Let's wait and see what that is."

Grainne quiets her sobs, agreeing with Clare that they need to await another message. Then, she reveals that the Extinction Rebellion Group has picked up intelligence that a militia formed by Moxxon Oil Company, now allied with Russian mercenaries and the Russian Navy, may have learned she is in Dún Aonghasa, and may be planning an attack to kidnap her.

"The Irish army, the Guardia, and the Travelers have vowed to defend us, but they may not be a large enough force to protect us. Many might be killed. I will either be killed or kidnapped."

Grainne starts to cry again and then composes herself to continue, "We will make a stand here at Dún Aonghasa. Some are saying this may be our Masada. You Message Bearers should leave to protect yourselves. You have done what you were called to do. You have delivered the message to me. This is not really your fight. So, maybe it's best for you to depart before this invasion happens. We can take your message from here. I will share it with all our people. We will discuss it and discern if it leads to some new plan. That is, unless the oil militia comes. If they do, we will do our best to fight them off, with the help of our marvelous Guardia."

She smiles at Superintendent O'Dowd, who manages a wan smile back at her.

The Message Bearers huddle together and discuss what to do. They unanimously decide to stay with Grainne at Dún Aonghasa. They will stand with her no matter what happens, waiting to see what is revealed next.

This time Aavani speaks for the group, "Grainne, we stand by you no matter what is to come. We have been told you are the key to what will happen next. Being here with you is part of our mission. God willing, there may be some reason to still hope. Perhaps Gaia will relent and give us humans one last chance. We have received some signs that give us hope. Devi is merciful, even when she is just."

Chooky then speaks up, reminding everyone of the warnings from her Alaskan humpback. She also describes to Grainne how the pod of humpbacks rescued them in the North Atlantic from the Blue whale, the orcas, the sharks, and the impending attack by the oil militia boat.

"There must be some reason we were saved. The universe seems to have a plan for us. Perhaps the message, and whatever else is revealed, is humanity's last, best hope. Or maybe a remnant of the human species is to survive. Or we might all be doomed. I don't know. But I agree that we want to stay here with you and your people, Grainne, and await the next development.

The warriors of the Oglala Lakota Nation had a saying they would shout before they went into battle, "It is a good day to die!" If it is to be, it is a good day, and this is a good place to die. Good people to die with. The right cause to die for. Perhaps, in making a stand here, we can defeat the forces of the climate deniers, and await the next part of the message. If not, we will have died a noble death for the sake of Mother Earth. And if this is the end of times for all of our human species, our deaths here will merely be a small part of the universe's plan to continue the evolution of life in the universe. We are, after all, only tiny particles on a tiny speck in the vastness of the universe.

Science tells us that no matter, no energy, is ever lost. It is simply transformed into another state. Same with us. Irrespective of what happens here, or what Mother Nature has in store for us, our lives and our mission will not end. It will be transformed—you might even say transubstantiated—into some new energetic form."

Chooky pauses for a moment, her eyes shifting to the left and up as she recalls something and considers whether it is relevant.

"I'm just now remembering this prayer from my father's funeral when I was twelve:

> "Life is eternal, love is immortal, and death is only a horizon;
>
> and a horizon is nothing save the limit of our sight.
>
> Lift us up, strong Son of God, that we may see further;

cleanse our eyes that we may see more clearly;
draw us closer to yourself that we may know ourselves
to be nearer our loved ones who are with you."

She pauses again, a surprised, bemused look spreading across her face, "Oh my God, listen to me! I'm starting to sound less and less like a scientist, and more and more like some kind of TV evangelist. Einstein, Darwin, please save me! Clare, Aavani, Mark, look at what you have done to me."

Woosh applauds. The whole group laughs along with Chooky.

Aavani yells, "Chooky, you are a spiritual muggle! Or at least you used to be. No matter. We still love you."

Chooky laughs again and continues, "Seriously, we stand with you, Grainne, and with your people, whatever may come. We have come too far, and seen too much, to stop now." Looking to the sky, Chooky concludes with what sounds like a scientist's prayer, "Gaia, we are yours. We surrender to your will. Guide us in your ways, not our ways. Lead us and grant us the fortitude to fulfill the mission you have given us."

Then Clare stands up and speaks for the rest of the Message Bearers, "Amen to what you just said, Chooky."

Turning to face the teenage leader, Clare declares, "Grainne, we have no desire to leave or save ourselves. We will stand with you, and if need be, fight and pray alongside you and your people. Now, darling, what do we need to do to prepare?"

Chapter Twenty-Seven

Grainne shows the Message Bearers to some vacant tents. Clare, Mark, and Aavani spend a lot of the next three days in prayer and meditation, hoping to hear or see what Gaia might reveal next.

Chooky and Woosh spend most of their time watching the ocean 400 feet below the back edge of the Dún. On the second day, Chooky notices a few whales swimming back and forth off the coast of Inishmore. She thinks they are humpbacks, but they are too distant to tell for sure.

After a couple hours siting at the cliff's edge watching the whales and staring out to sea, Chooky and Woosh return to their small backpack tent and snuggle into their borrowed two-person sleeping bag. They make slow, passionate love, and then fall asleep in each other's arms. When Chooky wakes up, she begins to read the international news on her laptop. Woosh wakes up and reads along with her.

Vesti Yamal (a Russian News Agency) – "Journalists flying over a remote region have spotted a monstrous 164-foot crater recently burst open in a desolate area of the Siberian tundra. Investigating Russian scientists have discovered sixteen more of these craters, called hydrolaccoliths. Their theory is that they were caused by the rapid thawing of the Siberian permafrost in response to global warming and the recent record heat in the Arctic. For several days this month, the temperature reached an unprecedented 100°F in a number of locations in Siberia.

This has led to sudden explosions of methane gas previously frozen in the permafrost, creating these massive craters. These explosions and other releases of methane from melting permafrost all around Earth's Arctic Circle are adding to the rapidly increasing rate of global warming. Methane is a greenhouse gas that causes twenty-one times more atmosphere warming than carbon dioxide, the most common greenhouse gas.

Atmospheric scientists have been cautioning for years that the rapid warming of the Arctic could release massive amounts of methane from the frozen soil, in turn accelerating the global warming that is causing the methane releases in the first place. Now the scientists investigating the Siberian craters are warning that one of these methane explosions could occur in populated areas or at an industrial site like an oil drilling or storage facility built atop permafrost. Such an explosion could be powerful enough to cause loss of life or a major petroleum spill and environmental disaster."

The Fairbanks Daily News-Miner – "Breaking News: Today at 10:23am there was a massive underground explosion in the middle of Pioneer Park in the heart of Fairbanks. Initial reports indicate that at least 26 people have been killed and 34 injured. There are also 15 reported missing. There is major damage to the Pioneer Air Museum, the Tanana Valley Railroad Museum, and the SS Nenana Sternwheeler Riverboat exhibit, all facilities within Pioneer Park. All three locations were crowded with tourists and locals at the time of the explosion, including a group of school-age children on a field trip from a

Fairbanks elementary school. First responders are still putting out the fires caused by the explosion and rescuing people who remain trapped in the rubble.

Initial reports from investigators just arriving on the scene indicate that the incident appears to be an eruption of a large cryovolcano, an explosion of methane and carbon dioxide gases suddenly released by the thawing of the mud and ice of the permafrost underneath the park. Similar eruptions have been reported in Siberia over the past months, but all of them occurred in remote areas. There were no witnesses to those explosions and no fatalities. If the preliminary theory is accurate, this would be the first such cryo-eruption in a populated area. Scientists have attributed this new phenomenon to the effects of global warming and the especially rapid rise of temperatures in the Arctic. More details will be forthcoming as reports from the scene are updated."

Klondike Sun Newspaper – "Breaking News: At 3:43pm the permafrost underneath buildings in the Dawson Historic District appears to have exploded, destroying several historic buildings, including Diamond Tooth Gerties Gambling Hall and the Red Feather Saloon. Both buildings, along with several other historic structures, are in shambles, leveled to the ground. Some of the flying debris was even flung into the nearby Yukon River. A fire has broken out at Gerties and a few other structures. Early reports are that there are multiple fatalities and injuries, but it is too early to report exact numbers.

The RCMP commander on the scene, Inspector Gerald MacDonald, commented that the explosion is very similar to the methane cryo-eruption that caused so much death and destruction this morning in Fairbanks.

"Strange things are happening here in the North as global warming rapidly changes our climate. This may be one of them. It may be an ice volcano, but it's too early to tell. We are not ruling out other possible explanations, including a natural gas leak or even terrorism."

RCMP arson investigators have already fanned out through the historic district to search for clues as to the cause. It will be several days before the results of their investigation can be released. Meanwhile, most of central Dawson, including the offices of the *Klondike Sun*, has been evacuated."

The Miami Herald – "The National Hurricane Center has announced the formation of the first named storm of 2025: Alexa. It is rapidly forming in the Caribbean Basin, south and east of Cancun. It is now a tropical storm with 65 mile-an-hour winds. It is projected to be a Category 1 hurricane when it strikes Mexico's Yucatan and Quintana Roo provinces.

It is then forecast to rapidly intensify into a monstrous Category 4 to 5 hurricane with winds up to 175mph after striking Mexico and moving into the waters of the Gulf of Mexico, already unusually warm for June. The current hurricane cone predicted by the NHC has Alexa striking the western shore of Louisiana near Cameron. This is the same location where two major hurricanes, Delta and Laura, struck in 2020.

Dr. Laura Dowd of the National Oceanic and Atmospheric Agency (NOAA) commented on the probability of this occurring again in 2025.

"In 2020, it was crazy that five named storms hit Louisiana, with eleven total striking the Gulf Coast. It was even crazier that two major hurricanes made landfall at almost the exact same spot in Louisiana. And then the same thing happened in Central America, when first Hurricane Eta and then Hurricane Iota made landfall at nearly the same spot within three weeks of each other. Both of them causing massive destruction and multiple deaths in the same regions of Guatemala, Honduras, and Nicaragua. These events are scientifically and statistically very improbable. But with Alexa it could happen again in a few days, since Cameron, Louisiana, is once again in the bull's-eye of the cone. I feel for the people of Lake Charles and that whole region. I understand that they still have not fully recovered from 2020."

The Guardian – "Scientists aboard the Russian research ship *Akademik Mstislav Keldysh* have found evidence that frozen methane deposits in the Arctic seas—known as the "sleeping giants of the carbon cycle"—have begun to be released over a large area of the under-ocean continental slope off the East Siberian coast. High levels of the potent greenhouse gas have been detected down to a depth of 350 meters in the Laptev Sea near Russia.

This is prompting concern among researchers that a new, dangerous climate feedback loop may have been triggered that would greatly accelerate the pace of global warming. The underwater slope sediments in the Arctic contain a huge quantity of frozen methane and other gases, known as hydrates. Methane has a warming effect eighty times stronger than carbon dioxide over twenty years. The discovery of potentially destabilized frozen methane raises concerns that a new tipping point is being reached, which could substantially increase the speed of global warming.

"The East Siberian slope methane hydrate system has been perturbed, and the process (of methane release) will be ongoing," said the Swedish scientist, Dr. Orjan Nilsson, of Stockholm University, in a satellite call from the Russian research vessel."

The Guardian – "A spate of bear attacks in Japan has prompted calls to stop the degradation of their natural habitat. Japanese media have reported a marked increase in incidents of "ursine terror." According to the environmental ministry, 46 people were killed and 157 people injured nationwide last year—the highest number on record.

Some of these bear encounters have been fatal to both humans and bears. In one incident, a 220lb bear attacked and killed a policeman, punctured the tire of his police car, and was shot dead by another policeman after invading a nearby home and threatening a family of four. This week another bear wandered into a shopping mall in Ishikawa, attacking and killing three shoppers, and seriously mauling four others. It then found a hiding place in the mall and was finally cornered and killed by authorities after a 13-hour search.

The attacks are being attributed to a shortage of acorns in the bear's natural habitat, forcing them into populated areas in search of food. "There is less to eat in the mountains and that is why they are coming down into villages and even into cities," said Yuko Kawasaki, president of the Japan Bear Society.

Conservationists are warning that encounters between bears and humans will continue and likely increase until the problem of bear habitat degradation is addressed. "We used to coexist with bears," Kawasaki said, "Bears are not naturally inclined to attack humans, but attacks like the recent ones strengthen my belief that we are tipping the scales, and altering the bears' habitat in such a drastic way that we are forcing them into these aggressive actions."

After they finish reading the news together, Woosh says to Chooky, "I hate what is happening to our Alaska. It is bad enough for our people that the salmon are disappearing. It's even worse for the Inuit up north. They are losing the sea ice from which they hunt their seals. They are finding it harder to perform their annual bowhead whale hunts, which they depend on for food to get through the winter. I heard some of the Inuit have had to go on Food Stamps after centuries of being fiercely self-sufficient.

And just like the Inuit, polar bears are slowly starving to death, and having fewer babies. They also depend on the sea ice to hunt. It's disappearing more each year and will probably be mostly gone in a few years. To add insult to injury, now the Inuit have to worry about the ground blowing up underneath them, or their homes simply collapsing around them as the permafrost melts. Then there are these insane, so-called "zombie fires" which now burn all winter under the snow, feeding on the underground peat layers, and exploding onto the surface in the Spring, starting another round of forest fires. Fire in the winter! Under the snow! How fucked-up is that?"

Chooky responds, "I know, Woosh, I know. I think our people's way of life in the North, as we have known it, is slipping away. It sounds like really all of humanity's way of life—or even our *very* lives—is threatened. But I am still holding onto the hope that Clare's intuition about a further revelation will give us some way out of this."

Woosh looks intently at Chooky and lowers his voice, "Chooky, you know we have had our ups and downs. But despite all of this craziness happening, I feel closer to you now than I ever have. I feel like I have gotten my amazing, beautiful Tlingit *Shawut* back. You are the only woman I have ever loved. I feel our spirits have become twinned again like they were when we were young and roaming around Pelican. Now, I know that no matter what happens next, we will be together forever. Nothing can come between us ever again. We are eternally soul-locked, soul-bonded to each other."

"Woosh, I feel the same way. Our spirits are so entwined that somehow, some way, we will always be joined together like the twin stars, Castor and Pollux, in the constellation Gemini."

Chooky kisses Woosh even more passionately than before, and they begin to make love a second time.

On their way to the teepee to pray, Clare and Aavani pass nearby, and begin giggling to each other as they notice the tent shaking. They smile at each other and walk on, leaving Chooky and Woosh to their lovemaking.

Nearing the teepee, they walk by Mark and Simon's tent which is also rocking and shaking like Chooky and

Woosh's. Clare and Aavani have to stifle their rising impulse to laugh until they get inside the teepee, where they both burst into uproarious laughter, tears running down their cheeks, like two schoolgirls sharing a secret joke.

When she is able to pull herself together, Clare asks Aavani with a big smile on her face, "Isn't it wonderful that there are so many ways to pray?"

Aavani smiles back and nods in assent.

Then they both sit down on the dirt floor in the lotus position, and enter into deep, silent meditation.

Chapter Twenty-Eight

Later that afternoon, Grainne assembles the environmentalists and the band of Irish Travelers in the central enclosure of the Dún. The Travelers are led into the encampment by their spiritual guide and spokeswoman, Shelta, a forty-year-old mother of five with long, bushy, dark hair and startingly brilliant sky-blue eyes. Superintendent O'Dowd and Colonel Padraig Quinlan Jr., the commander of the Irish Army units, also attend the meeting.

Colonel Quinlan is a grizzled veteran of several UN Peacekeeping missions in Africa, some of which involved fierce battles with warring tribal and rebel groups. He is the son of the Irish military hero famed for leading a small Irish UN unit in a courageous stand against a much larger Katangese force in the Congo in 1961. Like Superintendent O'Dowd, Colonel Quinlan is committed to protecting Grainne and her young followers, whatever it takes.

Grainne begins the meeting by playing the video of a speech Iona MacLeod delivered to the United Nations in New York, projected onto a white sheet stretched before the dark rock of the inner wall of the Dún. The assembly frequently cheers at Iona's powerful challenges to the world. The cheer is especially loud when the video plays her famous "How dare you" lines:

"Humanity is suffering, and is under threat;

people are dying, entire environmental systems are collapsing.

We are witnessing a mass extinction of many different species,

and all you can talk about is the world economy

and fairytales of eternal economic growth.

How dare you! How dare you!"

After the video is finished and the cheers die down, Grainne climbs atop the altar-like rock to one side of the enclosure. She has taken to calling this the *Seanchaí* stone, or Storyteller's stone.

From this circular stage, Grainne addresses the gathering, "My sisters and brothers, it is still so painful for me to see, and hear, our beloved Iona speak. I miss her courage and singlemindedness. I miss her boldness and vision. I miss her friendship, as all of you do. I have been lost and rudderless since her death. Drifting in grief and paralyzed by fear. You all decided a month ago to elect me to replace Iona as leader of our movement. I have been unable to accept your election—'til now. I felt no one could replace Iona, least of all me. I do not have the gifts for leadership she possessed. I lost all hope and confidence when she was assassinated. I felt the forces that killed her also killed all hope for saving the planet from the dire consequences of global warming.

But, as you have noticed, I'm sure, we have had guests here at the Dún the last couple of days. You will remember that Iona said her autism helped her to see things differently than other people, and this had enabled her to develop her powerful vision of the dangers of global warming. These four people I am about to introduce have also been given the gift of special sight. We call them the Message Bearers. They have shared with me a vision and a message that was given to them. It is a very frightening and disheartening message.

So, it is very strange, but their presence and their ominous message have brought me out of my despair. They have re-energized me. Their seemingly hopeless message has given me hope again. I feel Iona's spirit in them. I feel her presence here with us again. I feel now that I can accept your election as servant-leader, the least among equals. That is, if you still want me."

The whole assembly rises, clapping and shouting their support and once again unanimously endorsing Grainne by acclamation.

"Thank you, my brothers and sisters. I humbly—and I do mean humbly—accept your election. As I said, I am no Iona, but I have her same fire within me. It burns quieter in me, to be sure. And yet it burns just as intensely."

Grainne bows before the assembly as the applause and shouts of approval continue, then she kneels down atop the *Seanchai* stone. The Councilmembers make a circle around her and all reach up and silently lay their hands on her. They invite the Message Bearers to join them.

After a long silence, Grainne rises with tears in her eyes, and then continues to address the assembly, "Let me introduce the Message Bearers and their companions. Welcome, Old People!" The whole gathering laughs, especially the oldest, Sr. Clare. "We cherish your presence and your wisdom. *Céad Mile Fáilte.*"

Grainne introduces Clare, Aavani, Mark, Chooky, Woosh, Simon, and George. They each stand, and then the four Message Bearers climb up onto the *Seanchai* stone to join Grainne. The Message Bearers, each in turn, describe the vision and message they received, starting with Aavani, then Clare, Mark, and Chooky.

Aavani stands, now alone, on the *Seanchai* stone and begins speaking, "I was meditating one day in early April before the statue of the Divine Mother Goddess, Devi, in our temple at Haidakhandi Universal Ashram in the mountains near Crestone, Colorado. It was a very peaceful meditation. I had cleared my mind of all thoughts and was dwelling in the bliss of nothingness. I had sat there nearly an hour on my meditation cushion before Mother. Suddenly, an image popped into my emptied mind. It was a beautiful, peaceful scene of a mountain meadow on a sunny summer day. A crystalline mountain brook coursed gently through the meadow, softly burbling as it flowed around and over the rocks and boulders in its path, watering many different kinds and colors of mountain wildflowers. The glistening high peaks of our Sangre de Cristo mountains towered above the meadow.

Oddly, I noticed there were no birds, butterflies, dragonflies, or other small creatures you would ordinarily see in such a mountain clearing. The meadow looked much like the clearing where our ashram community gathers for our Navratri Fire Ceremonies in honor of Devi. This is a beloved and sacred place for me. I beheld this scene with the peace which had come over me during my meditation.

A large, four-generation family entered the meadow with picnic baskets and children's toys. There were twelve children of all different colors and ethnic groups—black, white, brown, red, and yellow—shepherded by parents, grandparents, and great-grandparents, also of all the different skin colors.

The adults proceeded to unpack the baskets and set up a large picnic on the grass in the middle of the meadow beside the stream. The children gleefully ran around chasing each other, playing touch and other children's games. The meadow was full of laughter and merriment.

Then, the beneficent visage of Devi appeared hovering above the meadow with Crestone Mountain and a dazzling double rainbow as her backdrop. She was dressed in blue robes lined with gold cloth, surrounded by rays of golden light. There was a large bouquet of red roses at her feet. She smiled at the family, and lovingly extended her four arms toward them, holding out flowers, food, and other gifts. I felt great peace with Devi's presence. She seemed to be blessing the family with her motherly love.

Suddenly, her appearance completely changed. She morphed into Kali, the Destroyer of Worlds. Her skin first turned black, then a dark blue. She was naked except for a garland of severed human heads and a short skirt made of human arms. Her jet-black hair fanned out over her entire back down to her upper thighs. In one of the hands of her four arms she held a scimitar red with blood. In another hand, she held the decapitated head of a man, his blood dripping into a bowl held by one of her other hands. Her dark eyes stared wildly at the family in the meadow. Her mouth was wide open, baring her ferocious canine teeth. Her fierce red tongue protruded out and down over her chin, like a Māori warrior challenging an enemy.

The family looked up just as benevolent Devi transformed into terrifying Kali. They had no time to react to her fearsome appearance before a large, dark swarm of ravens, golden eagles, various types of hawks, and stellar and camp-robber jays descended on them, and began attacking them, pecking at the heads and eyes of the children and adults alike. The family tried to fight them off, but there were too many powerful birds. The family was overpowered.

They attempted to flee from the clearing into the nearby grove of Aspen, but mountain lions, black bears and grizzly bears, wolves, coyotes, badgers, and porcupines suddenly emerged at the edges of the meadow and surrounded them. The animals slowly corralled the family into the center of the meadow.

The porcupines attacked first, shooting flurries of quills into the skin of the adults who had formed a protective circle around the children. The adults who were hit writhed in pain, but stoically maintained the human wall to shield the children. Then the bears, wolves, coyotes, and badgers all attacked together, very quickly overwhelming the circle of adults, killing the children first before turning on the adults.

The animals slaughtered the whole family. Mangled, bloodied bodies were scattered all over the grass and rocks of the meadow. The clear mountain stream flowed red with the family's blood. Then the attacking animals withdrew, blood dripping from their jaws, and returned to the surrounding forest. Kali oversaw the massacre and appeared to bless the birds and animals as they left the scene. Kali then summoned the scavenger birds, turkey and black vultures, who descended in greedy hordes onto the bodies of the children and adults, tearing them apart and devouring them.

Kali then turned to me and in a terrifying voice said, "This is what I must do to all of your kind."

After this horrific scene, a series of images—each more awful than the last—flashed before my eyes like a dreadful PowerPoint presentation of horror. I wanted to stop looking but I was not allowed to. Mount Vesuvius erupted and exploded without warning. Thousands of people in Naples and the surrounding cities, all the way down the coast to Sorrento, were swiftly covered with a suffocating layer of thick ash. They died agonizing, if mercifully quick, deaths gasping for breath, inhaling the caustic hot ash that cut their lungs like ground glass. Many other thousands were scalded and burnt to death by pyroclastic flows that roared down the slopes of Vesuvius into the city.

It was another Pompeii, yet on an even larger scale. At the same time, a string of volcanos in Guatemala erupted at once, sending pyroclastic flows down the mountainsides catching dozens of villagers unaware. Thousands were killed almost instantly. The historic town of Antigua was incinerated. Only a few dozen survivors were able to escape. There was another scene of the same kind of massive eruption happening on Mount Merapi, a volcano in Indonesia. Again, thousands of human lives were almost immediately snuffed out.

Then, I beheld numerous incidents of animals attacking and killing humans. Cats turning on their owners, scratching and biting at their jugular veins. Grizzly and black bears emerged from forests, attacking campgrounds in the middle of the night all over the U.S. and Canada, mauling thousands of people, including children. Packs of coyotes and wolves hunted down and killed humans all over the globe.

Hippos, Cape buffalo, elephants, monster crocodiles, along with multiple prides of lions, and groups of leopards and cheetahs, attacked towns and villages all over sub-Saharan Africa. Thousands of people, especially children and the elderly who could not run away, were slaughtered.

Huge gatherings of great white sharks cruised up and down the East and West coasts of the U.S. and the popular beaches of Spain, Portugal, South Africa, and Australia, systematically attacking and killing surfers and swimmers, even snatching some children from the shallow surf at the water's edge where they were playing. I could see thousands of people of all ages bleeding to death in the water or on the beach.

Gigantic sinkholes opened up in cities across the world swallowing whole neighborhoods. Houses, buildings, and cars disappeared into the open maw of these collapses. Thousands of people were reported missing. An intense swarm of 8+ earthquakes spread over the entire Pacific Ring of Fire, toppling buildings, fracturing streets and highways, collapsing bridges, and crushing millions of people in the rubble. Thousands of others were drowned in the multiple tsunamis that were generated all over the Pacific shorelines.

A series of Super-storm Category 5+ hurricanes and typhoons hit Louisiana, Florida, the Philippines, and Bangladesh all at once with 200+ mph winds and thirty-five-foot storm surges. They caused massive, widespread destruction and death. The warming oceans all over the planet brewed a toxic gas that emerged along the shorelines of the world and flowed onto the beaches, into the inlets and harbors, and crept along the streets of coastal cities and towns. Millions died a slow, agonizing death, as if gassed by chemical warfare munitions.

All of these horrors passed swiftly before my eyes, as if livestreamed on a deranged Facebook page. They all seemed very real, as if happening in real-time, or would be happening very soon. Then I heard a voice, the voice of Kali, "Behold how I am destroying my human children all over the planet. This is just a foretaste of the many ways I will hunt you down till I have exterminated all of you."

After that I was lifted into the sky like a human drone by Kali. I was shown scene after scene of bloodied human bodies, men, women and children of all ages and races, laid out on the open ground, a red harvest of carnage and death. I flew over the great cities of the world, and looking down, saw nothing but dead bodies in the streets, on the bridges, in the stadiums. There was no sign of human life or activity. I saw beaches full of the dead rotting in the sun or being washed out to see by the tides.

I flew over vast areas of the countryside and farmlands. Bodies were the only crop. The fields and forests and rivers were full of lifeless human bodies. Kali flew me over the whole world. The planet had become one massive slaughter and charnel house for all of humanity. There was no sign of human life anywhere. The planet was now totally free of the human species."

At this point, all of this became too much for me. I started to faint and lose consciousness. Just before I passed out, I heard Kali's voice once more, "This is what I shall do to my human children unless …."

Either Kali did not finish her sentence, or I was too overwhelmed to hear it. Then she said, "Tell no one what I have shown you today, until you find the young Irish woman. I will guide your way. You are my Message Bearer. There are three others, to whom I have also granted a revelation. These will accompany you."

At that point, I screamed very loudly and lost consciousness. Members of my ashram community heard my scream, came running, and found me lying on the floor in front of the statue of Devi, our Divine Mother Goddess. I awoke several hours later, unable to speak, but with the images of the vision very vivid in my mind."

Aavani steps down from the *Seanchaí* stone. Except for some murmured comments amongst the Travelers, the gathering has remained silent, stunned by what they have just heard.

Clare walks slowly to the *Seanchaí* stone, and with a boost from George, steps atop it, and starts her address to the assembly, "The vision that my sister, Aavani, just described came to me at the exact same time, 3:55pm, on the same Spring day, just a few miles down the road from her temple in Colorado. I was praying alone in our chapel sitting on my prayer cushion on the floor before the tabernacle of the Blessed Sacrament, under our large cross with the arms of Jesus reaching out to me.

I was just starting to complete my meditation hour when the vision was thrust into my mind. I saw everything Aavani just described to you, exactly the same. When I saw the vision of the holy woman hovering over the meadow, she looked to me like the Blessed Virgin Mary, similar to her appearances at Lourdes, Fatima, and Guadalupe. Well, except that she had four arms."

Clare laughs to herself a little and then continues, "I too felt great peace as the holy woman watched over the family and the meadow. I was very frightened when she morphed into the horrifying visage of Kali. I knew of both Kali and Devi from Aavani, so I recognized Kali as the goddess of Creation and Destruction. Everything in my vision was entirely the same as Aavani just described to you. Except for one thing: I was told by Kali that once we found the young Irish woman, and told her of our visions, something more would be revealed to us.

I have been meditating for hours each day since we arrived here, seeking this new revelation, but nothing has come. I have no idea what will be revealed next. I am thinking now that it will be revealed to all of us here, since we have told Grainne, and now all of you, of our vision. But I don't know anything for sure. I am also sensing there will be a message of hope in this next revelation despite the very dire warnings of our vision. But again, this just might be my wishful thinking. I simply don't know. I do believe we were given the vision for some purpose. That we were sent here on a mission. I don't yet know where that mission is leading us next, although I am heartened it has led us here to be with you.

Perhaps what we have been shown is just a warning about what could happen if we don't fight to save our planet. Perhaps there is still time to avert the disaster revealed to us, if we can just get humanity's attention and appeal to the better angels within us all, or even just appeal to humankind's survival instincts. Maybe we can yet deflect Gaia's wrath."

Pausing, Clare scans the whole gathering, looking into the eyes of each person, and then continues, "I believe all of us here, each and every one of you, are now being commissioned together as Message Bearers. The message we are being given is very simple and direct. If we don't change our ways as a species, we will die. All of us. Perhaps though, if we change, and change soon, we can still survive, and save the planet and her creatures from ourselves. Again, I don't know for sure what is to happen next. There is still so much uncertainty, but that is my hope and prayer."

As Clare steps down from the Storyteller's Stone, the whole assembly erupts in applause and cheers.

Now it is Mark's turn to ascend the *Seanchaí* stone.

"My brothers and sisters, on the same day, at the exact same time, just a few more miles up the road from Aavani's ashram and Clare's monastery, at the Crestone Mountain Zen Center, I received the same awful vision and message that Aavani and Clare just described. I was gathered with other retreatants and Zen monks in the meditation room. I had struggled for most of the hour's meditation with many intrusive thoughts from a trauma which I had recently endured, a mass shooting that happened several months ago at my church in St. Louis. I kept trying to focus on my breath as I had been taught by my Zen mentor, but the thoughts and images of the shooting kept coming back. I felt no peace, only turmoil and fear. To top it off, my back and knees were screaming in pain, and my butt was turning numb from sitting so long in the lotus position. To be honest, we Protestants are not used to meditation like this.

By some miracle, toward the end of the sitting hour, I was finally able to attend to my breathing. The traumatic thoughts and images, even the physical pain, disappeared. For the first time in months, I felt at peace. I was surprised and so grateful. At last, there was some relief from my PTSD and all the immense suffering my congregation and I had endured since the shooting. This only lasted a few minutes. Because suddenly, the images of the vision erupted into my mind, and I was shown, and told, all the same harrowing things Aavani and Clare have described to you.

But my reaction to the vision was different than Aavani's and Clare's. They quickly saw their vision as something spiritual. I simply assumed I was going crazy. I thought the images were some kind of hallucinations caused by my PTSD.

A few days later, I had a terrifying flashback to the vision in the middle of the mountains on my way back to St. Louis. This made me feel even crazier. I thought I must be falling apart. I thought I was having a nervous breakdown. Back in St. Louis, I immediately met with my psychotherapist. He also thought the terrible images of the vision were somehow related to my trauma and were the symptoms of some unusual form of PTSD.

In many ways I am the least likely—and I would add the least worthy—person to receive a vision like this. Even though I am a Christian pastor, I am a bit of a Doubting Thomas. You have to show something to me before I believe it. I need solid proof. My branch of Christianity does not have much of a mystical or contemplative tradition, so I had always been skeptical of such things as ecstasy and prophetic visions. My instinct is to interpret such events as just psychological.

I am a gay man and the pastor of a largely gay church. I have seen how people have used religion, and even the Bible, to justify discriminating against us and hating us. This has made me even more wary of supposed messages from God. My own father told me God instructed him to reject me when I came out to him.

It was only when Clare and Aavani came to St. Louis and described their visions that I began to believe in my own vision experience. I could see that their visions were exactly the same as mine, and they had come to them at exactly the same time, and only a few miles apart from each other. Only then could I begin to view my experience differently. I was now terrified in a whole new way. I was certainly relieved to find out I was not going bonkers! However, I still did not know what to make of our visions. Or why I was chosen to be one of the Message Bearers.

When we met with Chooky and heard her story of the encounter with the whale and the message she received, I started to become convinced we had all been graced with a true mystical experience. It particularly helped the Doubting Thomas part of me that she is a scientist and a natural skeptic like me. The earthquake and river tsunami we experienced in St. Louis, and the other unusual natural catastrophes reported around the world, sealed the deal for me. I'm now convinced that something very unusual is happening on our planet. All four of us have received something real and something very ominous. Why us—

particularly me—I have no idea. I think Gaia could have found a much better apostle for her message than me. But here I am.

Where this leads, I don't know either. Hopefully, we will be shown a way through. But maybe not. The visions are dire and the message is very foreboding, so perhaps this is the end of us. I have never put much stock in some Christians' End-of-the-World beliefs, the Rapture, the Mark of the Beast, the Anti-Christ, and all of the rest of these crazy misinterpretations of the Book of Revelation. But maybe this is it. This is the end. This is going to be how it ends. Maybe we four Message Bearers are really the Four Horseman of the Apocalypse. I pray not. I love life, I love humanity in all of its lunacy. I love this planet…"

Mark begins sobbing and can't continue. The Message Bearers climb back onto the *Seanchaí* stone and gather around him to console him. Simon climbs up onto the stone with them, wiggles into the middle of their circle, kisses Mark on the forehead, and holds him tightly in his arms. Many in the assembly weep along with Mark.

Mark finally composes himself, the Message Bearers step down from the stone altar, and he continues, "Like Clare, I still have a smidgeon of hope for humanity. I pray this further revelation she was told about comes soon. I hope it shows some way that we can repent, and convince Gaia to relent and give us a chance to redeem ourselves."

Mark jumps down from the stone into Simon's waiting arms. The assembly applauds. Many people embrace, consoling and comforting each other.

When the assembly grows quiet again, Chooky steps up onto the *Seanchaí* stone.

"As you all know, I am one of the four Message Bearers. But I am a different kind of Message Bearer than Clare, Aavani, and Mark. I was not given a vision, which is a good thing because I would have totally dismissed it. I am a marine biologist, and was taught to accept as reality only the things I could prove with solid scientific evidence. Instead of evidence, of all things, I was given a song-message from a humpback whale! Let me tell you the story."

Chooky first describes Woosh and herself rescuing the humpback from the fishing nets and crab pots. Then, Woosh steps up to the stone and hands Chooky her laptop. She first plays the humpback's song to the assembly. The strange, otherworldly moans, grunts, and shrieks of his singing, swinging quickly from incredibly low tones to high-pitched blasts, fill the enclosure with ethereal soundwaves which reverberate and magnify as they bounce off the ancient stone walls. The humpback's song echoes throughout Dún Aonghasa, down the bluff, and out to the ocean below.

Some people in the gathering think they hear other whales out in the Atlantic join in the song. It sounds and feels like a preternatural, epiphanic symphony of the mournful groaning of the whole of creation. The effect is overwhelming and mystical. Chooky then plays the translation of the song, the humpback's message to her, in an artificial computer voice that sounds like Siri's slightly deranged brother. The words of the humpback's song-message echo off the stone walls all around Dún Aonghasa and reverberate out to the ocean below.

Chooky plays the message three times so everyone clearly understands what the humpback is saying and warning:

> "Thank you for freeing me from those ropes. I was close to giving up. I am very grateful. Now I am going to do you a favor, because I can see some of your kind are good. You have stopped hunting us, and you try to rescue us when we are in trouble. Mother Gaia has told us not to reveal to any humans what I am about to tell you. So, you

must speak to no one, except for the one whom Mother has chosen, concerning what I am about to reveal to you.

Mother has spoken to my people and to all of her creatures in all of our languages and ways of knowing. Mother tells us she loves her human children, but her human children have greatly saddened her by their careless actions and are threatening the end of too many of her other creatures, even threatening Mother herself. So, with great sadness and increasing anger, Mother is turning against her human children, and is contemplating extinguishing them from the face of the Earth.

She would do this only to save her other children and herself. She has commanded us, and all creatures, and all of the forces of Nature to prepare for battle against you. Some creatures have even agreed to fight to their own death, offering their lives for Mother. If she chooses to do this, Mother will turn all of her might against you. There will be a mass human extinction. Mother will save a remnant of all of her other creatures, except for you humans.

It is nearly too late, but I offer this warning to you, because I felt your love today as you gently freed me. Go in peace."

After pausing to let the humpback's message sink in, Chooky continues, "Like Mark, I was very skeptical at first of this whole vision and message thing, even the message the humpback delivered to me personally. Scientifically, it made no sense to me. Even when I met with Clare, Aavani, and Mark, and heard parts of their vision, I still didn't believe. But when I saw with my own eyes phenomena that seemed out of the natural order, and read about them happening all over the planet, I began to see there was something going on in our world beyond the purely material. There is something strange happening in the realm of Spirit, as well as in the realm of matter.

As a scientist, I have been questioning how whatever is going on could be communicated to all of Earth's creatures and forces, except for us. How could this humpback be in touch with all of his fellow whales around the planet or with Mother Earth herself? I have been reflecting on that a lot. Then I remembered a scientific paper I recently read in neuroscience. There is a new theory that human consciousness is an energy field created by the electromagnetic waves given off by our brain's neurons as they fire and connect with each other. Information, free will, self-awareness, and other forms of consciousness are expressed in our brain's energy field.

So, I began to think, maybe the whole planet has such an energy field that sentient creatures all over the Earth can tap into, according to their capability. If that is so, probably the whole planet—and perhaps the universe itself—has some kind of consciousness energy field. That could explain what is going on right now. It also means we must quickly tap into humanity's consciousness energy field, and transform it in a way that enlists all of humanity to change our ways and save our planet."

Chooky pauses again, realizing she has just dropped a very esoteric concept on her audience, and then continues, "I am a Tlingit Indian from Southeast Alaska. But I had lost touch with my Tlingit roots. This whole experience has restored my Tlingit soul. My boyfriend, Woosh, tried to persuade me for years to not forgot our Tlingit traditions, especially our belief that Spirit lives in all of Nature, in all creatures. I refused to listen. I am listening now and what I am hearing is terrifying.

Like all scientists, I was trained to always be objective, and to only use my head, and ignore my heart. We can no longer afford to do this. We have to open our hearts to what is happening to our fellow creatures and to our planet. I know some of my fellow scientists also believe we have to move beyond scientific detachment to passionately advocate for change. Some scientists feel nearly helpless as they watch global warming steadily worsening. Some of my colleagues have described how they now feel like a doctor attending the bedside of a feverish planet, unable to break the patient's life-threatening, febrile inflammation. Or even like a hospice worker who can offer only palliative care to the dying species they study as they rapidly go extinct.

Scientists have been saying for several years now that we are in the middle of the Sixth Mass Extinction in the history of the Earth. Many species have already gone extinct in our time. Many more are threatened and will soon be extinguished unless changes are made. The previous five mass extinctions were all caused by natural events. This present extinction is entirely caused by us, by our assault on the planet and its species. So, now I am thinking that Mother Nature or Gaia, or whatever you want to call her, has decided that to save all the rest of her species, she has to get rid of one—us.

I would like to be hopeful like Clare. However, I have to be honest. I know my whale friend said there was still a chance for us. And maybe whatever future revelation Clare says is coming will provide some hopeful new information. But I have become very skeptical that the human race will wake up in time. I'm also doubtful we will be willing to make the sacrifices necessary to reverse our destructive impact on the planet and its many wondrous species. I don't see a common vision developing. Most of all I don't see many human beings looking unselfishly beyond their immediate personal needs and convenience, at the big, scary picture developing right in front of their eyes. I hope I am wrong. I don't want to be a gloom-and-doom pessimist. That really goes against my nature. However, I just don't see the evidence right now for any other conclusion."

Chooky steps down from the *Seanchaí* stone. The assembly has grown very quiet listening to Chooky's somber message. The only sound to be heard, as Grainne embraces each of the Message Bearers, is the distant roar of waves crashing at the base of the cliff, and a rising wind whistling through a few gaps in the rock wall.

Grainne ascends the *Seanchaí* stone, and again addresses the group, "Now you too know what our friends have seen and heard. You have heard the message they have been entrusted with. Nature, Mother Gaia, has decided that enough is enough. She is intent on destroying the human race to stop us from exterminating the rest of her children and destroying the planet. The next extinction is us. Who can blame her, eh?

We have been fighting to change the consciousness of the peoples of the world. To wake everyone up to the reality of what we are doing to our planet. To create awareness of the changes and sacrifices we must make to slow, and eventually reverse, the out-of-control warming of the planet. We have all run up against the resistance, disinterest, or myopic self-interest of so many. Some change is happening. More people are waking up, and demanding change, but we know it has not been enough, and it is coming much too slowly."

Mark interjects, shouting out, "You know Jesus ran into the same kind of resistance to truth and change. So, we are in good company."

Grainne nods and continues, "Yes, Mark, that's true. And we all know where that got him, don't we now? So, maybe Gaia has given up on us and we are doomed as a race. Perhaps this is necessary to save the planet for the rest of her creatures. If it is so, I am greatly saddened. And yet I accept the will of Mother Gaia, and I am ready to surrender my life to her."

More gasps ripple through the crowd.

One young man yells, "No! God have mercy! Gaia, please forgive us!"

A young woman cries out, "Grainne, I am with you. I too am willing to die for our planet, and for our sisters and brothers; the two-legged, four-legged, winged, finned, and rooted."

Grainne responds, "Thank you, Moira."

She pauses, stifles a few sobs, and then continues, "As I said, I am ready to accept that this is the end of our kind, if that is what is needed. But, hope against hope, I see what may be a glimmer in this darkness. The humpback told Chooky, "It is *nearly* too late" in his warning. Sr. Clare said she was told something else would be revealed after the Message Bearers brought the message to me. These things give me a tiny sliver of hope that there may still be a way to save our species and the planet too.

When I first heard of the visions, I told the Message Bearers I was ready to give up, go home to my family, and wait for the end. I now propose to you that we remain here and await the revelation Sr. Clare says is coming. Let's trust the word of the whale. Let's hope against hope, and stand together in our mission to save the world from ourselves."

The whole assembly rises to their feet shouting, cheering, and clapping.

"In a few minutes, I want us to break into our small working groups, discuss what we have heard, and come to a consensus about what to do."

Grainne pauses and gulps down a deep breath before continuing, "First, there is one more thing you must know:

Our friends from the Extinction Rebellion Group have sent us a warning. They have heard that a combined military force made up of an oil militia and Russian mercenaries may be planning to attack us here. They want to either kidnap or kill me. I don't know for sure what to believe about this report. It would surprise me that the climate deniers would be so brazen to attack us here on Irish soil, but I would not put it past them. All of us could be in danger. So, if any of you want to leave before something happens, I understand. There'll be no judgement on ya. You are free to go. No hard feelings. Everyone has to listen to their own soul and decide. If you need to go, the next ferry back to Galway leaves tomorrow at 15:00 hours.

As for me, I intend to stay and fight for our just cause, for the planet, and even for our crazy species—if we are allowed to redeem ourselves and survive. You may know I am named after Gráinne Ní Mháille (Grace O'Malley), the Pirate Queen of the West of Ireland who fought the English invaders in the 16th Century and considered herself the equal of the English Queen, Elizabeth I. I feel her spirit with me now. I also feel Iona's mighty spirit. I am ready to fight with the help of our Traveler friends and our comrades in the Guardia and in the Irish Army. I will do whatever it takes to bring our message to the world and save our planet."

Grainne raises her fist into the air and shouts, "Who is with me?"

A huge cheer rises from the group. Zoe, the American on the Council, climbs up to the top of the stone, stands by Grainne's side, raises Grainne's fisted hand into the air, and proclaims: "I think it's a consensus, Grainne. No need for a small-group discussion. It'd just be a waste of precious time, and we don't have much of that left. We are all with you. We are all in for the planet. We are all willing to fight for her. We will wait together for what else is to be revealed. We will stand with each other whatever comes."

Another great cheer fills the enclosure. For the moment, it drowns out the roar of the ocean waves pounding at the base of the cliff far below and the rising moan of the wind coursing over the dark circles of stones.

Chapter Twenty-Nine

That night, Grainne and the Message Bearers, along with the Councilmembers, Superintendent O'Dowd, Colonel Quinlan, and Shelta from the Travelers, gather around a cast-iron firepit, set in front of the teepee. It is one of those magical June nights in Ireland when twilight lasts till well past midnight, creating a prolonged dusk and a lingering soft glow in the sky. The usual wind off the ocean has subsided. The Atlantic is unusually calm, the sound of the waves hitting the rocky coast are muted and gentle.

Clare and Aavani are teaching the rest of the group how to make S'mores. Everyone is following their instructions, putting their concoctions on sticks and holding them in the fire. Grainne and Mark good-naturedly tease the teachers about being S'more perfectionists.

Grainne taunts Clare, "Sr. Clare, you are a remarkable woman but sometimes, like now, I see the nun come out in ya. Ya do get a little nunny about some things! You remind me of some of the Irish Sisters of Mercy that taught me back in school. Very strict and there was only one right way to think and act. Please don't tell me you keep a ruler handy to rap our knuckles if we get out of hand."

She and the rest of the group laugh.

Clare, playing along with the teasing, responds, "Darling, Grainne, yes I know some of the old teaching nun in me resurrects her habited head sometimes. But, you know, there *is* only one right way for some things. Like S'mores. That's why I readily confess to being a S'mores Nazi."

She laughs, adopting a stern nun face and pointing her finger at Grainne, "As for the ruler. Yes, of course, I always carry a hard metal-edged ruler in my pocket, next to my rosary, to bang some sense into rebellious children, such as yourself, young lady."

Clare softens her voice a little, but remains in her teaching nun mode, "Actually, I wish I could take a ruler to the climate deniers. Those people—whether from greed, lust for power, or sheer willful ignorance—continue ignoring all the signs from God, and from the Earth, that we are in deep trouble. I'd love to bang them on the heads and set them straight. Then, there are all of those who are just oblivious to what is happening, who want to go on with their lives exactly as they are. They remind me of the anti-vax people in 2020 and 2021. Tragic denial. So many of them died a totally avoidable, awful death from Covid. But I would only rap the climate deniers on the knuckles, because, as Jesus said, "Father, forgive them, for they know not what they do."

Mark replied, "Yes, Father, forgive them."

Grainne added, "Well, yes, Father, forgive them. But, as we say in Ireland, they're still "eejits." The whole lot of 'em."

They end their serious discussion and focus on toasting the S'mores in the firepit. Giggling, laughing, joking, and oohing and aahing over the S'mores like a group of kids at summer camp.

Someone breaks out a few bottles of Brunello di Montalcino that one of the Italian councilmembers had been saving for the right occasion, and passes them around. They distribute a few loaves of Irish Soda Bread and Irish Barmbrack Bread, along with some Irish and French cheeses. The S'mores round out the feast as the dessert.

Mark and Simon teach the group a few American camp songs, and Grainne leads the group in a few typically mournful Irish ballads. Everyone joins in the singing and general merriment, as if they hadn't a care in the world, as if the world wasn't threatening to end.

Around midnight, with the sky over the ocean still glowing with a soft, rosy light, the group grows quiet, everyone staring at the dying embers of the campfire. A somber spirit descends on the gathering. Mark breaks the spell, expressing the thought that is in everyone's minds, "Do you think this is really the end? Or is this our final warning, our last chance to prevent the end? What do you all think?"

Clare is the first to answer, "Mark, I don't know. It might be the end of humanity. But it sounds like there might still be a chance to save ourselves, if we only listen to what we are being told. Chooky's whale message, I think, gives us some slim hope. And, as I keep saying, I believe we need to wait on this promised revelation. Whenever it comes, it may give us some answers and provide some grounds for hope."

Chooky responds, "I want to believe the humpback that we may still have a chance, but honestly—as I said earlier—I'm not very hopeful. I've studied the five previous mass extinctions and the sixth extinction, which we are in the midst of now. The visions seem to say Nature has had enough, and the global warming we are causing will lead to our demise as a species, along with the many other species we are bringing down with us. It's like we are engaging in a mass murder-suicide, and nothing can stop us.

When the dinosaurs were wiped out by the asteroid impact in the Yucatan sixty-six million years ago, their extinction allowed mammals—and eventually us—to emerge and evolve. Maybe if we are part of this sixth extinction, we have to be eliminated so that evolution can bring forth a new, more intelligent, more evolved species. Like us, but better. Maybe that is Gaia's plan."

Aavani interjects, "Well, Chooky, I wouldn't mind being a part of this new and improved model. Maybe we all will, if reincarnation is real. I have these periodic talks with God about us humans. I ask her why she created such a glorious creature as a human being when we are also so deeply flawed. Why did she make us capable of such profound thoughts, creativity, compassion, and love, while at the same capable of inflicting such suffering on each other and on our fellow creatures? It's like we humans are some complex, contradictory mix of loving bonobo and aggressive chimpanzee, our nearest primate cousins.

I have this conversation with God—well, I guess, it's really an argument—every time somebody comes to our ashram wounded and traumatized by their family or by their spouse. Or someone devastated by a mass shooting; like you, Mark. Why did you create us this way, Lord, so wonderful and loving at times, yet so capable of hurting each other? This is what I ask, but I have yet to receive an answer."

Turning to Chooky Aavani adds, "Chooky, you scientists tell us our brains are the most complex, advanced organism known in the universe. But look at what we do with it. We find better and better ways to hate and kill each other. And now, our cleverness has led us to soil our own nest, and endanger our own home. If we are so bloody intelligent, what's up with that? So, perhaps you're right. We may need to be driven to extinction, so a saner, safer, more balanced species can emerge to replace us. Sort of the Human Race 2.0."

Grainne joins the discussion, "Well, perhaps we do need to be replaced. I guess we'll see. But, God willin', maybe we can evolve enough to be saved. We can evolve our own consciousness, can't we? We have about other things in our history, haven't we? It will take a profound change in humanity's consciousness, and it will have to be swift, because we don't have much time left. But it's in us to do it, if we only find the *misneach*—the pluck, the courage—to face reality, and make the necessary sacrifices to change how we live on this planet."

Clare chimes in, "I agree, Grainne, we are capable of incredible shifts in our consciousness, and that could save us if it happens. As I said when we were sailing across the Atlantic, we need a new environmental spirituality to inspire us to action. And we need a new paradigm that marries science and religion as equal partners in guiding us to a new way of living on our planet. We will fail without this. But we *are* capable of achieving it. The question is will we do it, and do we have enough time for it to happen? Our visions tell us Nature's patience with us is running out. We might have to go. I guess we will find out soon."

Mark responds, "Clare, I guess I am less than hopeful we will evolve fast enough. I see so many people living in denial and delusion. We have this magnificent brain and this vaunted intelligence, but as Aavani said, it has major weaknesses.

In my ministry I have seen so many addicts of all kinds in incredibly blind denial about what is clear to everyone else around them. I have also seen many people in my own community, in the U.S., and around the world, who develop these very passionate stubborn beliefs, based only on what they want to believe, or on whatever personal version of reality serves them. Facts, evidence, reality, other perspectives be damned. My therapist calls these delusions "emotional beliefs." The distortion is based on some psychological need to hold onto a way of thinking which serves some emotional purpose for the person, even if it is wrong and eventually destructive.

Think of people who "Drink the Kool-Aid" or "Inject the bleach." Remember all the resistance to wearing masks or getting vaccinated in 2020 and 2021? How many people were sickened or died, because so many held onto their ridiculous, selfish idea of "freedom" and refused to wear a mask or have a couple of jabs in the arm? Even though all the scientific evidence was that masks and vaccines could slow the spread of the virus, and save your life and the life of many others?

I'm afraid this weakness for emotional belief is too strong in too many people to get enough of us humans to evolve a new consciousness fast enough to save the planet. Sorry to be such a pessimist. I guess I see the glass half-empty with very muddy, murky water."

Bridget, an Irish member of the Council, raises her hand as if she is in school to get Clare's attention. Clare points to Bridget as if calling on her.

"Sr. Clare, what's the *craic* on God? How does he feature in all of this?"

Clare stands up and adopts her religion teacher mien, mostly in jest, "Well now, children, you won't find most of this in your Baltimore Catechism or even your current Catholic Catechism. The people who talk about God today, theologians, the best of them, integrate modern science with their God language, even when science questions some of our traditional understandings.

This is what I've gotten from them: The Universe is God's ecstasy, the outward expression of God's inner life of creativity, relationship, and love. This is the inner life of God that Christians call the Trinity. Remember St. Patrick using the three-leafed clover to explain the Trinity? This inner life of God exhaled, breathed out, and big-banged into existence the outer world we live in. This means all creation in some yet unknown way carries the divine DNA of the Creator.

What God has created is a self-creating world that, guided and informed by God's own DNA, creates itself through evolution, biology, quantum physics, and other natural forces. This means God has set all of this in motion, and then lets the universe develop by its own dynamics. God is not controlling everything like a divine puppet master. He is more like a parent who allows the child the space and freedom to grow into who they are meant to be, and who they choose to be.

God is present in Creation by the force field of Love. The universe is an ocean of divine love, and we are all fish swimming in that love. The water of divine love, though, is so clear and its energy so subtle, and we are so immersed in it, that like fish in the sea we cannot easily see what we are swimming in. We sometimes sense its movements, its tidal pull, the waves, and ripples. Perhaps we get a glimpse of love as it moves us along the reefs and beaches of our lives.

Yet, we are so *in* it, that—just as a fish is one with the ocean—we cannot perceive what we exist in, what surrounds, buoys, holds, and nourishes us. The force field of divine Love permeates all beings and is always present to us and in us. So, we are not alone. God is always present to us in his Infinite Love."

Shelta interjects, "We Travelers have always felt what you are describing, Sr. Clare. Since we are always on the move, with no one place to call our own, we have always had a special sense that we are traveling in God's enveloping love. That and our bond with each other has always been our security. We have always been on our own, outside of "normal" society, so we see things differently than most. Seeing with a third eye helps me to understand exactly what you are saying, Sr, Clare."

"Thank you, Shelta," Clare responds, "I deeply respect the special vision you and your people have about God and the world. I have enjoyed talking with you about spiritual matters and the wisdom of your people these past few days here in the encampment. We could all learn a lot from you, and, really, from all marginalized people."

Clare silently looks at everyone around the campfire, catching the eye of each, and—shifting to a gentler, less nunny tone of voice—continues, "I have more to add: This does not mean God micro-manages, or directly controls, the universe. A self-creating universe, begotten by God, means there is no *Deus ex Machina* coming to save us and our planet. In God's self-creating creation, it is our responsibility to do what it takes to save us and the Earth from ourselves. We can't wait for God to rescue us. The whole of humanity must have a metanoia—a complete change of heart, a total change of consciousness and change of direction.

So, my friends, it's up to us. It is up to the human race. God is with us and his Love is in our attempts to wake up humanity. The Spirit infuses our efforts with Divine energy and with the energy of the Universe. But we have to wake up and be the change—and soon!"

Clare pauses to let this sink in, "For now, we have to wait, and see if Creation can still tolerate us. Or if we have to go the way of the dinosaurs in order to save our planet, and make way for some new, more intelligent life form. No matter what happens though, remember God is with us, with each and every one of you. I can see his Love in each of you. We are not alone. We are all linked in the Web of Creation to one another and to Divine Infinite Love. God bless you all."

With tears in her eyes, Aavani blurts out, "Oh my sweet yoni! She must be tuned to Divine music. Clare, I get so turned on when you talk theology; it's even better than talking dirty."

The group around the campfire laughs and then applauds Clare. Clare blushes.

Aavani smiles at Clare and continues, "I agree with everything you said, Clare. God is the Creator. She empowers, permeates, and lives in all of creation. And creation is creating itself. So, we have to change, and align ourselves with that Life Force. God isn't going to swoop down to either destroy us or save us—whichever it's going to be—we will do it to ourselves. Either we keep altering the life of our planet and self-destruct, or we turn ourselves around, and reconnect to the creative Life Force of Nature and live in harmony with it. We can't wait on God or blame God. It's on us, and it's up to us."

Aavani pauses, tears welling up in her eyes again, and trickling into her voice.

"All of this theology is well and good—I love probing the Great Mystery—but I can't rid myself of this growing sadness and dread. I feel such deep sorrow. It's the same way I felt when I read the part of *The Lord of the Rings* where the Elves have to leave Middle-earth for another dimension. Is that going to be us?"

She begins sobbing. Clare and Mark embrace her and comfort her. The whole campfire circle, except for the superintendent and the colonel, breaks into loud crying and keening lamentation. They cluster in small groups, holding each other, and wordlessly crying in each other's arms.

Gradually, the grieving simmers down. It's 1am and the long Irish twilight is finally fading. It's dark in the East, and only a glimmer of reflected sunlight lingers in the clouds over the western horizon out to sea. One by one, each person gets up from the fire and walks silently to their tents. Finally, only Clare, Aavani, Mark, Simon, Chooky, and Woosh are left in the near dark. They embrace as a group, then separate, and find their way in the fading light to their tents.

Chapter Thirty

On the third day at Dún Aonghasa, Chooky walks to the cliff edge before dawn, and as the sun comes up, she sees a massive gathering of humpbacks—hundreds of them—forming a rough semi-circle from the base of the cliff to several miles out into the Atlantic. She runs back to their tent and wakes Woosh. Together they run back to the cliff edge. They stare at the gathering of humpbacks in disbelief, wondering how this great gathering of whales could be possible, and what it could mean.

Chooky finally turns to Woosh and speaks to him in an awed whisper, "I still don't know what to believe about spiritual signs and all of that, but my Tlingit spirit tells me the humpbacks are here to warn us again. Something is coming, something is about to happen. The humpbacks are here to sound an alarm or maybe even to protect us. We need to go tell Grainne and the rest of our group."

Chooky and Woosh rush around the encampment awakening Grainne, the Message Bearers, and the members of the council. They all hurry to the bluff and can see the huge assembly of humpbacks. Everyone agrees this is a sign, but of what? Clare, Aavani, Mark, Grainne, and Shelta gather in the teepee to meditate together. Maybe something will now be revealed to them.

On the way to the teepee, Grainne notices something, and comments to the group, "That's odd. It looks like all of our camp cats are gone. Only the dogs are still here. There were several dozen cats living here and about in the Dún when we arrived. Why would they all leave?"

No one has an answer.

They meditate in silence for a couple of hours. Finally, Sr. Clare speaks to the group, "The only thing I get from my prayer is the sense that nothing is going to be revealed to us now. We have to keep waiting. And, who knows, maybe the revelation isn't going to come to us through meditation this time, but in some different way. In any case, what I hear is to keep waiting."

They all agree to this. No one has received any guidance or revelation in their meditations, and they trust Clare's spiritual intuition. They leave the teepee disappointed and frustrated. Everyone feels a growing foreboding, but no one wants to speak it out loud. They drift back to the encampment and prepare a late breakfast, having fasted since dawn to sharpen their discernment.

Chapter Thirty-One

That night, under cover of darkness—amidst a furious Irish rainstorm—a combined force of Russian and Moxxon mercenaries, aboard four unmarked naval ships, invade

Inishmore. They swiftly, stealthily take control of the harbor and the villages of Kilronan. The soldiers unload several containers full of large animal cages from one of their ships. Deep roaring sounds come from the containers.

At the same time, large herds of feral and domestic cats, a horde of rats, hundreds of badgers, and hundreds of feral "super pigs" swim from the mainland to the island from all along the shores of Galway Bay. They are driven by an inner instinct to assemble for a great battle in Gaia's plan to save her creatures. They gather on the outskirts of the village near the soldiers and join the cats and the rats of the island who have already assembled in a large herd.

The super-pigs are feral hogs, a new invasive species in Ireland. They were introduced to the West of Ireland by an American billionaire developer who bought a large swath of land near Ballyconneely in Galway, and built a new golf course resort and personal estate.

He had grown up hunting razorbacks in Arkansas and wanted to be able to hunt them on his land. He secretly smuggled a small herd of the hogs from Arkansas onto his estate, thinking he could control and contain them there. Predictably, some escaped from the estate, bred rapidly, and spread throughout County Galway.

Being part European Wild Boar and part domestic pig—hence the name "super pigs"—they are highly intelligent, prolific, very large, and very destructive of the Irish countryside. They occasionally attack Irish farmers and hunters with their razor-sharp tusks. As was happening in the U.S., they quickly became a major nuisance and a threat to native species and vegetation. The Irish dubbed them "Yankee Pigs" and were especially incensed because they frequently dug up Irish potato patches. No one could stop their spread.

At dawn, large flocks of ravens, sea gulls, and bats gather in huge, dark swarms, whirling and gyring manically over the harbor like flocks of demonic spirits. They land near the cats, rats, badgers, and hogs, as if joining forces and awaiting an order or signal to begin an attack.

The ravens assume leadership of the animal army, being perhaps the most intelligent creatures there, like all of their Corvid cousins. The super-hogs are very smart as well, but, being ground grunts like the Marines, they lack the aerial overview of the battlefield afforded the soaring ravens.

One especially large, coal-black raven is the general, the leader of the congress of ravens on the Aran Islands. He is flanked by six other glossy, black ravens who act as his officer corps. Like all of the other animals and birds that have gathered on Inishmore, he has heard an inner instinctual voice directing him to Inishmore to join in a battle against humans, who Gaia has declared to be the enemy of creation. But he is confused.

Who does Gaia want killed? Which group of humans should they attack? The soldiers and militiamen, the environmentalists up at Dún Aonghasa, the Aran islanders, or all three groups?

Ravens, like crows, can distinguish between individual human faces. So, the general decides to fly over all three groups, examine their faces, and get a sense of who is most deserving of attack. He flies over the Russians and oil militia and is impressed by their rugged, handsome faces, their organization, and their uniforms. The Aran Islanders are familiar to him since he has known such people his whole life. They have usually been respectful to his people and seem the most innocent of the three.

When he flies to the Dún, he doesn't like what he sees. This group appears to the raven general to be the strangest, most unkempt of the three types of humans he has surveilled. The young peoples' bearded faces, their long hair, and strange, scruffy clothing, and the Guardia's and Irish Army's somewhat sloppy uniforms and irregular formations convince him they must be the right enemy to attack. They probably will also be easier to defeat in battle. Most of them don't look like they could put up much of a fight. Then he spies the Travelers, camped near the environmentalists. His people and theirs have a long history of mutual distaste and enmity. This confirms his decision. He flies back to his gathered forces intent on attacking the humans in Dún Aonghasa in alliance with the humans who have invaded the village.

Chapter Thirty-Two

The Inishmore villagers are awakened in the pre-dawn darkness by all of this noise and commotion on their usually quiet island. They are mystified and terrified by what they hear as they lay awake in their beds. Most stay hidden in their cottages. Amongst the other strange sounds in the night, some of the Aran Islanders are convinced they hear the wail and shriek of the fabled banshees, the harbingers of death.

Chooky is up at dawn and goes to the cliff edge to watch the sea. What she sees shocks her. There are a half-dozen naval ships of various sizes and shapes, standing a couple of miles off the coast. They are devoid of any insignia, but she thinks they might be Russian. A couple of hundred humpback whales have positioned themselves between the ships and the shoreline under Dún Aonghasa. Another group of humpbacks has formed a moving circle around the ships. Chooky runs to their tent to wake up Woosh. The two of them run through the camp sounding the alarm, rousing the Message Bearers, Grainne, and the environmentalists. Grainne alerts the Guardia, the Travelers, and the Irish Army brigade.

Superintendent O'Dowd sends back word that his scouts are reporting soldiers have invaded the harbor and the village of Kilronan and are moving toward Dún Aonghasa. He expects an imminent attack. The Guardia and the Irish Army units take up defensive positions behind the concentric stone walls of ancient fortifications.

Superintendent O'Dowd and Colonel Quinlan coordinate the defense and station themselves behind a large upright stone in the center of the third wall. Many of the young environmentalists volunteer to join the Irish defense forces and are issued rifles.

Led by Shelta, the whole Traveler band—including women and older children—arm themselves, ready to fight the invaders. Mark, Simon, Gustafson, Woosh, and Chooky also take up weapons, and position themselves atop the inner wall.

In the chaos of preparing for battle, George Gustafson seeks out Aavani across the central court of the Dún. He finds her near the teepee, deliberating with Grainne and Clare about what their role should be in the upcoming fight. George taps her on the arm, and asks her to come aside with him, and talk for a moment. Aavani is reluctant but agrees.

George looks Aavani in the eyes, and in a gentle voice, choked with emotion says, "Aavani, I don't know what is going to happen to us in this fight we're about to have, so I have to say this to you now. I have been thinking a lot about what you said to me that day back on *Ruach* about finally growing up. You were right. I have acted like a horny, immature teenager all my life. I realized I have been disrespecting and exploiting women like I used to do to the planet herself. I apologize that I tried to do the same thing to you.

I admire you for your courage in standing up to me. I have really taken your words to heart and have been trying to change. I haven't chased any women here at Dún Aonghasa—even though there are some pretty cute ones—

and I have even begun to pray as you suggested, although I really don't know what I am doing."

George smiles and chuckles briefly as he says this.

"Aavani, I have no right to ask you for forgiveness for harassing you. But I would feel more peaceful about going into this battle if we were friends—just friends—again. Can we be at peace with each other?"

Aavani answers with no hesitation, "Of course we can, George. I forgive you. And I'm very happy to hear you took my challenge so seriously. After this fight maybe we could sit down and talk more about it. I could even give you some meditation pointers."

"Thank you so much, Aavani," George says, extending his arms to her, "May I?"

When she nods, he pulls her into a warm, but chaste, Texas bear hug. They hold their embrace for a couple of minutes, and then George turns and joins the others taking up their defensive positions along the walls of the Dún.

He looks back once and waves. Aavani feels another great sadness come over her, as she waves back. She shakes it off, returning to her conversation with Grainne and Clare.

Grainne wants to join in the fight, but she is persuaded by Zoe to stay in the teepee in the center of the enclosure. Clare joins her there. Aavani is torn between fighting and praying, but finally decides to stay with Clare and Grainne. All three gather in the center of the teepee and start to pray. Aavani holds a rifle over her lap as she sits in the lotus position and chants.

"Clare, now I am officially a 'prayer warrior' as you Christians call it."

Aavani and Clare laugh. Grainne is too tight and tense to appreciate their humor. She remains silent, takes a rosary out of her pocket, and begins to quietly murmur her Hail Mary's, Our Father's, and Glory Be's, which she learned as a child at school in Lisdoonvarna.

A little after dawn, a dense fog—the same gray color as the stones of Dún Aonghasa—blows in from the sea. It blankets the whole island of Inishmore, reducing visibility to just a few feet. The defenders can hardly see the nose in front of their faces. The Irish soldiers had radioed the tiny Irish Air Corps for air cover, but that is not possible now. They will have to repel the invaders on their own. The fog also grounds the Russian ship-based, attack helicopters. The militia force had counted on their superior numbers and firepower and the helicopter gunships to make quick work of the environmentalists and their Irish defenders. Now they will also have to rely entirely on their ground forces.

Just before sunrise, a captain's gig leaves one of the Russian ships in the harbor carrying two men, one a burly, weathered man in his fifties, dressed in a military uniform with no insignia; the other a tall, athletically built forty-something man with a perfect military haircut and dressed top-to-bottom in designer camouflage, looking like the billionaire big-game hunter that he is. They creep through the fog to the harbor quay and disembark.

The two men are General Dmitry Ustinov, a retired Russian general and veteran of the shadowy Russian invasion of Ukraine, and Sam Burroughs, the CEO of Moxxon, a former Navy Seal and now the leader of the oil militia. It has been rumored that General Ustinov was the Russian officer who ordered the anti-aircraft missile to be fired which downed the Malaysian Airlines Flight 17 in July 2014, killing 298 passengers and crew. Burroughs and Ustinov are the co-commanders of the combined force of oil militia and Russian mercenaries.

The two commanders have been planning their attack together for the past week aboard the Russian vessels, training their forces to coordinate their strategies. They have devised a battle plan to attack and destroy the Irish and environmental defenders. They think it will be an easy task.

They also plan to capture Grainne and the Message Bearers, and imprison them secretly in a Siberian prison. Their goal is to silence their anti-fossil fuel message and their climate change warnings to protect the future of the oil industry in the U.S. and in Russia. Perhaps they can even be threatened and tortured into changing their story and speaking in support of the oil industry.

Burroughs and General Ustinov are driven to a crossroad in the village where their forces are gathered ready to attack. As they approach their soldiers, they notice large flocks of birds and bats swooping in and out of the fog. They also drive through dense herds of hundreds of cats, rats, badgers, and giant hogs.

Ustinov comments in heavily Russian-accented English, "That is quite strange. What are all of these birds and animals doing here? They look like they have gathered for something, but what? It is—how you say?—very creepy."

Burroughs just shrugs and remains silent. He really doesn't like the Russian general and would like it much better if he was in sole command of the forces. He resents Ustinov's imperious posturing, and is used to being the sole commander of any group he is leading. However, he knows he needs the Russians' firepower if this attack is to succeed.

In the impenetrable fog, the battle begins. Burroughs and Ustinov order their soldiers to begin the attack on Dún Aonghasa. To their surprise, an especially large raven swoops over them croaking very loudly, while his lieutenant's broadcast shrill alarm calls. Immediately, the birds and the animals form in rank, as if they had heard the general's orders. They move forward in front of the soldiers and begin to march toward Dún Aonghasa.

Sam Burroughs turns to General Ustinov and speaks in a heavy Texan accent, "Dimitri, what the hell is going on? It looks like these critters are going to help us. I'm not sure what's up here, but maybe Mother Nature is on our side for a change. In this damn fog, we can use all the help we can get. I'll be damned, if it doesn't look like they are going to join us in the attack. There sure have been some really bizarre things happening lately."

The ravens, seagulls, and bats lead the attack, swarming all around the Guardia, army, and environmentalists, pecking and biting as they emerge suddenly from the fog. The defenders are totally taken by surprise. They cannot see what is attacking them until the last minute. The birds and bats are on them, especially going for their eyes, before the Irish can even put up their hands in defense. The birds and bats swarm around the Guardia and the soldiers, dive-bombing and swirling around their heads. Their weapons are of no avail in fending off the fierce avian air-force.

Mark is injured by the bird attack, his head bleeding from multiple pecking wounds in his scalp and on his face. He can barely see because of the blood streaming down his face, but he manages to protect his eyes from the birds. Other defenders had not been so lucky and have had one, or both, eyeballs punctured and gouged out. Simon leaves his post to help Mark off the wall, and lead him back to the teepee where he and Aavani tend to Mark's wounds.

The rats, cats, badgers, and hogs attack next, coming in successive waves, infiltrating the Irish positions along the outer defensive walls. Rats swarm though crevices and over the rock walls, overwhelming the Guardia and soldiers by their sheer numbers. They scurry up their legs and jump from the rock defenses onto their faces, delivering numerous bites to their legs, arms, faces, and necks. The bites are not lethal, but some of the victims are so badly bitten with multiple rat bites all over their bodies they can no longer fight.

They have to retreat, many of them reporting to the emergency medical station Simon has set up near the teepee. Even this early in the battle, Simon is overwhelmed by the large number of wounded. He is the only doctor, and there are just a few young nurses among the environmentalists who have joined him at the hastily organized field hospital.

The defenders hear the terrifying sounds of the approaching cat attack. The sounds of hissing, spitting, howling, yowling, snarling, and growling eerily resound in the grey fog cloud and reverberate off the circles of the stone walls. Some of the defenders have heard these sounds during catfights they witnessed. Their skin tingles with fear, a primal amygdala chill shooting up their spines as they sense they are now the target of an imminent catfight.

Is this why all the cats suddenly disappeared from the compound? they wonder.

The cats attack the defenders in small groups, pouncing on their victims from the rocks, clawing at faces and eyes, and repeatedly biting their necks, attempting to rupture their jugular veins. There are too many of them attacking at once to push them off. Several defenders lie unconscious among the stones, bleeding out from their jugulars and carotids, torn open by the attacking cats. Some of the cats had been camp-cats up in the environmentalist's compound, fed and coddled by the humans who were now their victims. Their purrs of contentment and apparent affection had turned into snarls, growls, and whirling claws.

On their best days, badgers are an angry animal known to have a bad temper. Incited by Gaia's message to them, they become even more aggressive. They attack stealthily, hugging the rough ground with their short, powerful legs. Emerging from the fog, already at the defenders' feet before they realize it, the badgers lock their bite onto the legs and groins of the defenders with their teeth and powerful jaws. They rip their victims' flesh with their sharp, predator teeth. In a few cases, their vicious bite actually castrates the Guardia, the soldiers, and other male defenders, holding tight with their jaws until their victims bleed to death. They also horribly mutilate the genitals of a couple of the female defenders.

The super-pigs are a highly intelligent, adaptive hybrid species. They use their wit and speed to sneak up from behind, or feint an attack from one side, only to switch to the other before the human defender can react. A number of the defenders are outwitted and outflanked by the clever furious hogs and are badly mauled or killed. The feral hogs use their size and bulk to bowl over the defenders, slashing their legs as they do so. Once they have their victims on the ground, they employ their razor-sharp tusks to slice their abdomens open, leaving the hapless defender disembowelled, their guts and blood spilling onto the rocky soil.

Glimpsing some of these attacks from their stone command center through short breaks in the fog, Superintendent O'Dowd turns and comments to Colonel Quinlan, "Jaysus! Now even our *bagun* is attacking us. Are all those rashers I've eaten through the years getting their revenge? What in God's name is happening? I was prepared to fight human soldiers, but how do we defend ourselves against this? All these animals and birds, even cats, are attacking us unprovoked. The whole world is turning upside down."

Colonel Quinlan responds, "Maybe this is what the Message Bearers were warning us about. Nature herself is turning against us. But why are the birds and animals helping the Russians and oil militia? I don't understand what's going on anymore. None of it makes sense to me. All I know is that it's our job to make a stand, and protect these people, like my *Da* did in the Congo in '61."

O'Dowd and Quinlan look at each other, cock their heads, and shrug their shoulders in the way Aran Islanders do when they are non-verbally commenting on the shared mystery and absurdity of life. There is nothing else to be said. They return their focus to directing their forces, watching the tide of the battle begin to turn against them.

The Irish Travelers are the only ones not surprised or fazed by the attack of birds and animals. Their magical view of life has prepared them for such unnatural events. In their world, animals have spirits and sometimes superpowers. All of Nature talks to them. So they are not astonished in the least that animals would become soldiers and attack them.

The Travelers, accustomed to defending themselves from an often-hostile society, are especially fierce fighters. Shelta, armed with a rifle and a knife, fights as ferociously as any of the male Guardia or soldiers, fending off and killing attacking animals and Russians alike. When she sees the number of wounded lying exposed and vulnerable in the open, she organizes the Traveler women and a few of the men to rescue them. Many of them risk their lives to retrieve the wounded, pulling them up the hill, and hiding them among the rocks, if they cannot get them to Simon and his aid station.

The Guardia and Irish soldiers are able to shoot some of the animals but are overwhelmed by their sheer numbers. Many defenders are bitten and scratched and incapacitated. A number bleed to death from their wounds. Superintendent O'Dowd is bitten in the leg by a badger and his face scratched by two attacking cats, but he manages to fend them off. He and Colonel Quinlan decide to lead their forces in a strategic retreat, making a stand inside the third stone circle. As they retreat in the still-dense fog, they are harassed by the birds and the bats.

During their pullback, the Guardia come upon the limp body of Zoe, the American activist, her jugular vein torn open by a cat, her eyes plucked out by the birds. They carry her body up the hill through the passageway and into the enclosure to the field hospital tent which Simon has set up next to the teepee. Simon quickly sees it is too late to help her.

Grainne and Clare come out of the teepee to see Zoe. Grainne falls on her body, sobbing. Clare holds and comforts her. Between sobs, Grainne cries out, "Zoe, Zoe, I am so sorry! You have been a true friend to me and to Iona. You have been so brave, so committed. For you and for Iona, and for all that you believed in, we will keep fighting. I am so sorry!"

The Russian and oil mercenaries, led by Sam Burroughs and General Dimitry Ustinov, follow the momentum of the animals' attack and push the Irish back to the fourth, next-to-last defensive wall. There is much chaos and confusion in the swirling Irish mist. Shots are fired randomly into the fog without any clear targets. Neither side can see each other until the last minute. There are some chance casualties on both sides from bullets, but most of the carnage comes in fierce hand-to-hand combat all along the perimeters of the ancient rock circles.

The Irish and the environmentalists put up a surprisingly fierce resistance, but the oil militia and Russian mercenary force is considerably larger and better trained in close, H2H combat. They also possess superior firepower from their Russian weaponry, especially their heavy machine guns and RPGs. The advantage is to the oil forces and their bird and animal allies.

Seeing they are winning the battle, they press their attack. There are more and more Irish fatalities and wounded. Many of the young environmentalists, who have also fought fiercely despite their inexperience and lack of military training, also lose their lives. O'Dowd and Quinlan assess the situation the best they can in the fog, see they are losing, and order another retreat to positions behind the last thick inner wall of Dún Aonghasa. Grainne, Clare, and Aavani leave the teepee, and watch for a short time from the top of that thick inner wall. They cannot see much, but they can tell the battle is not going their way.

Suddenly, hundreds of dogs of many different breeds—some who were living with the climate protesters and others who swam over from Galway—come running into the battle. They pour through the passageway out of the fort and from their hiding places among the rock fortifications.

Organized in attack-packs of ten to twenty, the dogs decimate the rats and cats, and force the badgers and hogs to retreat. They push the surprised, suddenly outnumbered oil and Russian mercenaries back down to the bottom of the hill, biting at their heels as they retreat. The Irish forces, re-enforced by a band of Travelers and some of the environmentalists that had been held in reserve, counterattack, following the lead of the dogs. They push the oil forces out of the stone circles and back down to the bottom of the hill.

The raven general has been watching the battle perched on a tall stone in the fourth circle. He has been grounded by the thick Irish mist that largely kept him from soaring and circling over the battlefield as he had planned. He had hoped to monitor the battle and direct his forces from the air.

Despite the fog, he can see the battle is going against him, now that the dogs have entered the battle. He wonders whether he picked the wrong set of humans to attack. Perhaps the oil soldiers are the real enemy of Gaia?

He decides to call a strategic retreat while he reconsiders. He starts cawing loudly to his force of ravens. His cry is taken up by his officers and then the whole flock. The caw alarm is heard by the seagulls, cats, rats, badgers, and hogs as a command to retreat. They stop fighting the attacking dogs, pull back from their forward positions and follow the soldiers back into the village.

Burroughs and Ustinov retreat all the way to the harbor and with several other men begin unlocking a series of cages that were earlier unloaded from the Russian ships to the harbor quay in Kilronan.

Chapter Thirty-Three

General Ustinov radios Rear-Admiral Popov who is commanding the Russian naval flotilla out at sea to the west. Ustinov curses at Popov in Russian, demanding to know what happened to the amphibious force that was supposed to support the attack on Dún Aonghasa.

"Your men should have landed on Kilmurvey Beach by now to support our right flank and join us in the attack up the hill to the fortress. Where the hell are they? We have been pushed back to the harbor by a force of dogs and Irish who attacked us from your damned right flank. We need your units to land and counterattack now."

Admiral Popov replies, "We have been surrounded and harassed by these crazed humpback whales. They blocked our landing craft from leaving the flotilla and even capsized and sank two of them. Many men have been lost. But now the rest of the landing craft have broken through. They are rounding the south end of Inishmore and will speed up the east coast heading for Kilmurvey. They should be landing within the hour. They will be there to support you. Wait for them and then you can counterattack. We will win this day yet!"

General Ustinov grumbles a reply, "Popov, you damn well better deliver on your promise, or I'll make sure our dear President's poison squad finds you."

When the amphibious force comes within sight of Kilmurvey Beach, they see that another group of humpbacks has formed two circles across the mouth of the inlet leading to the white sands of Kilmurvey. The five remaining landing craft try to power their way through, ramming several of the humpbacks. Some of the huge whales are killed, but others dive, re-group into giant feeding circles, and blow a bubble-net around the ships laden with soldiers, as if they were merely a shoal of herring.

With incredible teamwork, they explode to the surface in their feeding circles, capsizing all five of the landing craft one at a time, drowning most of the heavily laden Russian soldiers. A few soldiers manage to struggle to shore and lie gasping for breath on the pristine white beach, normally full of American, British, and European tourists. The amphibious force is wrecked. They won't be rescuing the oil force after all.

Chapter Thirty-Four

The battle has now decidedly turned in favor of the Irish and the environmentalists. There have been numerous casualties on both sides. Grainne and the Message Bearers are starting to feel more confident when they hear blood-chilling, guttural growls, and strange huffing and woofing sounds reverberating through the fog from the bottom of the hill. They hear metal doors being opened and closed with loud clangs. Something fearsome is coming. The Guardia are the first to see them emerging from the fog. One hundred and fifty immense Kamchatka brown bears run up the hill toward them with astonishing speed for such large animals. The huge bears are followed by the Russian mercenaries and the oil militia.

The giant Kamchatka bears were collected and trained for battle by the Russian army, and supplied to the mercenaries by President Putin himself. The bear force was considered one of the most secret weapons in the Russian armory. They had previously been employed to intimidate anti-Putin protesters in the city of Khabarovsk in Russia's Far East but had never before been unleashed in a military action. General Ustinov is excited to see how they perform in battle. He is confident they will turn the tide back in favor of his forces, despite the decimation of the amphibious force.

This time the soldiers are not accompanied by the ravens, seagulls, bats, cats, badgers, and hogs. The raven general has decided to hold his forces back, remain neutral, and see which way the battle goes. The bird and animal forces follow behind the soldiers back up the hill toward the Dún, but don't engage in the attack. The rats, meanwhile, have all run off the battlefield, and are busy infesting the Russian ships in the harbor.

The flow of the battle again turns against the Irish and the environmentalists. The dogs try to fight the bears, but they are no match for them. The Irish force fires furiously through the fog at the onslaught of bears, but are then pinned down by cover fire from the mercenaries, and can only pick off a few of the Kamchatka giants.

The Irish and the dogs retreat behind the thick rock of the high, inner wall to make a last stand in the semi-circle keep of the Dún. They put up a courageous fight, but the bears and soldiers overwhelm them and begin to climb over the immense inner wall. They invade the enclosure and push the defenders to the edge of the Dún Aonghasa cliff that drops 400 feet into the ocean below.

Burroughs and Ustinov follow the bears and soldiers to the top of the inner wall to supervise the last stage of the battle. They are triumphant and gloating.

General Ustinov boasts, "Never underestimate the power of the great Russian Bear!"

They order their men and the bears to prepare to push everyone, except for Grainne and the Message Bearers— whom they plan to take hostage—off the cliff onto the rocks and into the ocean 400 hundred feet below.

Burroughs finds Gustafson among the now-defeated environmentalists and their defenders.

"Well, George, we meet again. The last time was at the Fossil Fuel Forum meeting. When you stopped attending, and turned tree-hugger, my colleagues and I decided you had gone Antifa or Extinction Rebellion Group and were a traitor to the cause. I wish we had put a bounty on your head then. I would happily collect on it now that you and your ilk are being defeated.

You were a brilliant oil engineer, George. Such a waste. But, if you would come back to our side now, I could save you. You could be very useful for us as a spokesman. Imagine how persuasive you could be as a petroleum executive who has seen the light about this phony global-warming conspiracy. We will see to it that you are well-rewarded for the rest of your life. Otherwise, you're going over the cliff with the rest of your fellow eco-terrorists."

Burroughs glares at Gustafson, hoping his offer will entice him to rejoin the carbon lobby.

"What do you say, George?"

"Sam, you can stuff an oil derrick up your ass! You can kill us today, but you can't kill the truth. It will always survive, re-emerge, and eventually catch up with people like you. I used to be your friend and was much like you until my eyes were opened, and I saw the truth of what we were doing to our planet. You and your crowd are committing murder-suicide, not just with us, but with the whole world.

You will push us over the cliff today. But you are going over the cliff yourself someday soon if you don't change. And you will take the entire planet with you. There may not be any hope for any of us. It may be too late. But these young people here, who you are going to murder, are the last hope we may have. Why can't you see that? Or do you see it and not care, because it's so profitable for you and your buddies to keep on pushing your delusional carbon fix?"

George glares back at him for a moment, then continues. "So, no Sam. I'm not coming back to your carbon cartel. As we say in Texas, "F, O, and D". Fuck Off and Die, Sam."

Sam becomes infuriated and orders his militiamen to seize George and immediately throw him over the cliff. Woosh is nearby and overhears the argument. He has been injured and badly mauled by one of the Kamchatka bears, blood streaming from a severe bite wound on his scalp. Simon is there attending to his wounds, attempting to stem the blood loss.

When Woosh sees Burroughs is going to kill George, he breaks away from Simon, and attacks the militiamen to try to stop them. He is too weak to have much effect, and the soldiers easily restrain him.

Sam commands his men, "Throw this red-skin over the cliff too. As they used to say in America, 'The only good Indian is a dead Indian.'"

The oil militiamen drag both George and Woosh to the edge of the cliff at the back of Dún Aonghasa and push them over. The Message Bearers, Grainne, Simon,

Superintendent O'Dowd, Colonel Quinlan, Shelta, and most of the surviving Guardia, soldiers, environmentalists, and Travelers watch with horror.

George and Woosh scream as they fall through 400 feet of air, then go silent as they hit the rocks below. Their bodies bounce off the sharp rocks and into the ocean. A large shiver of great white sharks is waiting there for them. There is an immediate, bloody feeding frenzy, and in minutes George and Woosh are gone. Everyone watching knows they will be next.

Watching this unfold right before her, Chooky screams, "No! No! Woosh, No!" and faints at the cliff's edge.

Clare, Aavani, and Simon rush to help her. Russian soldiers quickly stop them and push them to the ground. They have identified Grainne, Clare, Aavani, Mark, and Chooky as the Message Bearers, and herd them to the teepee, roughly carrying the unconscious Chooky with them. They tie each of them up and throw them into the teepee. They intend to hold them there until they can interrogate them, and torture them if needed. Their eventual fate depends on whether Burroughs and General Ustinov decide to hold them as hostages, and force them to make statements denying Gaia's message, or just kill them with the others.

Chapter Thirty-Five

As the oil and Russian soldiers prepare to push the whole Irish and environmental group over the Dún Aonghasa precipice, and feed them to the waiting sharks, without warning a fierce storm sweeps in from the ocean. A

200mph gust of wind knocks everyone, including the bears, to the ground. Burroughs and Ustinov are blown off the wall. Burroughs dies in the fall, his head split open on a rock. The ravens, gulls, and bats are blown out of the sky. Some of the Kamchatka bears take advantage of the chaos to turn on their Russian masters, getting revenge for their captivity by attacking and mauling a number of them to death.

The Irish and environmental forces are pushed back away from their precarious position on the edge of the great cliff by the wind. They flatten themselves on the ground, clinging to the dark stones, including the *Seanchaí* stone, at the center of the Dún. The teepee is toppled and blown away. Grainne and the four Message Bearers survive by holding onto each other, resisting the powerful force of the strange wind which threatens to tear them apart.

The wind continues to blow at a steady 185mph, forcing the mercenaries, militia, and the now-neutralized animal force to retreat back down the hill. As they run away, fierce forked lightning strikes and kills many of them. One of the first to be struck is Ustinov. He is electrocuted to death in a terrible forty seconds. Softball-sized hailstones kill many more. All this is accompanied by torrential rain which comes in massive sheets driven by the howling wind.

The invaders have been defeated. The survivors flee to the harbor town where some armed villagers pick off the stragglers. The remaining mercenaries and militia attempt to board one of the ships, but most are washed overboard, and drown in the monstrous, wind-driven waves.

The surviving animals run into the ocean, and either drown or swim back to the Irish mainland.

The raven general survives, fighting the wind to fly back up to the Dún with a small branch of a fuchsia bush in his beak with several deep red and purple flowers attached. He lays it at Grainne's feet as a peace offering and flies off.

When the wind and rain subside, Grainne and the Message Bearers, the survivors from the Irish force, climate activists, and Travelers stand on top of the inner wall of the Dún in wonder and awe at the power and destructiveness of the storm that has now passed them by. Nature has won the battle and saved them. They celebrate by breaking into dance and song on top of the wall and in the great semi-circle inside the fort.

After just a few minutes of celebration, the revelers hear a loud, continuous roar of thunder rumbling in from the ocean. The winds and storm clear the fog. Now the wind has completely stopped. The air is very clear and strangely still. They stop dancing and singing. An expectant silence comes over them. When the thunder is not booming, it is so quiet they can only hear the blood rushing in their ears. Strangely, there is thunder, but no visible lightning. They are now all standing, looking away from the wall and out to sea.

A tremendous black cloud, black-hole black—as if all light and matter are being sucked into its gravity force—rolls toward them from the North Atlantic, accompanied by nearly constant, ear-splitting thunder. Just as the cloud is about to enter the Dún, it stops and splits open, revealing a brilliant white light.

Emerging from the light, there she is. Gaia. At her right hand is Iona McCleod, looking as stern as she did the day she stood before the UN General Assembly, but also glowing from a soft, white light that emanates from within her, and, at the same time, envelops and surrounds her and Gaia. She remains silent, but stares intently at Grainne, the Message Bearers, and the young activists.

Gaia, at first, looks very similar to the fierce Hindu goddess, Kali, the goddess of Creation, Destruction, and Power. She displays this persona when she is warning and challenging. She is Kali, the Destroyer of Worlds. Her skin is a dark blue. She is naked except for a garland of severed human heads and a short skirt made of human arms. Her jet-black hair fans out over her entire back down to her upper thighs.

In one of the hands of her four arms she holds a scimitar red with blood. In another hand she holds the decapitated head of a man with his blood dripping into a bowl held by one of her other hands. Her dark eyes stare wildly at the gathering in the Dún. Her mouth is wide open, baring her ferocious canine teeth. Her fierce, red tongue protrudes out and down over her chin.

She then morphs into a benevolent mother goddess, like a cross between the mother goddess, Devi, and Catholic images of Mary, especially Our Lady of Guadalupe. She adopts this persona whenever she speaks gently and lovingly. In this guise, she is dressed in blue robes lined with gold cloth, surrounded by rays of golden light. There is a large bouquet of red roses at her feet. Her four arms extend to the gathering, her hands holding bread, wine, an olive branch, and other symbols of peace and abundance. She smiles beneficently, her face radiant with a warm, loving light that bestows instant peace to the beholder.

Gaia hovers in the air above the ocean almost at the brow of the great cliff. She is surrounded by an intense white halo of effulgent light. The thunder stops. There is complete calm. Everyone in the fort falls to their knees or lies supine on the ground. Many are terrified of what they are seeing, especially when Gaia has the visage of Kali. Simon and Chooky are stunned by what they see and confused about whether it is real or an hallucination. Aavani and Mark kneel in devotion. Only Sr. Clare and young Grainne remain standing, looking with great expectancy and peace at Gaia and Iona.

Then, Gaia speaks in a voice sounding alternately like thunder or a loud, fierce wind, shifting to a gentle breeze blowing lightly over a bubbling mountain stream. Her visage changes with each change of voice. As she speaks from the radiant white cloud, she changes back and forth between the goddess of death and destruction and a kind, beneficent Mother Nature, depending on what she is saying. Gaia manifests at first as the benevolent Earth Mother.

"I am Gaia, the Spirit and Soul of Planet Earth. My human children, I have come to save you for now, because you few have worked and fought so hard to save me and the rest of my children. I also come to warn you and all humanity. You are my children. I have always loved you and have given you special gifts and special opportunities. I love you still."

Gaia's appearance suddenly transfigures into fearsome Kali.

"But now I must destroy you! For the good of the planet and to save my creatures which you are threatening and driving to extinction, I must extinguish each and every one of you humans. You are now threatening me, your Mother, with unnatural and devastating changes. I cannot allow you to do this to me, your planet, and to the rest of my creatures. The next mass extinction is you, my human children!

I have sent you many warnings through your scientists and your prophets, and you did not listen. You have continued to pollute and overheat your planet. You are destroying my forests. You are stripping me naked. You are despoiling my special love, the great Amazon, and decimating the Pantanal, and many other places with your fires.

All over the planet you are ruining my creatures' habitats. You are driving them out of their homes. You are filling the land and the sea with your plastics and with all of your other toxic filth. My little ones eat plastic now, instead of their natural food.

I had hoped your so-called Paris Agreement would change your behaviors and begin to reverse global warming. But it was not enough, and it is much too slow. Too many nations have failed to fulfill their promises. Some are only paying lip-service to the efforts to reverse climate change and are not really trying at all. I can no longer tolerate this. You all must die.

You are pushing the planet ever nearer to what your scientists call a tipping point. Soon, you will arrive at the point of no return when it will be too late to reverse global warming and all of its disastrous effects. The sixth extinction of my creatures is already underway, and it will accelerate greatly if this milestone is passed. I must act now before we reach that point.

I have now come near to the tipping point myself with you humans. You have pushed my patience and love too far. So, I must tip the scales of life, and begin your extinction now before it is too late for the planet and for my other creatures. You have caused some of my creatures to go extinct in the past, but I forgave you, because I love you, and because I believed you would listen, learn, and change. I thought you would use the great intelligence I gave you to grow in understanding and compassion, and to reform your ways. Instead, you persisted in your selfish, foolish, murderous ways. How dare you reject my love and ignore all of my pleading and all of the signs I sent you! How dare you! God will forgive you, but I will not. I will not forgive you any longer for your sins against me and your planet."

Gaia-Kali pauses for several moments, glaring silently at the survivors with her intense eyes, reddened with unbounded rage, her blood-red tongue protruding and white fangs bared to show her unrestrained fury. Each person gathered in Dún Aonghasa feels her malevolent stare penetrating their chests and coursing, like a hot venom of rage and terror, through their whole body. Each of them is paralyzed by her stare, unable to move a muscle for what seems an eternity, until Gaia-Kali resumes her diatribe.

"You have been waging an undeclared war against me. I have not fought back out of my love for you. I have held back my fury in hopes that you would finally see what you are doing to me and repent. No more! I now declare war against you. I declare war on all human beings. I will marshal all of my forces and all of my creatures to wage this war against you until all of you are defeated, and the human species is eradicated from the face of the Earth.

You have seen reports from around the world about what I am starting to do to extinguish you. These phenomena will continue and expand. I will do everything in my power to destroy you. My legions of bats will spread a new, even deadlier virus over the whole planet, killing millions of you.

My pangolins will get their revenge. This virus which I have evolved is deadly only to you humans. It will move swiftly around the world before you can stop it with your medicines and vaccines.

Do you remember the Coronavirus of 2020, and what death and disruption it caused your societies? I sent that virus to warn you and give you a chance to repent and change. You even saw how the skies cleared, and how my atmosphere started to heal when you stayed home in quarantine and pumped less CO_2 and other pollutants into the air. But you ignored my warning and went back to your old ways. This new Coronavirus—your scientists will call it Covid-25—will be even more infectious and much more deadly. Many of you will die the horrible death of Covid-25, many more than died in 2020.

I will unleash my deadliest creature, the lowly mosquito, on you. I have been breeding great clouds of billions of mosquitos which will carry malaria, dengue fever, yellow fever, chikungunya, zika, West Nile, St. Louis Encephalitis. and numerous other deadly diseases. Global warming will lead to global swarming of legions of insects. Mosquitos will swarm all over your cities, biting and infecting and killing millions more of you.

The Pacific Ring of Fire will erupt all at once, spewing gigantic ash clouds into the whole atmosphere which will blot out the sun and kill all of your crops. Millions of you will slowly starve. The great Yellowstone Caldera will also explode, inflicting the same kind of devastation to the North American West and Midwest. Massive earthquakes will destroy the cities of the U.S. West Coast,

Japan, the Middle East, China, Indonesia, and Southeast Asia, unleashing terrible tsunamis that will wash away millions more.

My animals, at my command, have started to turn against you, and will hunt you down and attack you, no matter how big your armies or how powerful your weapons. You have seen here in this battle how your own cats and other animals turned against you and assaulted you. This will happen with all of my animal children all around the world. At my orders, every species will find ways to destroy you. You, who have preyed too long on my children, will now become the prey. You will be mercilessly pursued, attacked, mauled, and devoured.

The weather will turn more and more extreme with more powerful and destructive hurricanes, tornados, derechos, and thunderstorms. In some places I will so saturate my air that massive deluges of rain will descend in areas you would least expect. Your rivers will swell to one-thousand-year floods, over and over, every year, drowning many more millions of you. Your cities, towns, and villages will be swept away. I will catch you in your homes, in your subways, and along your roads and put you to a watery death.

In other places, I will suck the moisture from my skies so completely you will suffer years-long extreme droughts. Your crops will wither and fail. Many will starve. Your reservoirs will dry up, leaving your vaunted dams empty monuments to your folly. Drought-fed wildfires will incinerate your houses and torch your polluting cars. Smoke from these massive fires will turn the sun orange and red. The skies will turn from my brilliant blue to a dreary, dolorous grey. The smoke particles will enter your lungs, strangle your breathing, and slowly kill you.

The oceans are rising, and they will continue to rise ever faster. I will flood your coastlines and wash away your coastal cities. All of your low-lying islands, your fancy beach resorts, and your seaside hotels and mansions will be submerged and washed away. Because of you, all of my oceans are warming to dangerously high temperatures. Soon, my oceans will start to release poisonous gases, which I will blow inland to suffocate and kill millions more of you. All of this and more will continue until the whole human species is driven to extinction."

Gaia-Kali stops to stare again at her audience. She glowers at them as if seeing all of her human children before her. Her eyes are wild with fury and intoxicated with her vision of revenge. Blood starts to drip from the scimitar she holds in her upper right hand and from the severed human head she holds in her upper left hand. The blood begins to puddle at her feet, and flow away from her in bright red rivers toward the four directions.

After this pause, Gaia-Kali resumes her proclamation in an even more vehement voice, "You will reap the harvest of your unnatural warming of me. Many places on the planet will become too hot to live and work in. Many will die from the heat and from drought and famine. Wildfires will intensify and spread, killing thousands. Many more people will be forced to migrate. Global warming will lead to human swarming. As the climate warms, and many places become inhabitable, millions of people will flee their homelands, and swarm into the cooler North. National boundaries and borders will be overwhelmed.

This will lead to war, as you turn on each other. In these conflicts and wars millions will be killed. You will be doing my work of extinction when you kill each other in the name of nationality and race, scarcity and profit. You humans are already very good at making war and manufacturing increasingly better ways to kill each other. I will make you even better. This will help me to exterminate you. You will destroy each other on my behalf, as I work with the rest of my creatures and natural forces to annihilate you.

I have withheld my fury until now about your carbon-addicted ways. I have tried to be patient about your failure to hear my pain and the pain of your fellow creatures. Your hearts have hardened, and you have pursued only your self-interested, short-sighted desires. You have become carbon gluttons, solely interested in what you can consume of me, and the so-called profit you can make off of me. As a result, you have grown distant and alienated from me.

Unless you listen to my plea and the cry of my creatures immediately, you leave me no choice. I must destroy your species, so I can save the Earth and the rest of my children. Many of these creatures know they will die too in this extinction, but they are willing to sacrifice their lives to save the Earth and their fellow creatures by ridding the planet of you, my human children."

Just as suddenly as her previous transformation, Gaia changes back into the benevolent Earth Mother, Mary-like image, speaking now in a soft, melodic voice, "However, your loyal dogs, the big-hearted humpback whales, and the grateful sea turtles have pleaded with me to give your race one last chance. The dogs see your capacity for love and goodness and have thrived at your side for many millennia. Even though your hunting nearly wiped them out, the whales have forgiven you, and there are stories among them of your kindness in rescuing many of them. The sea turtles reminded me of the heroic efforts of some of the Texan humans who saved the lives of thousands of them during the cold snap of 2021—which, by the way, you humans caused.

I have also seen the purity in the hearts of your children and youth, and their desire to live a new kind of simpler life which honors and protects me. I have witnessed the devotion and determination of you, my Message Bearers, to spread my message to all humankind. I have just seen the willingness of all of you to risk your lives and fight for me. This is why I decided to intervene and stop the battle. Before this, I was willing to let you humans do my work and destroy each other. Because of your self-sacrifice and devotion to me, and because of your courage in defending me, I have decided to relent, hold back my fury for now, and give you humans one last chance."

Gentle Gaia pauses to look into the eyes of each of the survivors with love. She pauses longest to gaze into the eyes of Grainne, Clare, Aavani, Mark, and Chooky. When Gaia looks at Chooky, her eyes overflow with tears, and they fall out of the cloud like a warm rain onto Chooky's head. Chooky knows, without any words being spoken, that Gaia is grieving with her over the loss of her beloved Woosh. Everyone in the Dún feels a warm, palpable peace enter through their eyes and flow into the rest of their bodies. Later, most will comment that they had never felt so loved before in their lives, or so peaceful.

"This, though, is what you must do to earn back the right to continue as a species on my Earth. You have to persuade me by your actions. I care not for your empty words, and do not trust your promises and treaties. Show me by the transformation of your choices, policies, and behaviors that you repent of the way which you have been living at my expense. Only this will persuade me that you will cease warming my planet. I will only relent if I see you have listened to your scientists and to my messengers, and are learning to live on this planet without destroying it.

These are the actions I require from you for me to spare you. Every human person on the planet must go on a forty-day fast from carbon. It must be as complete as possible. You must turn off all of your lights and live only by the light of the sun. You will stop all driving, flying, and other polluting transportation. You will cease pumping oil and natural gas, close your coalmines, and stop burning any carbon for power. Any electricity you use has to be produced by wind, sun, or water. All businesses and factories must close for these forty days unless they supply or produce food, medicines, or other vital products. You will eat simply and only as much as you really need. By the way, many of you could lose some weight anyway, my children."

Gaia smiles, as if pleased with her own teasing, and then continues,

"There will be no TV, no internet, no cellphones. You will use this time to get to know me and your fellow creatures once again. You will meditate and reflect on what your short-sighted choices have done to me, to your planet, and ultimately to yourself. You will repent and learn to live in peace and harmony with me. You will renounce your carbon self-indulgence, and turn to me with open hearts and minds, embracing a new and simpler life, closer to me and my ways.

If you complete this fast, I command that Grainne and my messengers lead the youth of the world to convene a World Congress to be attended by all of the leaders of the Earth's nations, and leaders of major corporations, social, environmental, church, scientific and technical groups. The youth will be in charge. Grainne will be the president of the World Congress, and the Message Bearers will be her Advisory Council. There must be a genuine openness to real change, at whatever sacrifice, and an honest intention to find solutions to reverse the warming and the harming which you are inflicting on me.

This Congress will have six months to develop a plan to change your destructive human habits and achieve net-zero carbon emissions from all of your activities. All human nations and groups, the whole of humanity, must agree to this plan, and begin to implement it immediately after the Congress all over the world."

Gaia's visage instantly flashes back to the fearsome image of Kali.

"If your promises to create a net-zero carbon future are not kept this time, I will resume my war on you. So, if you fail to do this, you will perish. If you do not repent and return to my ways, you will surely die."

Gaia once again returns to the persona of loving Mary and kind-hearted Mother Earth. "I will withhold my wrath for now, and I will pull back all of my creatures and forces from attacking and destroying you, while I wait to see if you do what I ask of you. Remember, my children, I love you and I want to see you flourish and prosper on our beloved Earth. But, if you disobey my commands, and again refuse to heed my warning, my wrath and fury will be unleashed, and I will wipe you off the face of the Earth."

Gaia pauses and again looks deeply into the eyes of each person with a mixture of love and steely determination. She envelopes each individual in a golden wrapping of light, and then with the same light taps each of them gently on the forehead, as if to commission each of them to carry her Word to the rest of humanity. Gaia holds their gaze silently for several minutes, and then continues, "Now go and spread this Word to all of your human sisters and brothers, all across my cherished planet."

Immediately, the whitened cloud expands, and in the brilliant light the great wisdom figures of humanity appear, surrounding Gaia and Iona on all sides: Jesus, Buddha, Mary, Moses, Abraham, Mohammed, Mother Teresa, Gandhi, Socrates, Rumi, Confucius, Lao Tzu, the Dalai Lama, Martin Luther King, Luther, Francis and Clare of Assisi, Nelson Mandela, Einstein, Galileo, Newton, Theresa of Avila, John of the Cross, Thomas Merton, and many other unnamed wisdom figures of the ages. They stand in silent witness for several moments, staring intently at the survivors assembled at Dún Aonghasa. Without another sound the light dims, the cloud evaporates, and they are all gone. The terrifying visage of Gaia in the form of Kali is the last to fade, as if giving a final warning.

The assembled survivors stand silently in awe and wonder for some time after Gaia disappears, still looking out to sea, hoping for another glimpse. When the spell is broken, they cluster in small groups; the Guardia, soldiers, Travelers, and young environmentalists all mixed together. They speak in hushed whispers, embracing each other, amazed at what they have just witnessed, and astonished and grateful they are still alive. They ponder the words they have just heard and begin discussing how they are going to spread Gaia's message to humanity.

They realize their first duty is to tend to the wounded and minister to the bodies of the fallen, scattered throughout the stone circles of Dún Aonghasa. They organize teams to begin the grim work. Their excitement about Gaia's appearance is mingled with sorrow for their lost friends and comrades.

Clare turns to Grainne and Aavani, "That was it! That was the revelation we were told to wait for. Now we have our marching orders. We know what we must do to give humanity one last chance to survive."

Clare takes a deep breath and says with a sigh, half groaning and half pleading, "I only pray that the world will listen."

Chapter Thirty-Six

The young environmentalists, of course, had been recording Gaia's appearance on their cellphones. They immediately start sending their videos all over the world. In three hours, 90% of humanity has seen the apparition of Gaia, and heard her proclamation. Grainne also videos the Message Bearers recounting their visions and the message they received. These are sent out to the world less than two hours after the Gaia video.

All of this is disseminated worldwide through every possible news and social media platform. The videos are tweeted and re-tweeted millions of times. They are viewed one billion times on You Tube in just two hours. All the news outlets play the videos as Breaking News. All over the world people's cellphones sound notification alarms, buzzes, and banners, waking up many people on the night side of the planet with the startling news.

Le Monde – "Breaking News: A French panel of digital forensic experts have examined the videos from the incidents at Dún Aonghasa, Ireland, and have determined that the videos are authentic. They announce that they cannot find any evidence that the videos have been manipulated or photo-shopped in any way.

Similar panels in the U.K., the U.S., and South Korea have announced that their investigations yielded the same results. The leader of the French forensic group, Jean Charles Moreau, states in their report, "Of course, it is beyond our expertise to comment on the content of the videos. Except to say that they have not been artificially produced, and are a true recording of some type of real event or phenomenon."

L'Osservatore Romano, Vatican City – "Pope Francis II, the newly designated Dalai Lama, the Grand Imam of Egypt, the Chief Rabbi of Israel, and the Orthodox Patriarch of Constantinople have issued a joint appeal to the world to heed the message from Gaia and the Message Bearers. They call for an immediate forty-day carbon fast, as Gaia commanded. They plead with the people of the world to change their hearts, minds, and their carbon-producing habits to save humanity and the planet. Their joint statement reads in part:

"In the spirit of St. Francis of Assisi, the patron saint and inspiration for environmental spirituality, let all humanity see that Nature is our Mother, and all her creatures are our brothers and our sisters. Let us treat them accordingly. We are all intricately inter-related. Our survival and wellbeing are linked directly to the survival and flourishing of every creature on the planet, down to the smallest bird, reptile, insect, or plant threatened with extinction by our actions.

Gaia and her Message Bearers are clearly God's prophets. They are speaking God's Word to us. They warn us that we have one final opportunity to get it right. Nature and the Creator himself is angry at us, for good reason. We have sinned against Creation and its Creator. Let us repent, renounce our blindness and arrogant domination of Nature, surrender our destructive ways, and learn to live in harmony with God's creations.

We call on all humanity to honor the carbon fast Gaia has proclaimed. Let us slow down, listen, and reflect. May a new spirit of respect for our planet arise from these forty days. Pray that a new determination to change our ways will be kindled in us. God has given us this one last chance to be saved. If we do not heed the warnings of these prophets and repent, each and every one of us, we are doomed. We are truly in the "End Times" as predicted by many religions, but only if we do not act, and act now."

"Most world leaders, religious, scientific, and political, have endorsed the statement of these religious leaders, and have pledged that their organizations and countries will implement the fast as soon as possible. Only the leaders of Russia, the U.S. and China have remained silent."

BBC World News – "Two days after the joint statement of world spiritual leaders was released, under intense international pressure, the leaders of the U.S., Russia, and China have joined every other nation on the planet in calling for compliance to Gaia's demands. The United Nations General Assembly and Security Council met in an emergency session, unanimously endorsing a proposal to support the carbon fast, and to begin organizing the World Congress on the Environment which Gaia ordered. Russia, the U.S., and China initially were going to vote no or abstain. At the last minute, realizing they were going against overwhelming world opinion, including that of their own populations, the three world powers changed their vote to support the UN Declaration."

Washington Post – "The U.S. President, Rex Stout, has issued a statement in response to the declaration of religious leaders released in Rome about the Gaia videos and the current environmental crisis:

> "The U.S. government fully supports the Rome Declaration and will comply with the call for a so-called forty-day Carbon Fast. We will shut down all fossil fuel use and production during this period. However, we assert our sovereign right as a nation to

261

rescind this commitment at any time if it is in our national interest. We support the international efforts to conserve our world's resources and environment.

As a Judeo-Christian country, we Americans believe in the command of the Creator in the book of Genesis: "Be fruitful and multiply; fill the Earth and subdue it. Have dominion over all of the creatures of the Earth." This will be our guiding principle as we enter into the Carbon Fast and the World Congress on the Environment that is now in the planning stage. God bless America!"

"The response to President Stout's statement has been mixed. Evangelical Christian leaders have warmly endorsed it, especially Stout's reference to the Book of Genesis as a basis for future climate decisions. Predictably, Republican congressional leaders are unanimous in their support. Democratic leaders and more moderate and liberal religious leaders have been more critical in their reactions. Most are appreciative that President Stout is agreeing to the Carbon Fast and the World Congress, but question his commitment to actually reducing reliance on carbon-producing fossil fuels.

They also express their vigorous disagreement with his interpretation of the book of Genesis. Namely, his assertion that mankind is called by God to subdue and dominate the Earth and its creatures. Rabbi Judith Tockman, spokesperson of the Rabbinical Council of America, represents the sentiments of many religious leaders:

"We are grateful for President Stout's support for the Carbon Fast and the World Congress. However, his continued misuse of the words of scripture in the book of Genesis, greatly concern us. President Stout, and some other people of faith, are still clinging to old beliefs about our relationship to Creation. These are the beliefs that have put us in this predicament in the first place. The Hebrew word for "dominion" does not mean "domination" over nature. It is more closely translated as "having skilled mastery among or with respect to all creatures." We are called to skillfully live in harmony with nature, not control it for our own selfish and short-termed benefit."

National Catholic Reporter – "Most of the U.S. Catholic bishops have been silent in response to President Stout's proclamation, frustrating many American Catholics. Many commentators consider this lapse predictable, but inexcusable, especially considering how outspoken Pope Francis has been about the climate emergency. The one exception is Bishop Robert McNary of San Diego, who has issued this statement:

> "I am happy to hear President Stout endorse the Rome Declaration. However, his appeal to American sovereignty over the needs of the planet, and his continued use of old, widely discredited concepts of biblical teaching about our relationship with Creation should give all of us pause. I pray he truly and fully supports Pope Francis and the other world religious leaders, who are urging us to heed Gaia's clarion call for repentance and heartfelt, effective change to end global warming and protect our environment. I believe this is a call from God as well."

New York Times – Analysis by Laura McCarthy, special correspondent to the NYT: "Extremists on the right have attempted to protest the Rome Declaration and the United Nations' endorsement of the Carbon Fast and the World Climate Congress. They claim the so-called 'Deep State' has now gone international, infecting even the Churches, and is attempting to impose a socialist or even Marxist world government. For once, they are being largely ignored, and their attempts to stop the Gaia Message have gained no traction. It is as if the spiritual power of the Message and the obvious existential threat to our survival has profoundly shifted the consciousness of humanity.

The whole world is finally waking up to the danger and reality of what we are doing to our own planetary home. The whole of humanity is finally facing the facts of global warming and the reality of impending environmental collapse and disaster, as well as the very real threat of mass human extinction. Let's hope this apparently widespread, profound paradigm shift is not coming too late to save us. Let's also hope the absurd, baseless claims of the climate deniers on the far-right continue to be disregarded and denounced by world opinion and by our political, scientific, and religious leaders. We now know our very survival as a species depends on it."

Chapter Thirty-Seven

Grainne, the Message Bearers, Shelta and her Travelers band, and the surviving environmentalists leave Dún Aonghasa in an array of horse-drawn jaunty carts, organized by Fergus Connelly, the harbormaster, and his cousin, Columbkille.

Fergus greets them as they board the carts, "Sure, didn't I know you Americans were up to something good. I knew you weren't tourists, for God-sakes. Now I see you on my mobile along with most of the rest of the world. Sr. Clare, the vision you saw, it wasn't your usual Knock or Lourdes kind of apparition, now was it? It was terrifying, is what it was. But I think it was from the Lord himself. Don't you?"

"Yes, Fergus," Clare responds in a soft voice, "I think it was most definitely from God. I hope it puts the fear of God in all of us. The Lord wants us to be saved; if we only will listen."

"God bless you then, sister, and God bless all of you. May your road ahead rise to meet you, and may all the rest of them Irish blessings be upon ya. May God bless each of you and the mission you are on to save us all. God willing, you will win out."

He makes the sign of the cross over the whole group. Clare, Mark, and even Aavani make the sign of the cross on their own faces to receive the blessing. Chooky, in shock and desperate grief, keeps her head buried in her hands, barely even hearing Fergus' blessing.

The jaunty carts then bring them slowly down the hill to the harbor at Kilronan. No one looks back up at Dún Aonghasa; its dark rock now forever imbued with the memory and blood of their fallen friends and comrades, the trauma of the terrible battle, and the terrifying warning from Gaia.

After arriving at the harbor, they travel by ferry-boat to Galway City. They have an Irish Navy escort, the navy's flagship patrol boat, *LÉ Eithne*. The bay is unusually calm, and their passage is uneventful under a clear, sparklingly blue sky. The mountains of Connemara, the Twelve Bens and behind them Croagh Patrick, are a patchwork of grey and green, standing guard over the land of Grace O'Malley. After a brief stopover in Galway, they are driven to Dublin in a small fleet of electric vans, loaned to them by the Taoiseach himself. They are escorted by Superintendent O'Dowd, Colonel Quinlan, and their battered units. Shelta travels with them to Dublin, but most of her surviving Travelers return to their caravan community outside of Galway near Clifden to rest and heal from the battle.

The whole entourage is grieving the deaths of Woosh, George Gustafson, Zoe, and the rest of their friends and compatriots who sacrificed their lives in what is now being called the Battle of Dún Aonghasa. Chooky is nearly inconsolable, sobbing and weeping every few minutes during the three-hour drive to Dublin. Clare, Aavani, and Mark comfort her the best they can. Aavani is surprised at how much she misses George considering her run-ins with him. She feels a deep sadness that she could not have been friends with the spiritually maturing man who was emerging at the end. She is very grateful they had reconciled just before the battle began.

The entourage is met in Dublin with a hero's welcome. A large parade is organized in the heart of Dublin, marching down O'Connell Street, past the O'Connell Monument, over the River Liffey Bridge, and ending at St. Stephen's Green. There a hastily arranged Earth Day Festival is celebrated in their honor in the central plaza of the park. Thousands of Dubliners and people from all over the world have gathered for the festival, and fill the park with colorful signs, banners, and flags. Some of the banners and flags feature reproduced images of Gaia herself, displaying both her Mother Earth and her fearsome Kali icons.

Grainne, Clare, Aavani, and Mark all stand before the large crowd and give speeches. Despite being almost disabled with grief, Chooky also speaks. She is determined to honor Woosh by continuing the mission he died for. She gets through her speech, barely holding her tears at bay, until the end of her talk. She comes undone when two banners are unfurled with photos of Woosh and Gustafson, captioned "Heroes of Humankind and Martyrs for the Earth."

Chooky starts to sob uncontrollably once again. All of the Message Bearers and Grainne gather around her at the podium, holding her as she cries.

The crowd cheers for Chooky, Grainne, and the rest of the Message Bearers. They cheer just as loud when Grainne introduces Shelta, Superintendent O'Dowd, Colonel Quinlan, their Guardia officers and Irish soldiers, and all of the young environmental defenders of the battle of Dún Aonghasa. There is a half-hour standing ovation.

A young Dubliner in the crowd, with a clear Irish tenor voice, spontaneously starts to sing the American Civil Rights anthem *We Shall Overcome*. After a few bars, the whole crowd joins in, holding hands and swaying to the rhythm of the music. A Trad musical group in the crowd joins in with their fiddle, tin whistle, harp, Uilleann pipes, and bodhran, turning the African-American protest song into a jaunty Irish hymn of solidarity and hope. Some people link arms and begin to dance. As the Irish are wont to do, by the end of the song many in the crowd are vacillating between mournful sobs and joyous laughter and cheers.

After the celebration, Grainne and the Message Bearers return to Trinity College in Dublin, where they have been invited to set up a headquarters to continue to spread Gaia's message and prepare for the World Congress. The group meets several hours a day to discuss their next steps.

Chooky cannot bring herself to attend these meetings. She stays alone in her room in the Trinity College dormitory they are all sharing. She can't focus her mind on Gaia, the future of the planet, or even the humpback's message to her. The mental video of Woosh being thrown off the cliff at Dún Aonghasa, bouncing off the rocks into the ocean, and into the mouths of the sharks, plays over and over in her mind. She hears Woosh's scream as he falls. She can see Woosh's and George's blood churned by the ferocious feeding frenzy. She can't stop these horrible images from playing in a continuous feedback loop in her brain.

Clare and Aavani try to draw Chooky into their discussions, and to comfort her, but there is nothing they can do, or say, that consoles her. They worry Chooky may never recover from her grief. They worry too that she may have been permanently lost to the team of the Message Bearers. They are especially concerned about losing Chooky, because she represents the scientific part of the message and vision. They had been counting on her to convince and reassure the skeptical intellectual and scientific communities of the world.

Each evening, while the others are meeting, Chooky leaves her room and the campus, and walks alone through Dublin the three miles to Sandy Mount Strand on the coast of the Irish Sea. She walks the long, wide beach searching for some connection to Woosh. She has lost the sense of his presence, something she had always felt, even when they were separated during her academic days in the Lower 48. Chooky scans the twilight skies searching for the constellation Gemini. She keeps hoping that spotting its twin stars will help her to feel Woosh's presence, and to believe his promise that they would be together forever, as eternal twin souls. But the summer twilight is too bright to reveal any stars.

On the second night walking the strand, Chooky remembers it is nearly Summer Solstice, and Gemini will soon sink below the horizon and not be seen again until the winter skies return. She starts to sob, inconsolable that she cannot even have this visual reminder of Woosh's love for her.

She weeps as she walks back through the streets of Dublin to Trinity College, feeling entirely empty and bereft of any consolation. She begins to fear she will eventually lose her memories of Woosh's smile, the feel of his hands on her body, and the safety of being held in his arms.

Simon is the only one of the group who notices Chooky returning from her nightly walk, tears streaming down her face. He mentions it to Mark, but they are unsure how to comfort her. On the third evening, the night of the Summer Solstice, Simon decides to follow Chooky to make sure she is alright, keeping his distance to respect her privacy. He follows her up the strand till she stops and turns to the west to watch the sunset. When he sees her sobbing, he cannot hold himself back, and approaches her.

Chooky recognizes him and falls into his arms, crying even harder, "Oh, Simon, I can't find Woosh! I can't feel him. I can't feel his love," Chooky manages to stutter out between sobs. She tells Simon what Woosh said about the twin stars of Gemini. She describes how she had been searching the skies for them to find her lost connection to Woosh, until she realized Gemini was now below the sunset, below the horizon, and no longer visible at night until winter.

Simon keeps holding her, feeling powerless to alleviate her pain. After several moments of uncomfortable silence—while struggling for the right words to say to Chooky—an idea finally comes to him. He pulls away from Chooky's embrace, takes his cellphone from his pocket, and says, "Maybe this will help."

He opens up his astronomy app, Night Sky, holds it up to the western sky, and then points it down toward the ground in the direction of Dublin. He shows it to Chooky.

"Chooky, there," he says, pointing to a spot on his cellphone, "just underneath the Sun, a little below the app's horizon-line, there's Gemini, with Castor and Pollux at the head of the constellation."

Chooky takes Simon's phone and stares intently at the Night Sky app.

"Oh, my God! Gemini is still here, it's just below the horizon." Then she recalls the funeral prayer her grandmother back in Hoonah taught her. Chooky whispers it into the screen, "Life is eternal and love is immortal, and death is only a horizon, and a horizon is nothing save the limit of our sight…"

She starts to weep again, but it's a different type of crying, softer and less desperate,. "Woosh, my love, I can feel you with me again. What you promised is true. We will always be together, like these twin stars. Whether I can see you or not, you will always be just over the horizon, not visible, yet always with me."

Chooky pauses to let the tears flow gently down her cheeks.

"Woosh, I know you want me to fulfill the mission Gaia and the humpback gave us. I just couldn't do anything before. I was paralyzed by your death. Now I feel your spirit with me again, I can fight, like you did, to do what Gaia has commanded us to do to save the planet, and— maybe—us humans too."

Chooky stops weeping and turns to Simon.

"Simon, I know you probably don't believe in these sorts of things—I didn't either—but you have saved my soul and returned Woosh's spirit to me. Thank you!"

Simon takes Chooky's hand, and they turn back toward Dublin. "Simon, let's get back to the group. We have a lot of work to do." They walk hand-in-hand through the darkening streets of Dublin until they reach the green space of the Trinity College campus.

That same evening, all the Message Bearers gather together in the magnificent Trinity College Library, a shrine to the written word, surrounded by towering dark wood shelves of historic books. They are given permission to hold their meetings right next to the exquisite Book of Kells, the colorfully illuminated manuscript of the Four Gospels from 800 AD displayed in its glass tabernacle. Clare, Aavani, and Grainne are surprised and thrilled to see Chooky walk into the library. She nearly looks like her old self again. They rush over to greet her with a tight group hug. Mark and Simon join them.

Chooky speaks to the encircling huddle, "Thank you all for your love and prayers. I'm still pretty fragile, but I feel connected to Woosh again, thanks to Simon. My mind is fairly clear now, and I'm ready to fight for Gaia's message again. I know this is what Woosh would want. I feel his spirit right here with us now." She stifles a sob, breaks free of the comforting scrum, and continues in a strong, commanding voice, "So, let's get back to work. What do we need to do?"

Aavani responds, "It's so good to have you back, Chooky. The four musketeers of Gaia are back in the saddle again. Alleluia! Praise Devi!"

They arrange the library chairs in a circle in front of the Book of Kells display and begin their daily meeting. Each shares their reflections on what they experienced together, discussing the work ahead to fulfill Gaia's mandate. The Carbon Fast is scheduled to begin in five hours at midnight Greenwich Mean Time, as determined by the vote of the United Nations General Assembly. Most of the group is excited and hopeful. All the peoples of the world and all of the world governments appear for once to be united in their commitment to the Carbon Fast and to the World Congress to follow. Initially, there was much discussion and some resistance and dissent, even a few protests. Eventually, humanity became convinced that, if it was to survive, it had to obey Gaia's commands.

Grainne rises and stands in front of the Book of Kells. "My sisters and brothers, we have traveled a long journey together, and gone through much suffering to get to this day. Some of our friends and comrades have given their lives for us to arrive at this point. For the first time in years, I am hopeful we can reverse global warming and save our planet. We have a lot of work to do at the World Congress to achieve this. But I believe the world has finally awakened, and is at last ready to change its relationship with Nature, and stop assaulting and exploiting her. It will take even more sacrifice. Yet I believe we are finally able as a species to accept the reality of global warming and climate change, and do what it takes to save ourselves and all of Gaia's children." She pauses and injects a stern tone into her voice, "We are all real eejits, as we Irish say, if we don't do this. And dead eejits to be sure."

Clare rises from her chair with a grave look on her face and stands with Grainne.

"Grainne, I pray you are right. I am hopeful too. I am amazed at the world's response to Gaia's appearance and message. But, despite my faith, I am a world-class worrier. It is looking good so far, but a lot could go wrong. So, let's not count our solar panels and our wind turbines till they are hatched...I mean installed."

Everyone giggles nervously. Clare continues, "I would suggest we spend the next hours in prayer and meditation until midnight when the Carbon Fast begins. Let's do a silent vigil and prepare our hearts and souls for what is ahead."

The whole group agrees. They arrange the library chairs in a circle. Each one prays in their own fashion and tradition. Chooky remembers her tribal spiritual practices, and silently chants in the Tlingit language, alternating with the Russian Orthodox prayers her grandmothers taught her.

Simon focuses on his breathing as Mark instructed him when he returned from the Zen Center in Crestone. Mark softly chants the Jesus Prayer Clare shared with him. Clare joins him. Aavani summons to her mind's eye the statue of Devi back at her Crestone ashram, and silently repeats her mantra. Grainne, Clare, Aavani, Mark, and Chooky each sink into a deep, meditative trance.

A palpable spirit of peace descends on the group. Clare feels it as well. Yet, she senses some disturbance deep in her soul. She dismisses it as resistance from the worrier part of her personality and tries to let it go. She re-centers and returns her focus to the Jesus Prayer. But the disquiet in her soul keeps resurfacing.

Chapter Thirty-Eight

Outside of the Trinity Library, the world begins to respond. With astonishing swiftness, the carbon fast begins all across the planet. All lights and all power are turned off at midnight GMT. Many people go out to marvel at the night sky, seeing stars and planets they have never seen before. People stay home and talk to each other, meditate, and pray. They fast and begin to eat more simply. They go for walks in nature and begin experiencing a peace that has long eluded them. They walk or cycle to wherever they really need to go. Travel and most commerce ceases. The stock markets of the world predictably crash, and the world economy goes into a nosedive. Unlike the Covid-19 crisis of 2020, most people seem to believe the hardships and sacrifices required are necessary and acceptable.

The sky is eerily free of all planes, like in the days after 9/11. Polluted skies again begin to clear, and the air becomes more breathable, just as happened in the shutdown of 2020. The world is so much quieter. The noise and all of the other distractions of modern life are gone. The screens of billions of digital devices go dark and blank. There are no texts, tweets, emails, phone calls, videos, TikToks, Instagrams, or Facebook posts. Every app, computer program, streaming service—everything based on carbon—disappears for forty days. Everything that had grown like a metastasizing cancer in everyone's daily lives distracting and disturbing the spirit of humanity, and anesthetizing the soul, vanishes.

This time social distancing and self-quarantining is not required. People leave their homes and gather in the streets all over the world to reassure each other and discuss the amazing events. There are gigantic, mostly peaceful protests and gatherings in support of the environment and the carbon fast in cities all over the world. More and more people begin hearing whispers from deep inside, from the quiet voice of their souls, that they had never heard or even noticed before.

Churches, temples, synagogues, and mosques overflow with frightened congregants seeking spiritual consolation and guidance. Their leaders preach a message of reassurance and hope. They almost universally start to teach a new eco-spirituality, calling for repentance for humanity's eco-sins against Creation. They challenge their people to engage in a massive change of the world's energy consumption, and to end humanity's wasteful, polluting habits.

Whether from fear for their own survival, or a new realization of what is happening to the Earth, the peoples of the world open their hearts and minds and repent, like Ninaveh hearing the prophecy of Jonah. They start to turn away from everything they had been doing that hurts or threatens Mother Gaia. The carbon fast becomes universal. Every nation on Earth mandates that the carbon fast be scrupulously observed. For a change, there is little resistance or protest. A few extremists—some on the left, as well as from the right—maintain their belief that Gaia's apparition at Dún Aonghasa is a hoax or conspiracy. They are mostly ignored.

All the governments of the world, the churches, NGOs, universities, science and tech groups, and many other organizations use the fast to prepare for the upcoming World Climate Congress. The video of Gaia's appearance and message and the broadcasts of the Message Bearer's visions have filled most of the world's population with fear and remorse. A new determination grows to halt and reverse global warming, and to end all the other ways humankind has been abusing Nature.

BBC World News – "Analysis by Dr. Trevor Somerset, Professor of Modern Philosophy at Cambridge University":

"To many peoples' surprise, threatened with extinction, humanity has nearly universally responded in the positive to the message from Gaia, the purported feminine spirit of Planet Earth. As has been often said, nothing focuses the mind like an impending hanging. The people of every nation can now see the noose hanging before their eyes.

Whether caused by fear or a long overdue awakening to the effects of global warming, the reports from all over the world, east and west, north and south, verify that an overwhelming majority of humankind is heeding Gaia's warning and commands. This is a huge surprise to a skeptic like myself. I always expect there will be contrarians, rebels, and extremists among us, no matter what the issue or the evidence might be. I usually count myself among these cynics and doubters.

I have always been very "stroppy," as we English call it. I was diagnosed with ODD, Oppositional Defiant Disorder, when I was a lad. I think this is why I became a philosopher. I have long questioned everything. I have come to believe ODD is actually a part of human nature, fallen or not. We are all oppositional and defiant to some degree. This is both a blessing and a curse, as I well know.

So, I, and many other dubious commentators, have been quite astonished to see that humanity has reached such a swift consensus about global warming, and so quickly implemented Gaia's demands. Seeing the near-universal acceptance of Gaia's message and commands, I have come to rethink my skeptical stance about our human race.

Perhaps, we are, after all, capable of truly awakening to a new consciousness, developing a new paradigm, and making major changes in our choices and behaviors. We are certainly capable of creating the necessary technologies, as has been demonstrated in the last few years. I am starting to believe we can also adopt the mindset and spirit necessary to make the difficult policy decisions to implement the technologies, and make the sacrifices that reversing climate change requires.

There are, to be sure, still extremists— right and left, climate deniers, and other assorted trolls—still around who are resisting Gaia's message and making a bit of noise. But without an audience, and lacking any evidence to back their rebellion, even they are starting to grow silent.

Because there is such widespread acceptance of Gaia's message, I am chastened in my normal cynicism, and have developed a renewed hope in humanity. I now believe we can act, and change enough that Gaia's rage will be assuaged, and her revenge averted. We can stop—even reverse—global warming. Humanity and the planet might yet both be saved, if we as a species continue on this current path to redemption. I, for one, am finally ready to give up my Jaguar carbon-spewer, and go electric or hydrogen. I am even starting to pray."

Chapter Thirty-Nine

On the International Space Station, astronauts Anatoly Invanivich, Oleg Sharapova, Jessica Christie, Andrew Cassidy, Christina Morgan, and Luca Parisi have been following the events on Earth. NASA in Houston, ESA in Paris, and Roscosmos in Star City, Russia, their respective space agencies, have been keeping them abreast of the developments unfolding below them. The astronauts have been able to upload and view the videos of Gaia's appearance and the Message Bearers' accounts of their visions along with the rest of the world. They play them over and over.

As they go about their daily ISS duties, they discuss Gaia's appearance and message. As engineers, pilots, and scientists they are fairly skeptical. But they wonder, if it is true, what it will mean for them? Will they be stranded in space and slowly die as humanity is extinguished beneath them? Will they be the last humans? If they can return to Earth, what will they find left? They know Earth and their home countries will be greatly changed no matter how things unfold.

As a group of science-minded astronauts, they had long accepted that the planet outside their windows was in trouble. But like most people they assumed it would be decades before climate change greatly impacted the human race. They thought humanity still had time, and might just change enough to forestall, or prevent, the worst of global warming. But now they had awakened to the fact that the doomsday future forecast by climate scientists was already upon them.

They debated what to do. Should they remain on the ISS? Request that a rescue mission be sent up to return them to Earth? If what they were hearing was true, and if humanity didn't respond to Gaia's plea, would it better to die back on Earth, or survive a while longer on the Space Station until their food and oxygen ran out? If humanity is wiped out, there would be no one left to launch a SpaceX Dragon 2 capsule to rescue them. They will be abandoned and orphaned in the dark void of space. Their own lives slowly being snuffed out as they watch the human-emptied planet turn below them. For several days, they fervently discuss their options over and over, but can't come to a consensus about what to do.

On the day the carbon fast is to begin, they lose all communication with their Earth command centers. Honoring the fast, Houston, Paris, and Roscosmos shut down and are silent. The astronauts are now on their own, circling in the emptiness of space, two-hundred-fifty-five miles about the Earth, orbiting their home planet at seventeen-thousand-one-hundred miles per hour. The astronauts stop all of their work, and gather in the cupola module, the seven-windowed dome installed on the space station in February 2010. The cupola provides a panoramic view of the Earth spinning below them. For a long time they are all silent, weightlessly floating in the zero-gravity, as they watch the incredible beauty of their blue-green planet turning majestically beneath them.

The cupola is bathed in varying color light as they pass over different regions of the planet. There is a pink-red glow as they pass over Australia, its iron-red soil reflecting into space. A gleaming blue iridescence fills the cupola during their transit of the Pacific Ocean. The great Sahara in North Africa projects a soft golden-orange glow onto the assembled astronauts. A stark white light penetrates harshly into the cupola as they pass over what remains of the great ice-fields, ice shelves, and glaciers of Antarctica.

The many shapes and colors of water and land masses appear, and then fade from their view. From their orbital perch—what astronauts call "the orbital perspective"—they can see some evidence of humanity's imprint on the planet, but national boundaries are not visible at all. These artificial human lines and divisions simply do not exist in the perspective from space. The Earth, from the astronauts' point of view, is one, unified super-organism.

As the astronauts orbit the Earth, they look for signs of what is happening on their planet. As the Carbon Fast takes hold, they watch the lights go out in each country in the night zone. Eventually, they see all of the lights on the whole planet have been turned off. All of the urban and rural lights go out as the Earth turns below them. First North and South America, then Europe, Africa, the Middle East, Russia, Asia, Australia, New Zealand, and the Pacific

Islands. All the lights blink off. Eventually, the whole Earth is dark in the night zone, with no human lights visible anywhere. The great cities around the globe, usually glowing bright clusters of light in the night, are now completely dark.

The astronauts leave the cupola and gather in the Unity module where they eat meals together. They give each other weightless high-fives. They all voice their relief that it appears humanity will obey Gaia and survive. They toast each other with squeeze bottles of orange and apple juice. The Russian cosmonauts have sneaked little squeeze bottles of vodka on board. They share these with their colleagues. The Carbon Fast looks to be successful. Humanity will be spared. They will not be the last orphans of the human race, lost and abandoned in space, after all.

One astronaut, Luca Parisi from Italy, doesn't join the celebration. He lingers in the cupola, gazing at the Earth turning below him. On the fifth orbit since the blackout, he has a view of the United States at night. Orbiting from West to East, he sees the West Coast, the Southwest, the Plains states, the Middle West, the South, and the Northeast are all completely dark.

As he observes the Earth turn, Luca notices a pinpoint of light blinking on in the Mid-Atlantic region. It looks like Washington, D.C. From his past visits to Washington, Luca guesses the light is coming from one large, white house in the center of D.C. He reaches for his binoculars to get a clearer view. As he watches, numerous other lights surrounding the house flicker on. Then the lights of all of the public buildings and public spaces of D.C. come on at once. The White House, the Capitol Building, the National Mall, and most of federal Washington D.C. are ablaze with defiant light.

Luca's heart sinks.

He debates with himself whether he should go and tell his fellow astronauts, spoiling their celebration. He decides to wait and watch. As the Earth turns far below him, he holds a silent, solitary vigil, a lone sentinel, anxiously vigilant for signs of any more ominous lights on the darkened planet.

Acknowledgements

It takes more than a village to raise a book. It requires a small city. So many people have inspired, influenced, and supported me through the years up to the writing of this book. Most will remain nameless, and I am grateful to them all. Many life experiences also come together to create a writer. I want to acknowledge Pogo (the late 40's – mid 70's comic strip whose most famous line was "We have met the enemy and he is us.") for instilling a love of playing with words and creative language. I wish to thank my stutter of 25 years for teaching me to listen to people and to their speech, and for, often painfully, challenging me to be creative in finding the best words. I attribute my love for science to my parents' childhood gift of a telescope and a chemistry set which spawned my fascination with cosmology and things that can blow up. I am also grateful for my faith and spirituality for constantly expanding my mind, heart, and soul to embrace ever deeper truths, even when they are inconvenient and personally challenging. I thank my God for his love and for her eternally unfolding creativity, mystery and inspiration. God transformed a year of intense personal suffering battling breast cancer, mental collapse, and global warming induced extreme weather into the idea for this book.

I am most grateful to several people who contributed so much to the writing of *Gaia's* Revenge. They read my drafts, and provided me with both encouragement and constructive critiques: Bart Baker, a remarkable screenwriter and novelist, who also gave me invaluable guidance through the maze of the publishing business; Lou Jobst, friend and English teacher extraordinaire; Chris Scherer, my nephew and fellow writer; Chris Lauber, my excellent science consultant and grandson, an aerospace engineer and future Martian, for his scientific review of the manuscript; and Michelle and Nicole Gutierrez, my multi-talented twin granddaughters, future photo-journalists. They provided excellent YA advice about the manuscript, and also designed and created the cover art. I'm grateful for my outstanding editor, Jessica Keet, who helped refine and redirect my wandering sentences and paragraphs. Thank you to Joe McGlynn for his legal consultation and for his encyclopedic knowledge of all things Irish.

I wish to thank my family: my sisters, Joan and Andy, my brothers, Rocky and Jack, our ten grandchildren, three great-grandchildren, my nieces and nephews, and the rest of my amazing family for their support and excitement about my writing these past 15 years. Also, thank you to the Lauber family for embracing me as one of them. I want to express my gratitude to my friend and co-writer Victoria Schmidt, who has shared so much of my writing journey. Finally, and most of all, I thank Sue, my best friend and lover, partner-wife, co-writer, and muse for her challenging, yet unconditional love and belief in me. Sue, you are the greatest gift of my life. "And we will make of our love a bright, impossible rainbow."

Made in the USA
Monee, IL
07 November 2021

81593535R00157